新曙光 XINSHUGUANG

现代商务英语系列教材

高职高专适用

现代商务英语 下

Contemporary Integrated **Business English** ②

综合教程

主　编◎李荣庆　李全福

副主编◎雷淑雅　李红兵

天津大学出版社
TIANJIN UNIVERSITY PRESS

内 容 提 要

《现代商务英语综合教程》(下)是高等职业教育商务英语专业高年级学生的主干课程教材。本教材内容涵盖工商领域产、供、销和对外贸易的各个环节。各单元由精读文本、词汇注释、课文详解、练习题目及辅助阅读短文组成。

教材各练习环节均为以学生为中心的教学模式而设。比如,每单元专设学生展示(PPT presentation)环节,教师可因势利导,安排互动教学。

本系列教材重视整体构建,另编有《现代商务英语听力教程》、《现代商务英语口语教程》。这些教材各单元的主题与《现代商务英语综合教程》基本一致,形成呼应关系,数种教材同时使用,可以产生课程间教学合力,为迄今比较先进的教材组合设计。本教材附带教师教学用PPT演示文稿,其中收入每单元练习题目的答案以及每篇英语文本的汉语译文,方便教师使用。

图书在版编目(CIP)数据

现代商务英语综合教程.下/李荣庆,李全福主编.—天津:天津大学出版社,2010.11
新曙光现代商务英语系列教材.高职高专适用
ISBN 978-7-5618-3718-4

Ⅰ.①现… Ⅱ.①李…②李… Ⅲ.①商务–英语–高等学校:技术学校–教材 Ⅳ.①H31

中国版本图书馆 CIP 数据核字(2010)第 212625 号

出版发行	天津大学出版社
出 版 人	杨欢
地 址	天津市卫津路 92 号天津大学内(邮编:300072)
电 话	发行部:022-27403647 邮购部:022-27402742
网 址	www.tjup.com
印 刷	昌黎太阳红彩色印刷有限责任公司
经 销	全国各地新华书店
开 本	185mm×260mm
印 张	14
字 数	402 千
版 次	2011 年 1 月第 1 版
印 次	2011 年 1 月第 1 次
印 数	1 – 3 000
定 价	36.00 元

前　言

　　新曙光现代商务英语系列教材是根据教育部"以服务为宗旨,以就业为导向"的高等职业教育战略方针,针对我国高等职业教育商务英语教学状况以及我国经济高速发展的实际情况而编写的一套系列教材。随着我国经济的快速发展和快速融入全球经济体系,各地高等职业教育的商务英语专业的设置和在校学生人数已经初具规模,商务英语专业的教材建设也越来越受到重视。教学实践经验表明,与时俱进的新型现代商务英语教材的开发对于培养出具有国际商务综合能力的学生有着十分重要的意义。新曙光现代商务英语系列教材的组织策划者和编者在该教材的开发设计和编写中就如下几个方面达成共识。

　　一、本套现代商务英语系列教材的建设必须以培养具有外语能力的商务技能型人才为目标。除了重视传统的听、说、读、写、译等英语专业的基本技能外,学生的商务专业技能的培养应放在突出的地位。本套教材的设计和编写注重学生的设计能力、沟通能力、交际能力、团队能力、想象能力、创新能力、批评能力、审美能力、动手能力和计算机操作等具体的技能培养。

　　二、本套现代商务英语系列教材应该成为推进教学改革的平台。本套教材的设计和编写融入了近年来世界范围内先进的教学理念,使创新性学习(Creative Learning)、主动性学习(Active Learning)、批判性学习(Critical Learning)、分析性学习(Analytical Learning)的求知模式能够得以实现。本套教材的编写还致力于推进以教师为中心的教学模式向以学生学习为中心的教学模式的转变。

　　三、本套现代商务英语系列教材的建设以就业为导向。商务英语专业具有跨学科性、专业覆盖面宽、就业面广等特点。因此,本套教材的配套设计专门考虑到几个就业岗位群的需要,这些岗位群包括涉外管理岗位群、涉外贸易岗位群、涉外服务岗位群、外语师资岗位群。本套教材的设计开发以"基础技能主干教材＋岗位方向配套教材"的理念面向这些岗位群。

　　四、本套现代商务英语系列教材的建设吸收了近年来新的科学技术成果。本套教材采取多维立体化教材存在模式,每种教材都配有数字化辅助教学资源,从而使这套教材实现了立体化,发挥出高效的施教与学习效果。

　　新曙光现代商务英语系列教材在相关专业教学指导委员会、相关行业协会、学会、企业、事业单位和相关学校的关怀和支持下,必定能够成为21世纪商务英语专业的优秀教材。

《现代商务英语综合教程》（下）编写说明

　　《现代商务英语综合教程》是为高职高专商务英语专业学生量身打造的新曙光现代商务英语系列教材之一。它适应于高职高专商务英语专业高年级同学使用。本书为《现代商务英语综合教程》的下册。共计12个单元。每单元按6学时授课，可满足一个学期72学时的教学工作量。本教材各单元的主题分别为：国贸理论、国贸组织、市场营销、市场组合、促销活动、品牌战略、工商伦理、职场女性、股票债券、经济周期、保护主义、知识产权。这些主题承接上册主题，使工商领域各个环节的内容在教材中都得到体现。其中一些单元的内容较上册难度程度有所增加，体现了学习上先易后难的理念。

　　《现代商务英语综合教程》（下）编写人员如下。

主　　编：李荣庆，李全福

副主编：雷淑雅，李红兵

参　　编：林丹燕，李春风，李东，王英华

　　其中李荣庆编写第4章、李全福编写第10章、雷淑雅编写第1章、李红兵编写第2、3章、林丹燕编写第5、6章、李东编写第7、8章、李春风编写第11、12章、王英华编写第9章。

Contents

现代商务英语综合教程（下）

Unit One   The Theory of International Trade

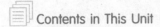 Contents in This Unit

1. Two pre-reading discussion questions.

2. A text on comparative advantage.

3. New words and expressions.

4. Explanatory notes for the text.

5. Some exercises to build up your skills both in English and business.

6. A PPT hands-on assignment to give you space for creation.

7. Further readings on the theory of international trade.

Pre-reading Discussions for the Text

Please discuss these questions in pairs. You may talk over the topics either in English or in Chinese according to your teacher's instruction.

1. Do you often shop at local markets or at large shopping centers downtown? Discuss and explain your choice to us. You may write down some key words and phrases before you talk.

_____

_____

_____

2. "Every man has his gift." What does this proverb mean? Discuss why some people can succeed in their lives. You may write down the key words and phrases before you talk.

_____

_____

_____

Text: The Theory of Comparative Advantage — Historical Overview

The theory of comparative advantage is perhaps the most important concept in international trade theory. There is a popular story told amongst economists that once when an economics skeptic asked Paul Samuelson (a Nobel laureate in economics) to provide a meaningful and non-trivial result from the economics discipline, Samuelson quickly responded with "comparative advantage". Comparative advantage suggests that each country is relatively good at producing certain products or services.

Paul Samuelson

The original idea of comparative advantage dates to the early part of the 19th century. Although the model describing the theory is commonly referred to as the "Ricardian model", the original description of the idea can be found in *An Essay on the External Corn Trade* by Robert Torrens in 1815. David Ricardo formalized the idea using a compelling, yet simple, numerical example in his 1817 book, titled *On the Principles of Political Economy and Taxation*. The idea appeared again in James Mill's *Elements of Political Economy* in 1821. Finally, the concept became a key feature of international political economy upon the publication of *Principles of Political Economy* by John Stuart Mill in 1848.

The theory of comparative advantage is also one of the most commonly misunderstood principles. The sources of the misunderstandings are easy to identify. First, the principle of comparative advantage is clearly counter-intuitive. Many results from the formal model are contrary to simple logic. Secondly, the theory is easy to confuse with another notion about advantageous trade, known in trade theory as the theory of absolute advantage. The logic behind absolute advantage is quite intuitive. This confusion between these two concepts leads many people to think that they understand comparative advantage when in fact, what they understand is absolute advantage. Finally, the theory of comparative advantage is all too often presented only in its mathematical form. Using numerical examples or diagrammatic representations are extremely useful in demonstrating the basic results and the deeper implications of the theory.

The early logic that free trade could be advantageous for countries was based on the concept of absolute advantages in production. Adam Smith wrote in *The Wealth of Nations*, "If a

David Ricardo

foreign country can supply us with a commodity cheaper than we ourselves can make it, better buy it of them with some part of the produce of our own industry, employed in a way in which we have some advantage. "

Because the idea of comparative advantage is not immediately intuitive, the best way of presenting it seems to be with an explicit numerical example as provided by David Ricardo. Indeed some variation of Ricardo's example lives on in most international trade textbooks today. In his example Ricardo imagined two countries, England and Portugal, producing two goods, cloth and wine, using labor as the sole input in production. He assumed that the productivity of labor (i. e. the quantity of output produced per worker) varied between industries and across countries. If Portugal is twice as productive in cloth production relative to England but three times as productive in wine, then Portugal's comparative advantage is in wine, the good in which its productivity advantage is greatest. Similarly, England's comparative advantage good is cloth, the good in which its productivity disadvantage is least. This implies that to benefit from specialization and free trade, Portugal should specialize and trade the good in which it is "most best" at producing while England should specialize and trade the good in which it is "least worse" at producing. If appropriate terms of trade (i. e., amount of one good traded for another) were then chosen, both countries could end up with more of both goods after specialization and free trade than they each had before trade. This means that England may nevertheless benefit from free trade even though it is assumed to be technologically inferior to Portugal in the production of everything.

All in all, this condition is rather confusing. Suffice it to say, that it is quite possible, indeed likely, that although England may be less productive in producing both goods relative to Portugal, it will nonetheless have a comparative advantage in the production of one of the two goods.

Adam Smith

As it turned out, specialization in any good would not suffice to guarantee the improvement in world output. Only one of the goods would work. Ricardo showed that the specialization good in each country should be that good in which the country had a comparative advantage in production. To identify a country's comparative advantage good requires a comparison of production costs across countries. However, one does not compare the monetary costs of production or even the resource costs (labor needed per unit of output) of production. Instead one must compare the opportunity costs of producing goods across countries. The opportunity cost of cloth production is defined as the amount of wine that must be given up in order to produce one more unit of cloth. A country is said to have a comparative advantage in the production of certain product if it can produce that product at a lower cost than another country.

Note that the trade based on comparative advantage does not contradict Adam Smith's notion of advantageous trade based on absolute advantage. In fact, the theory of comparative advantage is the upgraded version of the theory of absolute advantage. Advantageous trade based on comparative advantage, then, covers a larger set of circumstances while still including the case of absolute advantage. Hence, it is a more general theory.

 *Vocabulary*

1. amongst [ə'mʌŋst]　　　*prep.* in the midst of; among
　　　　　　　　　　　　　　　在……之中，在……之间

2. skeptic ['skeptik]　　　*n.* someone who habitually doubts accepted beliefs
　　　　　　　　　　　　　　　怀疑者，怀疑论

3. laureate ['lɔ:riət]　　　*n.* someone honored for great achievements
　　　　　　　　　　　　　　　得奖人

4. meaningful ['mi:niŋful]　　*adj.* having a meaning or purpose
　　　　　　　　　　　　　　　意义深长的，有意义的

5. trivial ['triviə]　　　　*adj.* of little substance or significance
　　　　　　　　　　　　　　　琐碎的，不重要的

6. formalize ['fɔ:məlaiz]　　*vt.* to be or make formal; to express in the symbols
　　　　　　　　　　　　　　　of some formal system
　　　　　　　　　　　　　　　使成为正式；使具有一定形式

7. title ['taitl]　　　　　　*vt.* give a title to a book or music, etc.
　　　　　　　　　　　　　　　（给书籍、乐曲等）加标题，定题目

8. contrary ['kɔntrəri]　　　*adj.* opposed in nature, position, etc.
　　　　　　　　　　　　　　　相反的，相违背的

9. notion ['nəuʃən]　　　　*n.* a vague idea, concept or opinion
　　　　　　　　　　　　　　　观念，概念，看法

10. diagrammatic [,daiəgrə'mætik]　*adj.* shown or represented by diagrams
　　　　　　　　　　　　　　　图式的

11. demonstrate ['demənstreit]　*vt.* provide evidence for; stand as proof of; show by
　　　　　　　　　　　　　　　one's behavior, attitude, or external attributes
　　　　　　　　　　　　　　　证明，演示

12. intuitive [in'tju:itiv]　　*adj.* resulting from intuition
　　　　　　　　　　　　　　　有直觉力的；凭直觉获知的

13. explicit [iks'plisit]　　*adj.* precisely and clearly expressed or readily observable; leaving nothing to implication
　　　　　　　　　　　　　　　明确的，详述的，明晰的

14. numerical [nju:'merikəl]　*adj.* measured or expressed in numbers
　　　　　　　　　　　　　　　数字的，用数字表示的

15. sole [səul]　　　　　　　*adj.* being the only one; single and isolated from others

　　　　　　　　　　　　唯一的;单独的

16. assume [ə'sjuːm]　　　　*vt.* take to be the case or to be true; accept without proof

　　　　　　　　　　　　假定,设想

17. productivity [prɔdʌk'tiviti]　*n.* (economics) the ratio of the quantity and quality of units produce to the labor per unit of time

　　　　　　　　　　　　生产率,生产能力

18. vary ['vɛəri]　　　　　　*vi.* make or become different in some particular way, without losing one's or its former characteristics or essence; change

　　　　　　　　　　　　变化

19. imply [im'plai]　　　　　*vt.* express or state indirectly

　　　　　　　　　　　　暗示,意味

20. benefit ['benifit]　　　　*vi.* derive a benefit from; profit; gain

　　　　　　　　　　　　得益

21. inferior [in'fiəriə]　　　　*adj.* not as good as sb./sth. else

　　　　　　　　　　　　不如的;较差的

22. suffice [sə'fais]　　　　　*vi.* be sufficient; be adequate either in quality or quantity

　　　　　　　　　　　　足够

23. monetary ['mʌnitəri]　　*adj.* relating to or involving money

　　　　　　　　　　　　货币的,金钱的

24. define [di'fain]　　　　　*vt.* give a definition for the meaning of a word

　　　　　　　　　　　　定义,解释

25. contradict [kɔntrə'dikt]　*vt.* be in contradiction with

　　　　　　　　　　　　与……矛盾, 同……抵触

26. upgrade ['ʌpgreid]　　　*vt.* rate higher; raise in value or esteem

　　　　　　　　　　　　提高,改善

27. version ['vəːʃən]　　　　*n.* a variant form of something; type

　　　　　　　　　　　　版本;形式

28. circumstance ['səːkəmstəns]　*n.* a condition that accompanies or influences some event or activity

　　　　　　　　　　　　环境, 条件, 情况

29. cover ['kʌvə]　　　　　　*vt.* include or deal with

　　　　　　　　　　　　涉及, 包含

30. hence ［hens］   *adv.* therefore, thence, thus

因此，所以

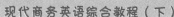

1. date to 追溯到

2. be contrary to 与……相矛盾

3. confuse with 把……和……混淆

4. live on 继续存在；靠……为生

5. vary between 在……之间变化

6. end up with 以……而结束

7. be inferior to 在……之下；次于；不如

8. turn out 结果是……；原来是……

9. all in all 总而言之

10. suffice it to say 只要说……就够了；无须多说；可以肯定地说

1. The theory of comparative advantage is perhaps the most important concept in international trade theory.

译文：比较优势理论也许是国际贸易理论中最重要的概念。The theory of comparative advantage 即比较优势理论，其创始人是大卫·李嘉图（David Ricardo）（1772—1823），他是最有影响力的古典经济学家之一。1817 年他发表了《政治经济学及赋税原理》，集中讨论了国际贸易问题，提出了著名的"比较优势贸易理论"。

2. There is a popular story told amongst economists that once when an economics skeptic asked Paul Samuelson (a Nobel laureate in economics) to provide a meaningful and non-trivial result from the economics discipline, Samuelson quickly responded with "comparative advantage".

译文：经济学家当中有一个众所周知的故事，一次有位经济学怀疑论者请保罗·萨缪尔森（诺贝尔经济学奖得主）就经济学准则提供一个言简意赅的结论，萨缪尔森迅速回应说，"比较优势"。保罗·萨缪尔森（Paul Samuelson）（1915—2009）是第一位获得诺贝尔经济学奖的美国经济学家，他的经典著作《经济学》1948 年首次出版，是全世界最畅销的教科书。本句包含了一个 a popular story 的同位语从句，以 that 引导到句子结束。同位语从句中又有一个 when 引导的时间状语从句，主语从 Paul Samuelson 到句子结束。

3. The original idea of comparative advantage dates to the early part of the 19th century.

译文：比较优势最初的概念可追溯到 19 世纪初。短语 date（back）to 意为"追溯到……"。例：Oxford and Cambridge date back to the thirteenth century. 牛津和剑桥的历史可追溯到 13 世纪。

4. Although the model describing the theory is commonly referred to as the "Ricardian model", the original description of the idea can be found in *An Essay on the External Corn Trade* by Robert Torrens in 1815.

译文：虽然描述该理论的模型通常被称作"李嘉图模型"，但这一观点的原始描述可以在罗伯特·托伦斯 1815 年写的《玉米的外部贸易》一文中找到。本句是主从复合句，由 although 引导让步状语从句，其中 describing the theory 为现在分词短语作 the model 的后置定语。to be referred to as 意为"被称作……"。例：A tax will be referred to as progressive where the tax rate increases as the base increases. 当税基增长，税率亦增长时，这个税就是累进税。

5. David Ricardo formalized the idea using a compelling, yet simple, numerical example in his 1817 book, titled *On the Principles of Political Economy and Taxation*.

译文：1817 年，大卫·李嘉图在他的《政治经济学及赋税原理》一书中，用令人信服且显而易见的数值例子正式确立这一理论。本句为简单句，using 是现在分词短语作谓语 formalized 的方式状语，其中 compelling, numerical 为形容词作 example 的并列定语，yet simple 为插入语。句中 titled... *Taxation* 是过去分词短语作为先行词 book 的非限制性定语。

6. The idea appeared again in James Mill's *Elements of Political Economy* in 1821.

译文：这一概念又一次出现在詹姆斯·穆勒 1821 年所写的《政治经济学的元素》一书中。詹姆斯·穆勒（1773—1836），英国经济学家，在经济学史上占据显著地位。其子约翰·斯图亚特·穆勒也是英国经济学家，通常称其为"老穆勒"，其子为"小穆勒"。

7. Finally, the concept became a key feature of international political economy upon the publication of *Principles of Political Economy* by John Stuart Mill in 1848.

译文：最后，这一概念随着约翰·斯图亚特·穆勒在 1848 年《政治经济学原理》一书的出版而成为国际政治经济的主要特征。约翰·斯图亚特·穆勒（1806—1873），19 世纪英国著名经济学家，詹姆斯·穆勒的长子。

8. First, the principle of comparative advantage is clearly counter-intuitive.

译文：第一，比较优势原则显然是违反直觉的。句中 counter-intuitive 意为"反直觉的"，是复合形容词；counter 为副词时意为"反方向地，对立地"。例：counter-attack 意为"反攻"；counter-strike（CS）意为"反恐（一种网络游戏）"。

9. Many results from the formal model are contrary to simple logic.

译文：从正规的模型看，许多结果是违反简单逻辑的。短语 be contrary to 意为"与……相矛盾；与……相违背"。例：The details in the movie are contrary to the historical facts. 这部影片的细节违背历史事实。

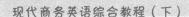

10. Secondly, the theory is easy to confuse with another notion about advantageous trade, known in trade theory as the theory of absolute advantage.

译文：第二,这个理论很容易与另一个赢利贸易方面的概念相混淆,也就是贸易理论中的绝对优势理论。短语 confuse with 意为"把……和……搞混"。例:Don't confuse value with prices. 不要将"价值"和"价格"混同了。I always confuse John with his brother Peter; they are very much alike. 我总是分不清约翰和他的哥哥彼得,他们长得太像了。

11. This confusion between these two concepts leads many people to think that they understand comparative advantage when in fact, what they understand is absolute advantage.

译文：这两个概念之间的混淆导致许多人认为他们了解了比较优势,而事实上他们理解的是绝对优势。本句中 to think that...是不定式短语,其中 that 引导的宾语从句作 to think 的宾语;整个不定式短语是宾语 many people 的宾语补足语。句中 when 意为"然而",是转折连词,连接前后两个并列分句。例:We have only five books when we need ten. 我们只有5本书,可是我们需要10本。

12. The early logic that free trade could be advantageous for countries was based on the concept of absolute advantages in production.

译文：早期的逻辑,即自由贸易对贸易国有利,是基于绝对优势概念这个基础上的。句中 that...for countries 是同位语从句,其先行词为 the early logic。短语 be based on 意为"以……为基础;基于"。例:Judgment should be based on facts instead of hearsay. 判断应该是基于事实,而不是道听途说。Action should be based on solid facts. 行动应有确凿的事实为依据。

13. Adam Smith wrote in *The Wealth of Nations*.

译文：亚当·斯密曾在《国富论》中这样写道。亚当·斯密(1723—1790),经济学鼻祖,他所著的《国民财富的性质和原因的研究》简称《国富论》,是第一本试图阐述欧洲产业和商业发展历史的著作。他在这本书中最早提出了绝对优势理论,发展出了现代的经济学学科,也提供了现代自由贸易、资本主义和自由意志主义的理论基础。

14. "If a foreign country can supply us with a commodity cheaper than we ourselves can make it, better buy it of them with some part of the produce of our own industry, employed in a way in which we have some advantage."

译文："如果另一个国家可以提供给我们比我们自己生产的更便宜的商品,最好的做法就是用我们自己生产的有优势的产品来换取他们的商品。"

15. Indeed some variation of Ricardo's example lives on in most international trade textbooks today.

译文：事实上,今天多数国际贸易教科书中的例子仍然是由李嘉图算例演变而来的。句

中 lives on 意为"继续存在"。例：He's ninety, but still he lives on. 他90岁了,还健在。

16. In his example Ricardo imagined two countries, England and Portugal, producing two goods, cloth and wine, using labor as the sole input in production.

译文：在李嘉图的算例中,假设两个国家——英国和葡萄牙,生产两种商品——布匹和葡萄酒,并且以劳动作为唯一生产投入。本句是个简单句,England and Portugal 是宾语 two countries 的同位语;producing two goods, cloth and wine 为现在分词短语作宾语 two countries 的定语,cloth and wine 是 two goods 的同位语;using labor as... 是现在分词短语,是 producing two goods 的方式状语。

17. He assumed that the productivity of labor (i. e. the quantity of output produced per worker) varied between industries and across countries.

译文：他假定劳动生产率(即每个工人的产出量)在不同行业与不同国家之间各有不同。短语 vary between 意为"在……之间变化"。例：Members in each class vary between 30 and 60. 各班的人数从30人到60人不等。注意区别：vary with 意为"根据……而变化"。例：The menu varies with the season. 菜单随季节而变化。

18. If Portugal is twice as productive in cloth production relative to England but three times as productive in wine, then Portugal's comparative advantage is in wine, the good in which its productivity advantage is greatest.

译文：如果葡萄牙布匹的生产效率是英国的2倍,但葡萄酒的生产效率是英国的3倍,那么,葡萄牙的比较优势在葡萄酒,该产品的生产力优势最大。本句为主从复合句。在 If 引导的条件状语从句中,twice as productive... relative to... (as) 是表示倍数的比较级。倍数的比较级结构为"倍数/half + as much/many + as +被比较方"。例：The price was very reasonable; I would gladly have paid three times as much as he asked. 那个价格很合理的,我愿意出他索要的三倍价钱。句中 then Portugal's... is greatest. 是主句;其中 the good 是 wine 的同位语,in which... 是 the good 的定语从句。

19. This implies that to benefit from specialization and free trade, Portugal should specialize and trade the good in which it is "most best" at producing, while England should specialize and trade the good in which it is "least worse" at producing.

译文：这就意味着各自要从专业化生产和自由贸易中受益,葡萄牙要专门生产并交换的产品应该是生产优势"最最好的",而英国专门生产和贸易的产品应该是生产劣势"最最小的"。本句中 that 引导两个并列宾语从句,while 为转折连词;to benefit... free trade 是不定式短语作目的状语;in which 引导的定语从句限制先行词 the good。

20. If appropriate terms of trade (i. e., amount of one good traded for another) were then chosen, both countries could end up with more of both goods after specialization and free trade than they

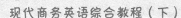

each had before trade.

译文：如果选择一个适当的贸易条件（即，一种产品与另一种产品贸易的数量），然后进行交易，这两个国家最终可能拥有两种产品比专业化生产及自由贸易以前更大的贸易量。本句是主从复合句，If 引导条件状语从句。短语 end up with 意为"结果是……，以……而结束"。例：Someone who sells short the shares may end up with very substantial losses if the price rises by a large amount. 要是价格大幅度上升，卖空股票的人士可能会蒙受巨大亏损。We had a banquet, which end up with soup. 我们举行了一个宴会，最后一道菜是汤。

21. This means that England may nevertheless benefit from free trade even though it is assumed to be technologically inferior to Portugal in the production of everything.

译文：这意味着英国仍可从自由贸易中受益，即使英国两种产品的生产技术都不如葡萄牙。本句为主从复合句，even though 引导让步状语从句。短语 be inferior to 意为"在……之下；次于；不如"。例：Actual products are inferior to the sample. 实际产品比样品差。I would not wish to be inferior to others. 我不希望自己比别人差。

22. All in all, this condition is rather confusing.

译文：总的说来，这种情况是相当令人费解的。all in all 意为"总的说来"。例：He has his faults, but, all in all, he is a good helper. 他虽有缺点，但总的说来，他是一个好帮手。All in all, it was a great success. 总之，那是很大的成功。

23. Suffice it to say, that it is quite possible, indeed likely, that although England may be less productive in producing both goods relative to Portugal, it will nonetheless have a comparative advantage in the production of one of the two goods.

译文：可以肯定地说，虽然英国相对于葡萄牙可能两种商品的生产效率都不高，但就两种商品其中之一它是具有比较优势的，这是相当有可能的，也的确有可能。句子中 that it is quite possible, indeed likely 均为插入语，表示肯定的语气。Suffice（it）to say（that）... 意为"只要说……就够了；可以肯定地说；一句话"。例：Suffice it to say that his success will bring his family great hope. 一句话，他的成功将给全家带来巨大的希望。

24. As it turned out, specialization in any good would not suffice to guarantee the improvement in world output.

译文：实际结果表明，任何商品的专业化生产都不足以保证世界商品产量的提高。As 在此是关系代词，引导一个非限制性定语从句。例：She opposed the idea, as could be expected. 正如所预料到的，她反对这个意见。As you know, Betty is leaving soon. 你是知道的，贝蒂马上要离开了。短语 turn out 意为"结果是……，证明是……；原来是……"。例：Contrary to our expectation, the examination turned out to be a piece of cake. 出乎我们预料的是，这次考试容易极了。suffice to do sth. 意为"足够做某事"。例：One example will suffice to illustrate the point. 举

一个例子就足以说明这一点。

25. Only one of the goods would work.

译文：只有其中一种商品可以做到这点。句中 work 意为"起作用；产生影响"。例：The medicine worked. 药物奏效了。

26. Note that the trade based on comparative advantage does not contradict Adam Smith's notion of advantageous trade based on absolute advantage.

译文：需要指出的是，基于比较优势的贸易理论与亚当·斯密的赢利贸易基础上的绝对优势概念并不矛盾。句中 contradict 意为"与……发生矛盾，与……抵触"。例：They contradict each other all the time. 他们总是相互抵触。The facts contradict his theory. 那些事实与他的理论相悖。

Exercise

I. Text comprehension questions.

1. What is a brief description for comparative advantage?

_____

_____

2. When did the original idea of comparative advantage appear?

_____

_____

3. Who established the theory of comparative advantage?

_____

_____

4. Why is it said that the theory of comparative advantage is one of the most commonly misunderstood principles?

_____

_____

5. What is the relationship between Adam Smith's absolute advantage notion and David Ricardo's theory of comparative advantage?

Ⅱ. **Decide whether each of the following statements is true（T）or false（F）or not mentioned（NM）in the text.**

1. Paul Samuelson was a great American economist who formalized the theory of comparative advantage.

2. The original description of the idea of comparative advantage can be found in *An Essay on the External Corn Trade* by Robert Torrens.

3. *The Wealth of Nations* was written by Adam Smith.

4. The best way of presenting the idea of absolute advantage seems to be with an explicit numerical example as provided by David Ricardo.

5. In his example Ricardo imagined two countries, England and Australia producing two goods, wool and cloth, using labor as the sole input in production.

6. To identify a country's comparative advantage product requires a comparison of production costs across countries.

7. Although England may be less productive in producing both goods（cloth and wine）relative to Portugal, it will nonetheless have a comparative advantage in the production of one of the two goods.

8. The core content of the theory of comparative advantage is to choose the greater of two advantages and to choose the lesser of two disadvantages.

Ⅲ. **Choose the best answer to each question with the information from the text.**

1. Who was awarded the Nobel Prize in Economics according to the passage?

A. David Ricardo.　　B. Paul Samuelson.　　C. Adam Smith.　　D. James Mill.

2. Which statement is FALSE according to the passage?

A. The idea of comparative advantage is not immediately intuitive.

B. The logic behind absolute advantage is quite intuitive.

C. The theory of absolute advantage is often presented in its mathematical form.

D. There is some confusion between the concepts of comparative advantage and absolute advantage.

3. Which statement is TRUE in Ricardo's example?

A. Portugal's comparative advantage is in cloth.

B. England's comparative advantage is in wine.

C. Both Portugal and England could benefit from specialization and free trade.

D. England may not benefit from free trade since it is technologically inferior to Portugal in the production of everything.

4. To identify a country's comparative advantage good requires a comparison of _____ across countries.

A. the monetary costs of production

B. the resource costs of production

C. the opportunity costs of production

D. all the costs above

5. Advantageous trade _____ .

A. is based on the principle of comparative advantage

B. is based on the principle of absolute advantage

C. does not include any case of absolute advantage

D. can only exist in the two countries, England and Portugal

IV. Choose the word or phrase that is closest in meaning to the underlined one.

1. The agreement will <u>formalize</u> a longstanding commitment (义务;承诺).

A. make something to be a form   B. make something to be former

C. make something to be formal   D. make a form for something

2. The lease is <u>explicit</u> in saying the rent must be paid by the end of every month.

A. implicit   B. overt   C. distinct   D. vague

3. We can <u>define</u> the core content of the theory of comparative advantage as choosing the greater of two advantages and choosing the lesser of two evils.

A. give a definite explanation   B. refine

C. give a defective explanation   D. deflect

4. An assembly line was imported to enhance <u>productivity</u>.

A. productive force   B. the quantity of production

C. the efficiency of production   D. the quality of production

5. Advantageous trade can occur between countries <u>assuming</u> the countries differ in their technological abilities to produce goods and services according to Ricardian Model of Comparative Advantage.

A. whether   B. though   C. although   D. if

6. The prices of some goods <u>vary</u> with the season.

A. change   B. adjust   C. shift   D. adapt

7. The <u>inferior</u> handicrafts are now in transit.

A. humble rank   B. bad name   C. low quality   D. small size

8. "Every man has his gift." <u>implies</u> that every person may have his or her comparative advantage in a certain aspect.

A. includes   B. signals   C. points   D. indicates

9. Their behavior seriously <u>contradicts</u> international trade practices.

A. is in contradiction with   B. is compatible with

C. is in accordance with   D. cooperates with

10. If you cannot send me the sample with a quotation of prices, a fax copy will <u>suffice</u> right now.

A. be superficial   B. be sufficient   C. be superfluous   D. be satisfactory

11. I have <u>upgraded</u> my computer so I can run better software.

A. promoted   B. increased   C. improved   D. raised

12. Developing countries have continuously enhanced their economic strength, <u>hence</u> raising their international status.

A. from then on   B. from now on   C. therefore   D. in the future

V. Fill in the blanks with the phrases and expressions from the text. Change forms where necessary.

> be inferior to   vary between   be contrary to   suffice it to say   turn out

1. Any party whose acting _____ the contract should be legally responsible for all the possible losses.

2. The cost of transaction usually _____ the purchase price and sale price of the bond（债券）.

3. He told us a lot of local customs in Tibet. It _____ that he was never there.

4. Most teenagers consider that traditional games _____ computer games.

5. _____ that the 29th Olympics in Beijing was a great success.

VI. Match the words with their definitions.

1. a person honored with an award for art or science

2. therefore, thus

3. give a definition for the meaning of a word or a concept, etc.

4. of little importance; ordinary

5. to raise in value, importance, esteem, etc.

6. to express or indicate by a hint; suggest

7. someone who habitually doubts accepted beliefs; doubter

8. make formal or official

9. precisely and clearly expressed, leaving nothing to implication

10. of or relating to money or currency

(   ) skeptic   (   ) explicit   (   ) trivial

(   ) upgrade   (   ) laureate   (   ) formalize

(   ) hence   (   ) define   (   ) imply   (   ) monetary

VII. Translate the following sentences into English.

1. 大卫·李嘉图的比较优势理论与亚当·斯密的绝对优势概念并不矛盾。(be contrary to)

_____

_____

2. 发展中国家的劳动生产率普遍比发达国家的要低。(be inferior to)

_____

_____

3. 对两种优势产品实行专业化生产和自由贸易以后，两个国家的两种产品的产量及贸易量较之以前大大地增加了。(end up with)

_____

_____

4. 李嘉图的数值算例今天在大多数国际贸易教科书中仍然发挥着作用。(live on)

_____

_____

5. 一句话，绝对优势理论与相对优势理论是对外贸易中的两个重要理论。(suffice it to say)

_____

_____

VIII. Oral exercises.

Students in groups of two will make conversations about the theory of comparative advantage. In the conversation practice, some sentence patterns will be used. In this unit, students will use the following two sentence patterns:

In my opinion/view...   我认为……

It is wrong to...   ……是不对的

Please follow example (1) and complete the following dialogue exercises. Student A and B will exchange roles upon completion.

For example (1):

Student A: <u>In my opinion</u>, the concept of comparative advantage is very useful in every aspect of life.

Student B: I agree with you (or That seems too absolute).

Student A: <u>In my opinion</u>, (Adam Smith, David Ricardo, Robert Torrens, James Mill, Paul Samuelson) contributed really a lot to the development of international trade.

Student B: You are absolutely right.

Please follow example (2) and complete the following dialogue exercises. Student A and B will exchange roles upon completion.

For example (2):

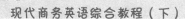

Student A：It is wrong to think that Ricardo's theory is contrary to Adam Smith's theory.

Student B：You are quite right.

Student A：It is wrong to think that the reason for advantageous trade only includes（differences in technology, differences in resource endowments, differences in demand）.

Student B：You are absolutely right.

IX. **Writing skills. Please look at the pictures, the words and phrases coming from the pictures in relation to the concept of comparative advantage below. And then write 3 – 5 sentences to describe each of the pictures.**

The expressions in the brackets may help you to start your writing.

（*First, let's look at the picture in the top left corner; There is/are ... in the picture; They are... ; The man on the left is... ; Then let's look at the next picture in the upper right corner; This picture is about... ; The lady on the right... ; Others are... ; The picture in the center is... ; The picture suggests that... ; The picture in the bottom left corner shows two men... ; From their facial expressions, we can figure out that... ; Lastly, look at the picture in the bottom right corner; The lady in the picture may be a... ; She is... ; Therefore, ... see the advantages and disadvantages*）

Picture 1 (group discussion, general manager, assistants, sales program)

Picture 2 (output analysis, president, project managers, the advantageous product)

Picture 3 (two CEOs, shake hands, agreement, cooperate in trade, both benefit)

Picture 4 (stock expert, compare with line graphs, ups and downs, advantages, disadvantages)

Picture 5 (globe, money, international trade, benefit)

X. PPT presentation. Two students in a group will work together to prepare 4 –5 pages of PPT slides to be presented in class. The topic for this unit is about what are some of the traditional Chinese goods for export; what are the comparative advantages they used to have; in today's world market, what are challenges they are meeting. You may choose one of the products to explain(for example: tea, silk, chinaware).

Further Reading One: Reasons for Trade

The first theory section of this course contains explanations or reasons that trade takes place(发生) between countries. The five basic reasons why trade may take place between countries are summarized(总结) below. A variety of(各种各样的) models(模型) are described, which offer a reason for trade and the expected effects(预期的影响) of trade on prices, profits, incomes and individual welfare(个人福利).

Differences in Technology. Advantageous trade can occur(发生) between countries if the countries differ in(在……不同) their technological abilities to produce goods and services. Technology(技术) refers to(指的是) the techniques(技能) used to turn resources(labor, capital, land) into outputs. The basis for trade in the Ricardian Model of Comparative Advantage is differences in technology.

Differences in Resource Endowments(资源禀赋). Advantageous trade can occur between countries if the countries differ in their endowments of resources. Resource endowments refer to the skills and abilities of a country's workforce(劳动力), the natural resources available(现有的) within its borders(国界)(minerals, farmland etc.), and the sophistication(先进程度) of its capital stock(资本存储)(machinery(机械), infrastructure(基础设施), communication systems). The basis for trade in the Pure Exchange model and the Heckscher-Ohlin Model(赫克歇尔－俄林模型) is differences in resource endowments.

Differences in Demand. Advantageous trade can occur between countries if demands or preferences(偏好) differ between countries. Individuals(各个人) in different countries may have different preferences or demands for various products. The Chinese are likely to demand more rice than Americans, even if facing the same price. Canadians may demand more beer, the Dutch(荷兰人) more wooden shoes, and the Japanese more fish than Americans would, even if they all faced the same prices.

Existence of Economies of Scale in Production(生产中规模经济的存在). The existence of economies of scale in production is sufficient to generate(产生) advantageous trade between two countries. Economies of scale refer to a production process(过程) in which production costs fall as the scale of production rises. This feature of production is also known as "increasing returns to scale"(规模报酬递增).

Existence of Government Policies. Government tax and subsidy programs(财政贴息项目) can

be sufficient to generate advantages in production of certain products. In these circumstances, advantageous trade may arise solely due to (由于) differences in government policies across countries.

Exercise

I. Choose the best answer to each question with the information from the text.

1. How many basic reasons are there for advantageous trade according to the passage?

A. Five.   B. Four.   C. Less than five.   D. More than five.

2. What is the basis for trade in the Ricardian Model of Comparative Advantage?

A. Differences in Demand.   B. Differences in Technology.

C. Existence of Government Policies.   D. Differences in Resource Endowments.

3. What is the basis for trade in the Pure Exchange Model and Heckscher-Ohlin Model?

A. Differences in Demand.   B. Differences in Resource Endowments.

C. Differences in Technology.   D. Existence of Economies of Scale in Production.

4. What demand preference may the Chinese have even if facing the same price?

A. Fish.   B. Beer.   C. Rice.   D. Wooden shoes.

5. What does the term "increasing returns to scale " mean?

A. It means that the scale of production falls as production costs rise.

B. It means that the resource costs fall as the output rises.

C. It means that production costs fall as the scale of production rises.

D. It means that the opportunity costs rise as the monetary costs fall.

II. Decide whether each of the following statements is true (T) or false (F).

1. Advantageous trade may happen between countries if the countries are different in their technological abilities to produce goods and services.

2. Resource endowments refer to the natural resources available within its borders.

3. The basis for the Ricardian Model is differences in resource endowments.

4. Even if facing the same prices, Canadians may demand more beer than Americans.

5. Advantageous trade may occur due to differences in government policies across countries.

Further Reading Two: International Trade and Investment

In order to understand international business, it is necessary to have a broad conceptual understanding of why trade and investment (投资) across national borders take place. Trade and investment can be examined in terms of (在……方面) the comparative advantage of nations.

Comparative advantage suggests (表明) that each nation is relatively good at producing certain products or services. This comparative advantage is based on the nation's abundant factors of production (丰富的生产要素)—land, labor, and capital (资本)—and a country will export those products/services that use its abundant factors of production intensively (密集地). Simply, consider on-

ly two factors of production, labor and capital, and two countries, X and Y. If country X has a relative abundance of labor and country Y a relative abundance of capital, country X should export products/services that use labor intensively, country Y should export products/services that use capital intensively.

This is a very simplistic（简单的）explanation, of course. There are many more factors of production, of varying qualities（不同的质量）, and there are many additional（额外的）influences on trade such as government regulations（政府的法令法规）. Nevertheless, it is a starting point for understanding what nations are likely to export or import. The concept of comparative advantage can also help explain investment flows（投资流动）. Generally, capital is the most mobile（流动的）of the factors of production and can move relatively easily from one country to another. Other factors of production, such as land and labor, either does not move or are less mobile. The result is that where capital is available（可得到的）in one country it may be used to invest in other countries to take advantage of（利用）their abundant land or labor. Firms may develop expertise（专门技能）and firm specific advantages（独特优势）based initially on abundant resources at home（国内）, but as resource needs change, the stage（阶段）of the product life cycle matures（成熟）, and home markets become saturated（饱和）these firms find it advantageous to invest internationally.

I. Choose the best answer to each question with the information from the text.

1. A nation's factors of production mainly include _____ .

A. labor and capital   B. varying qualities of products

C. land, labor and capital   D. government regulations

2. A country will export the products or services _____ .

A. that use its abundant factors of production intensively

B. that use its abundant factors of production extensively

C. that use its scarce factors of production intensively

D. that use its scarce factors of production extensively

3. Which is the most mobile of the factors of production?

A. Land.   B. Labor.   C. Capital.   D. Product.

4. As resource needs change, the stage of the product life cycle matures, and home markets become saturated, firms find it advantageous to invest _____ .

A. in their own countries   B. in other countries

C. in expertise and specific advantages D. in their home markets

5. What is the best title for this passage?

A. International Business

B. Production Factors

C. The Conceptual Understanding of Comparative Advantage

D. International Trade and Investment Based on the Comparative Advantage of Nations

II. Decide whether each of the following statement is true (T) or false (F).

1. Trade and investment can be examined in terms of the absolute advantage of nations.

2. Only two factors of production, labor and capital, and two countries, X and Y are considered in the passage.

3. If country X has a relative abundance of labor, country X should export products/services that use capital intensively.

4. Capital is the most mobile of the factors of production.

5. If a country has a relative abundance of capital, it may invest in other countries to take advantage of their abundant land or labor.

现代商务英语综合教程（下）

Unit Two   World Trade Organization

Contents in This Unit

1. Two pre-reading discussion questions.
2. A text on World Trade Organization.
3. New words and expressions.
4. Explanatory notes for the text.
5. Some exercises to build your skills both in English and business.
6. A PPT hands-on assignment to give you space for creation.
7. Further readings on the World Trade Organization.

Pre-reading Discussions for the Text

Please discuss these questions in pairs. You may talk over the topics either in English or in Chinese according to your teacher's instruction.

1. Do you think there should be an international organization to control or guide world trade? Why?

_____

_____

_____

2. Can you name some regional trade organizations?

_____

_____

_____

Text: What Is the World Trade Organization?

Simply put it, the World Trade Organization (WTO) deals with the rules of trade between nations at a global or near-global level. But there is more to it than that. There are a number of ways of

looking at the WTO. It's an organization for liberalizing trade. It's a forum for governments to negotiate trade agreements. It's a place for them to settle trade disputes. It operates a system of trade rules. But it's not Superman, just in case anyone thought it could solve — or cause — all the world's problems!

Above all, it's a negotiating forum. Essentially, the WTO is a place where member governments go, to try to sort out the trade problems they face with each other. The first step is to talk. The WTO was born out of negotiations, and everything the WTO does is the result of negotiations. The bulk of the WTO's current work comes from the 1986 – 1994 negotiations called the Uruguay Round and earlier negotiations under the *General Agreement on Tariffs and Trade* (GATT). The WTO is currently the host to new negotiations, under the "Doha Development Agenda" launched in 2001. Where countries have faced

trade barriers and wanted them lowered, the negotiations have helped to liberalize trade. But the WTO is not just about liberalizing trade, and in some circumstances its rules support maintaining trade barriers—for example to protect consumers or prevent the spread of disease. It's a set of rules. At its heart are the WTO agreements, negotiated and signed by the bulk of the world's trading nations. These documents provide the legal ground-rules for international commerce. They are essentially contracts, binding governments to keep their trade policies within agreed limits. Although negotiated and signed by governments, the goal is to help producers of goods and services, exporters, and importers conduct their business, while allowing governments to meet social and environmental objectives. The system's overriding purpose is to help trade flow as freely as possible—so long as there are no undesirable side-effects—because this is important for economic development and well-being. That partly means removing obstacles. It also means ensuring that individuals, companies and governments know what the trade rules are around the world, and giving them the confidence that there will be no sudden changes of policy. In other words, the rules have to be "transparent" and predictable. And it helps to settle disputes. This is the third important side of the WTO's work. Trade relations often involve conflicting interests. Agreements, including those painstakingly negotiated in the WTO system, often need interpreting. The most harmonious way to settle these differences is through some neutral procedure based on an agreed legal foundation. That is the purpose behind the dispute settlement process written into the WTO agreements.

The WTO began life on 1 January 1995, but its trading system is half a century older. Since 1948, the *General Agreement on Tariffs and Trade* had provided the rules for the system. The second WTO ministerial meeting, held in Geneva in May 1998, included a celebration of the 50th anniversary of the system. It did not take long for the *General Agreement on Tariffs and Trade* to give birth to an unofficial, de facto international organization, also known informally as GATT. Over the years GATT evolved through several rounds of negotiations. The last and largest GATT round, was the Uru-

guay Round which lasted from 1986 to 1994 and led to the WTO's creation. Whereas GATT had mainly dealt with trade in goods, the WTO and its agreements now cover trade in services, and in traded inventions, creations, designs and intellectual property.

 *Vocabulary*

1. organization [,ɔːgənaiˈzeiʃən]
   n. a body of administrative officials, as of a political party, a government department, etc.
   组织；机构

2. global [ˈgləubəl]
   adj. covering, influencing, or relating to the whole world
   全球的，全世界的

3. negotiate [niˈgəuʃieit]
   v. to work or talk (with others) to achieve (a transaction, an agreement, etc.)
   谈判；协商；商定

4. negotiation [ni,gəuʃiˈeiʃən]
   n. the act or process of negotiating
   协商，谈判，磋商

5. agreement [əˈgriːmənt]
   n. a settlement, esp. one that is legally enforceable; covenant; treaty
   协定，协议，契约

6. essentially [iˈsenʃəli]
   adv. in a fundamental or basic way; in essence
   本质上；根本上，基本上

7. Uruguay [ˈurugwai]
   n. a republic in South America, on the Atlantic
   乌拉圭（国家名,位于南美洲）

8. tariff [ˈtærif]
   n. a tax levied by a government on imports or occasionally exports for purposes of protection, support of the balance of payments, or the raising of revenue,a system or list of such taxes
   关税，关税表

9. agenda [əˈdʒendə]
   n. also called agendum, a schedule or list of items to be attended to
   议事日程,(会议的)议程表

10. launch [lɔːntʃ]
    v. to start off or set in motion,to put (a new product) on the market
    开始从事,发起,发动

11. barrier [ˈbæriə]
    n. anything that prevents or obstructs passage, or progress
    障碍，隔阂

12. bulk [bʌlk]
    n. volume, size, or magnitude, esp. when great; the main part

主体,绝大部分

13. environmental [in,vaiərən'mentəl] *adj.* of or relating to the external conditions or surroundings

环境的

14. overriding [,əuvə'raidiŋ] *adj.* taking precedence

最重要的;高于一切的

15. obstacle ['ɔbstəkl] *n.* a person or thing that opposes or hinders something

障碍(物),妨碍

16. transparent [træns'perənt] *adj.* easy to see through, understand, or recognize; obvious

透明的,含义清楚的

17. predictable [pri'diktəbl] *adj.* possible to foretell

可预言(预报)的,可预见的

18. conflicting [kən'fliktiŋ] *adj.* clashing; contradictory

相矛盾的;冲突的

19. painstakingly ['peinz,teikiŋli] *adv.* in a fastidious and painstaking manner

刻苦地;煞费苦心地

20. harmonious [hɑ:'məunjəs] *adj.* having agreement or consensus

和谐的;协调的

21. ministerial [,minis'tiriəl] *adj.* of or relating to a government minister or ministry

部长的,大臣的,公使的

22. celebration [,seli'breiʃən] *n.* a joyful occasion for special festivities to mark, some happy event

庆祝;庆祝会(仪式)

23. anniversary [,æni'və:səri] *n.* the date on which an event occurred in some previous year

周年纪念,周年纪念日

24. de facto [di:'fæktəu] *adj.* in fact

实际上存在的

25. intellectual [,inti'lektjuəl] *adj.* of or relating to the intellect, as opposed to the emotions

需用智力的;用脑力的

26. property ['prɔpəti] *n.* something of value, either tangible, such as land, or intangible, such as patents, copyrights, etc.

所有权;版权

1. deal with 　讨论，处理，涉及，对付

2. at a global level 　在世界级别上，在全球一级上

3. in case 　假使，以防（万一），以免

4. above all 　首先，尤其是，最重要的是

5. sort out 　整理；弄清楚，解决

6. in some circumstances 　在某些情况下

7. within agreed limits 　在商定的范围内

8. conflicting interests 　利益冲突

9. give birth to 　生（孩子），产生

10. intellectual property 　知识产权

Notes for Text

1. Simply put it, the World Trade Organization (WTO) deals with the rules of trade between nations at a global or near-global level.

译文：简单地说，世界贸易组织（WTO）涉及全球或将近全球国家之间的贸易规则。Simply put it 是 to put it simply 的另一种表达法，意为"简而言之"或"简单地说"。其中 put 在这句话中的意为"当……说"。例：口语中有句话是"Let me put it this way"，意为"让我们这样来说吧"，此句中的 put 与上句中的 put 意思是一样的。

2. Essentially, the WTO is a place where member governments go, to try to sort out the trade problems they face with each other.

译文：从本质上讲，世贸组织是一个场所，各成员国政府来这里试图面对面地理清它们之间的贸易问题。本句中 they face with each other 是定语从句，修饰先行词 the trade problems，这里省略了引导词 that，因为它在定语从句中作宾语。essentially 意为"本质上；基本上"，在本句中是一个插入语。短语 sort out 意为"整理；弄清楚"。

3. The WTO is currently the host to new negotiations, under the "Doha Development Agenda" launched in 2001.

译文：根据 2001 年发起的"多哈发展议程"，世贸组织现在是新谈判的主办机构。句中 host 为名词，意为"主人，东道主，主办方（机构；组织）"。be/play host to sb. 意为"（作为主人）招待或款待某人"。例：The college is (playing) host to a group of visiting Russian scientists. 这所学院接待了一批来访的俄罗斯科学家。

4. But the WTO is not just about liberalizing trade, and in some circumstances its rules support maintaining trade barriers — for example to protect consumers or prevent the spread of disease.

译文：但是世贸组织不只是让贸易自由化，在某些情况下它的规则支持维护贸易壁垒——例如，保护消费者或防止疾病的蔓延。本句中 support 是及物动词，后跟动名词短语 maintaining trade barriers 作它的宾语。例：The majority of Americans support sending troops into the region. 多数美国人支持向该地区派遣军队。

5. They are essentially contracts, binding governments to keep their trade policies within agreed limits.

译文：它们基本上是契约合同，用来约束各成员政府，使他们的贸易政策保持在各方议定且符合各方利益的限度之内。本句中 binding governments to... 是现在分词短语作定语，修饰 contracts。

6. Although negotiated and signed by governments, the goal is to help producers of goods and services, exporters, and importers conduct their business, while allowing governments to meet social and environmental objectives.

译文：虽然这些文件的谈判和签署属于政府行为，但是其宗旨是帮助商品生产者、从事服务业劳动者、出口商及进口商开展业务，与此同时政府也实现了社会和环境方面的目标。本句中 Although 引导的状语从句是一个省略结构，省略了 they/these documents are，主句主语 the goal 指 the goal of these documents；现在分词短语 allowing governments... 中的逻辑主语也是 they 或 these documents。

7. The system's overriding purpose is to help trade flow as freely as possible — so long as there are no undesirable side-effects.

译文：该体系的首要目的是帮助贸易尽可能自由地流动——只要没有不良的副作用。短语 so long as 意为"只要"，本句中 so long as there are no undesirable side-effects 作让步状语从句。

8. That partly means removing obstacles.

译文：这在某种程度上也意味着消除障碍。句中 mean 意为"意味着"，后接动名词短语。例：To a certain extent, to raise wages means increasing purchasing power. 在一定程度上，提高工资意味着增加购买力。

9. Trade relations often involve conflicting interests.

译文：贸易关系常常涉及利益冲突。句中 involve 为及物动词，意为"包含，使卷入，牵涉"。例：Painting the room involved moving out the piano. 粉刷房间就要把钢琴搬出去。

10. The last and largest GATT round, was the Uruguay Round which lasted from 1986 to 1994 and led to the WTO's creation.

译文：关贸总协定最后一轮也是规模最大的一轮谈判是从 1986 年至 1994 年的乌拉圭回合，它促成了世界贸易组织的创建。本句中 The last and largest GATT round 是句子的主语，which lasted from 1986 to 1994 是定语从句，修饰表语 the Uruguay Round。

Exercise

I. Text comprehension questions.

1. What does the World Trade Organization deal with in brief?

2. What are the main functions of the WTO?

3. What is the most important goal of the WTO system?

4. What is the most harmonious way to settle disputes between member countries?

5. How does GATT differ from the WTO?

II. Decide whether each of the following statements is true (T) or false (F) or not mentioned (NM) in the text.

1. The World Trade Organization (WTO) is the only international body dealing with the rules of trade between nations.

2. All that the WTO does is the result of negotiations conducted among member countries.

3. The WTO is just about liberalizing trade.

4. The WTO agreements are a set of rules that lay the foundation for international commerce.

5. The rules that the WTO deals with ought to be clear, unambiguous, and easy to follow.

6. There shouldn't be changes of policy for the WTO system.

7. Lowering trade barriers is one of the most obvious means of encouraging trade.

8. The WTO and the GATT have different trading systems and are dealing with different world trade problems nowadays.

III. Choose the best answer to each question with the information from the text.

1. Which of the following statements about the WTO is FALSE?

A. The WTO is an organization for liberalizing trade.

B. The WTO tells government how to conduct their trade problems.

C. The WTO is a place for governments to settle their trade disputes.

D. The WTO is a forum for governments to negotiate trade agreement.

2. What functions do the contracts serve?

A. Binding governments to keep their trade polices within agreed limits.

B. Helping traders to conduct their business.

C. Allowing governments to meet social and environmental objectives.

D. A, B and C.

3. Which of the following statements is NOT what the liberalizing trade involves?

A. Ensuring individuals, companies and governments know what the trade rules are around the world.

B. Removing obstacles.

C. Causing conflicting interests.

D. Giving individuals, companies and governments confidence that there will be sudden changes of policy.

4. How are the WTO agreements negotiated and signed ?

A. By its member governments.   B. In the WTO system.

C. A and B.   D. By most of the world's trading companies.

5. Which of the following statements related to the WTO is TRUE?

A. The WTO came into being just after Uruguay Round negotiations (1986 – 1994).

B. Freer trades are more important than other principles of the WTO system.

C. The WTO tells governments how to encourage their national trade and commerce.

D. Small countries are powerless in the WTO.

IV. Choose the word or phrase that is closest in meaning to the underlined one.

1. It was transparent that her pride was hurt.

A. true   B. serious   C. obvious   D. easy

2. Ballet is essentially a middle-class interest.

A. basically   B. specially   C. particularly   D. mainly

3. Finally the two sides have reached an agreement.

A. achievement   B. arrangement   C. solution   D. belief

4. On a global scale, AIDS may well become the leading cause of infant death.

A. worldwide   B. earthly   C. large   D. worldly

5. She painstakingly explained how the machine worked.

A. heatedly   B. carefully   C. hardly   D. seriously

6. I wouldn't have expected to find you in such comfortable circumstances.

A. surrounding   B. situation   C. environment   D. circles

7. The police have launched an investigation into the incident.

A. started   B. conducted   C. sent   D. made

8. He had the intellectual capacity of a three-year-old.

A. academic   B. knowledgeable   C. mental   D. mindful

9. The jury heard conflicting evidence from three different witnesses.

A. disliking   B. confronting   C. arguing   D. contradictory

10. Their overriding aim was to keep costs low.

A. chief   B. only   C. solely   D. whole

11. It now seems unlikely that it will be possible to negotiate a peaceful settlement of the conflict.

A. involvement   B. agreement   C. end   D. condition

12. Mankind has been trying every means to maintain the balance of nature.

A. lose   B. support   C. provide   D. keep

V. Fill in the blanks with the phrases and expressions from the text. Change forms where necessary.

> deal with   in case   sort out   be a/the host to   above all

1. Never waste anything, but _____ never waste time.

2. They then moved on to _____ the agenda point by point.

3. _____ the 2010 World Expo, Shanghai is busy preparing for the big event.

4. You need a professional to _____ your finances.

5. Leave a message for him _____ he forgets to return the files to the secretary.

VI. Match the words with their definitions.

1. the activity of buying and selling goods and services

2. characterized by visibility or accessibility of information especially concerning business practices

3. relating to the natural world and the effect that human activity has on it

4. relating to the ideas and ways of thinking that are developed by intelligent people in a society

5. an argument or a disagreement between two people, groups or countries; discussion about a subject where there is disagreement

6. a party or special event at which you celebrate something such as a birthday or a religious holiday

7. in a way that shows you have taken a lot of care or made a lot of effort

8. something that prevents people from communicating, working together, etc.

9. (of relationships, etc.) friendly, peaceful and without any disagreement

10. to make certain that something happens or is done

(　　) environmental　　(　　) harmonious　　(　　) painstakingly

(　　) celebration　　(　　) ensure　　(　·　) barrier

(　　) dispute　　(　　) trade　　(　　) intellectual　　(　　) transparent

VII. Translate the following sentences into English.

1. 如果我回来前他就到了,请叫他等我。(in case)

_____

_____

2. 你可有限度地信任她。(within limits)

_____

_____

3. 设身处地替他想想,在那种情况下,你还能怎样做?(in the circumstances)

_____

_____

4. 只要你不提他的伤心事,他是没有什么的。(so long as)

_____

_____

5. 简的妈妈刚刚生了一对双胞胎。(give birth to)

_____

_____

VIII. Oral exercises.

Students in groups of two will make conversations about the World Trade Organization. In the conversation practice, some sentence patterns will be used. In this unit, students will use the following two sentence patterns:

Personally, I think /believe /feel...　　我个人认为/相信/感觉……

You are (not) allowed to...　　(不)允许你……

According to...　　依照/根据……

Please follow example (1) and complete the following dialogue exercises. Student A and B will exchange roles upon completion.

For example (1):

> Student A：<u>Personally，I think</u> the WTO is the only international organization dealing with the rules of trade between nations.
>
> Student B：There is more to it than that.
>
> Student A：<u>Personally，I think</u> the WTO is (a forum for governments to negotiate trade agreements，a place to settle trade disputes，an organization for liberalizing trade，a system of trade rules).
>
> Student B：There is more to it than that.

Please follow example (2) and complete the following dialogue exercises. Student A and B will exchange roles upon completion.

For example (2)：

> Student A：<u>You are not allowed to</u> hurt the trade interests of other countries <u>according to</u> the WTO rules.
>
> Student B：Yes，that's right.
>
> Student A：<u>You are not allowed to</u> (go against the WTO agreements，have sudden changes of trade policy，cause any undesirable side-effects to the world trade) <u>according to</u> rules of the WTO system.
>
> Student B：Quite right.

IX. Writing skills. Please look at the pictures，the words and phrases coming from the pictures in relation to the World Trade Organization below. And then write 3 – 5 sentences to describe each of the pictures.

The expressions in the brackets may help you to start your writing.

(*There is/are . . . in the picture*; *In the middle of the picture*; *Then let's look at the next picture*; *This picture is about. . .* ; *The person on the right. . .* ; *From the picture*, *you can see. . .* ; *The central focus of this picture is. . .* ; *In the top left corner /bottom right corner of the picture*, *a man/woman/boy/girl. . .* ; *From her/his facial expression*, *I can assume that. . .* ; *From the. . .* , *I can tell that. . .* ; *Perhaps this man is about to. . .*)

Picture 1 (China's accession to the WTO, signing ceremony, the Representative of China)

_____
_____
_____

Picture 2 (light truck tyres, 2009, trade dispute, the United States, China)

_____
_____
_____

Picture 3 (a demonstration against the WTO, march, thousands of people)

_____
_____
_____

X. PPT presentation. Two students in a group will work together to prepare 5 – 8 pages of PPT slides to be presented in class. The topic for this unit is about a trip to the WTO.

Further Reading One: World Trade Organization

The World Trade Organization (WTO) is an international organization founded in 1995 to promote global trade in goods, services, and intellectual property. It is the successor to the *General A-*

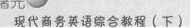
greement on Tariffs and Trade（GATT）, which since 1947 sought to promote international economic growth through the establishment of legally binding rules governing trade between countries. In 1993 GATT held its Uruguay Round negotiations at which it was decided that its final act would further liberalize trade measures and establish a permanent（永久性的）structure, the WTO, to manage international trading procedures and protocols（议定书）. Ministers meeting in Marrakesh, Morocco, in 1994 agreed to the final act. Concurrently（同时地）in Marrakesh, a majority of GATT countries approved the establishment of the WTO. In 1998, 132 countries, including the United States, belonged to the WTO. The WTO provides a framework used by national governments to implement trade legislation and regulations and the WTO provides a forum for collective debate, negotiation, and adjudication of trade disputes. In this regard the WTO has five essential functions: to administer and implement the multilateral（多边的）and plurilateral（多边的）trade agreements that make up the WTO; to provide a forum for trade negotiations; to provide a forum for the resolution of trade disputes; to monitor trade policies of member countries; and to cooperate with other international organizations involved in global trade, commerce, and economic policy making.

Exercise

I. Choose the best answer to each question with the information from the text.

1. When was the World Trade Organization founded?

A. In 1947.　　　　B. In 1993.　　　　C. In 1994.　　　　D. In 1995.

2. How did *General Agreement on Tariffs and Trade*（GATT）seek to promote international economic growth since 1947?

A. Through the establishment of a new world trade organization.

B. Through the establishment of legally binding rules governing trade between countries.

C. Through the negotiation of the trade agreements.

D. Through the abolishment of the trade barriers.

3. At which round negotiation was the WTO decided to be created?

A. *General Agreement on Tariffs and Trade*.

B. Doha round negotiations.

C. Uruguay round negotiations.

D. Tokyo round negotiations.

4. Which of the following functions doesn't the WTO have?

A. To administer and implement the multilateral and plurilateral trade agreements that make up the WTO.

B. To provide a forum for trade negotiations.

C. To provide a forum for the resolution of trade disputes.

D. To dictator trade policies of member countries.

5. What does the WTO provide a forum for?

A. Negotiation.　　　　　　　　　　B. Collective debate.

C. Adjudication of trade disputes.　　　D. A, B and C.

II. Decide whether each of the following statement is true (T) or false (F).

1. *General Agreement on Tariffs and Trade* (GATT) was the predecessor of the WTO.

2. In 1995 GATT held its Uruguay Round negotiations.

3. The GATT provides a framework used by national governments to implement trade legislation and regulations.

4. The WTO provides a forum for collective debate, negotiation, and adjudication of trade agreements.

5. The WTO has a function to cooperate with other international organizations involved in reginal trade, commerce, and economic policy making.

Further Reading Two: Regionalism: Friends or Rivals?

The European Union, the North American Free Trade Agreement, the Association of Southeast Asian Nations, the South Asian Association for Regional Cooperation, the Common Market of the South (MERCOSUR), the Australia-New Zealand Closer Economic Relations Agreement, and so on. By July 2005, only one WTO member—Mongolia—was not party to a regional trade agreement. The surge(激增) in these agreements has continued unabated(不减弱的) since the early 1990s. By July 2005, a total of 330 had been notified(通知) to the WTO (and its predecessor(前身), GATT). Of these: 206 were notified after the WTO was created in January 1995; 180 are currently in force; several others are believed to be operational(运转的) although not yet notified.

One of the most frequently asked questions is whether these regional groups help or hinder(阻碍) the WTO's multilateral trading system. A committee is keeping an eye on developments. Regional trading arrangements(区域贸易安排)—they seem to be contradictory(相矛盾的), but often regional trade agreements can actually support the WTO's multilateral trading system. Regional agreements have allowed groups of countries to negotiate rules and commitments(承诺) that go beyond what was possible at the time multilaterally. In turn, some of these rules have paved the way for agreement in the WTO. Services, intellectual property, environmental standards, investment and competition policies are all issues that were raised in regional negotiations and later developed into agreements or topics of discussion in the WTO. The groupings that are important for the WTO are those that abolish(消除) or reduce barriers on trade within the group. The WTO agreements recognize that regional arrangements and closer economic integration can benefit countries. It also recognizes that under some circumstances regional trading arrangements could hurt the trade interests of other countries. Normally, setting up a customs union or free trade area would violate(违背) the WTO's principle of equal treatment for all trading partners ("most-favoured-nation"). But GATT's Article 24 allows regional trading arrangements to be set up as a special exception(例外), provided(假如) certain strict criteria are met. In particular, the arrangements should help trade flow more freely among the countries in the group without barriers being raised on trade with the outside world. In oth-

er words, regional integration(一体化) should complement(补充) the multilateral trading system and not threaten it. Article 24 says if a free trade area or customs union is created, duties and other trade barriers should be reduced or removed on substantially(基本上) all sectors of trade in the group. Non-members should not find trade with the group any more restrictive than before the group was set up. Similarly, Article 5 of the General Agreement on Trade in Services provides for economic integration agreements in services. Other provisions(条款) in the WTO agreements allow developing countries to enter into regional or global agreements that include the reduction or elimination(消除) of tariffs and non-tariff barriers on trade among themselves.

On 6 February 1996, the WTO General Council created the Regional Trade Agreements Committee. Its purpose is to examine regional groups and to assess whether they are consistent with WTO rules. The committee is also examining how regional arrangements might affect the multilateral trading system, and what the relationship between regional and multilateral arrangements might be.

Exercise

I. Choose the best answer to each question with the information from the text.

1. How many regional trade agreements had been notified to the WTO by July 2005?

A. 180.　　　　　B. 206.　　　　　C. 330.　　　　　D. 386.

2. What is the relationship between the WTO's multilateral trading system and regional trade agreements?

A. Supplementary.　　B. Additional.　　C. Contradictory.　　D. Complementary.

3. Why do regional trade agreements support the WTO's multilateral trading system?

A. They allow groups of countries to negotiate rules and commitments that go beyond what was possible at the time multilaterally.

B. Some of these rules have paved the way for agreement in the WTO.

C. The issues that were raised in regional negotiations were later developed into agreements or topics of discussion in the WTO.

D. A, B and C.

4. How can the regional arrangements complement the multilateral trading system and not threaten it?

A. It should encourage the free trade in the group without raising trade barriers with other countries.

B. It should help trade flow more freely among the countries in the group.

C. It shouldn't hurt the trade interests of other countries.

D. It benefits countries.

5. Which of the following statements is not the purpose of the Regional Trade Agreements Committee?

A. To examine how regional arrangements might affect the multilateral trading system.

B. To examine the reason why a free trade area or customs union is created.

C. To examine what the relationship between regional and multilateral arrangements might be.

D. To examine regional groups and to assess whether they are consistent with WTO rules.

II. Decide whether each of the following statement is true (T) or false (F).

1. The surge in the regional trade agreements has continued unabated since the last decade of the last century.

2. All the duties and other trade barriers should be reduced or removed in the group.

3. Regional trading arrangements could hurt the trade interests of other countries.

4. Non-members would find trade with the group more restrictive than before the group was set up.

5. The WTO agreements don't allow developing countries to enter into regional agreements.

Further Reading Three: WTO Rules: Regional Trade Agreements

WTO rules say regional trade agreements have to meet certain conditions. But interpreting the wording of these rules has proved controversial(有争议的), and has been a central element in the work of the Regional Trade Agreements Committee. As a result, since 1995 the committee has failed to complete its assessments of whether individual trade agreements conform(符合) with WTO provisions. This is now an important challenge, particularly when nearly all member governments are parties to regional agreements, are negotiating them, or are considering negotiating them. In the *Doha Declaration*, members agreed to negotiate a solution, giving due(应有的) regard to the role that these agreements can play in fostering (促进) development.

The declaration mandates(要求) negotiations aimed at "clarifying and improving disciplines and procedures under the existing WTO provisions applying to regional trade agreements. The negotiations shall take into account the developmental aspects of regional trade agreements."

These negotiations fell into the general timetable established for virtually all negotiations under the *Doha Declaration*. The original deadline of 1 January 2005 was missed and the current unofficial aim is to finish the talks by the end of 2006. The 2003 Fifth Ministerial Conference in Mexico was intended to take stock of(对……估价) progress, provide any necessary political guidance, and take decisions as necessary.

Exercise

I. Choose the best answer to each question with the information from the text.

1. What has been a central element in the work of the Regional Trade Agreements Committee?

A. Providing necessary political guidance for member governments.

B. Interpreting the wording of these rules in the regional trade agreements.

C. Improving disciplines and procedures under the existing WTO provisions.

D. Fostering economic development.

2. What has the committee failed to achieve since 1995?

A. To complete its assessments of whether individual trade agreements conform with WTO provisions.

B. To meet certain conditions.

C. To reduce barriers on trade within the group.

D. To help trade flow more freely among the countries in the group.

3. What should be given due to the *Doha Declaration*, agreed by member governments?

A. Free trade.

B. The rules of the WTO system.

C. The role that the regional agreements can play in fostering development.

D. The role of the worldwide agreements.

4. What time was the original deadline of the regional agreements negotiation?

A. At the end of 2006.   B. 1 January 2005.

C. 1 January 2006.   D. 1 January 1995.

5. What was the 2003 Fifth Ministerial Conference in Mexico intended to do?

A. To take stock of progress.   B. To provide any necessary political guidance.

C. To take decisions as necessary.   D. A, B and C.

II. Decide whether each of the following statement is true (T) or false (F).

1. The rules in the regional trade agreements are transparent and uncontroversial.

2. The committee has succeeded to complete its assessments of whether individual trade agreements conform with WTO provisions.

3. All member governments are parties to regional agreements, are negotiating them, or are considering negotiating them.

4. The negotiations shall take into account the developmental aspects of global trade agreements.

5. The current unofficial aim of the regional trade agreements is to finish the talks by the end of 2006.

Unit Three　Marketing

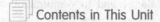 Contents in This Unit

1. Two pre-reading discussion questions.
2. A text on target marketing.
3. New words and expressions.
4. Explanatory notes for the text.
5. Some exercises to build your skills both
   in English and business.
6. A PPT hands-on assignment to give you
   space for creation.
7. Further readings on marketing.

Pre-reading Discussions for the Text

Please discuss these questions in pairs. You may talk over the topics either in English or in Chinese according to your teacher's instruction.

1. Could you list some differences between the concepts of marketing and selling?

_____

_____

_____

2. What is your own definition about a market?

_____

_____

_____

Text: Target Marketing

A target market is a set of buyers sharing common needs or characteristics that a company decides to serve. A company identifies a target market in order to organize its tasks and cope with the particular demands of the marketplace. Target marketing forms the foundation of a modern marketing strategy because doing it well helps a company be more efficient and effective by focusing on a cer-

tain segment of its market that it can best satisfy.

Targeting also benefits consumers because a company can reach specific groups of consumers with offers carefully tailored to satisfy their needs. To do so, a company has to evaluate the various segments and decide how many, and which one, to target. There is no single way to segment a market. A company needs to research different segmentation variables alone, and in combination with others, to find its target market. There are four main variables that can be used in segmenting consumer markets: geographic segmentation, demographic segmentation, psychographic segmentation, and behavioral segmentation.

Geographic segmentation calls for dividing the market into different geographic units, such as nations, regions, states, counties, cities, or neighborhoods. Many companies today are localizing their products—as well as their advertising, promotion, and sales efforts—to fit the needs of individual cities, regions, and neighborhoods. For example, clothing stores sell clothes targeted to their geographic markets. In January, the Gap clothing store sells winter clothing in Portland, Maine, such as mittens, scarves, and winter jackets. A Gap located in Clearwater, Florida, will sell more T-shirts, shorts, and bathing suits.

Demographic segmentation divides the market into groups based on such variables as age, gender, family size, family life cycle, income, occupation, education, religion, race, and nationality. Demographics is the most popular basis for segmenting customer groups because consumer needs, wants, and usage rates often closely reflect demographic variables. Even when a market segment is first defined using other factors, such as psychographic or geographic segmentation, demographic characteristics must be known in order to assess the size of the target market and to reach it efficiently. This information is also the easiest and least expensive to retrieve because it is secondary data; that is, it comes from research that has already been conducted. An example of successful demographic target marketing is that of cosmetic companies that have responded to the special needs of minority market segments by adding products specifically designed for black, Hispanic, or Asian women. For example, Maybelline introduced a highly successful line, called Shades of You, targeted to black women, and other companies have followed with their own lines of multicultural products.

Psychographic segmentation is the process of dividing markets into groups based on values, social class, lifestyle, or personality characteristics. Individuals in the same demographic group may fall into very different psychographic segments. Psychographic segmentation involves qualitative aspects—the "why" component of consumer buying patterns. Therefore, a company must conduct its own research, which can become very time-consuming and expensive. Marketers, however, are increasingly focusing on psychographic characteristics. *Redbook* magazine, for example, targets a lifestyle segment calls "*Redbook* jugglers", defined as 25 to 44-year-old women who must juggle family, husband, and job. According to a *Redbook* ad, "She's the product of the me generation, the thirty-something woman who balances home, family, and career—more than any generation before her, she refuses to put her pleasures aside. She's old enough to know what she wants, and young enough to get it. " According to *Redbook*, this consumer makes an ideal target for marketers of health foods and fitness products. She wears out more exercise shoes, swallows more vitamins, drinks more diet

soda, and works out more often than do consumers in other groups.

Behavioral segmentation divides a market into groups based on consumer knowledge, attitude, use, or response to a product. Many marketers believe that behavior variables are the best starting points for building market segments. Why does one consumer drink Coke, and another Pepsi, and a third iced tea? Demographics and psychographics can provide many clues, but it is often helpful to consider additional factors as well. Individuals act differently depending on their situation or the occasion for using the product. For example, a woman who shops only at discount stores for clothing may nonetheless think nothing of spending $100 on a bathing suit at a specialty shop for her Caribbean vacation. Some holidays, such as Father's Day and Mother's Day, were originally promoted partly to increase the sale of flowers, candy, cards, and other gifts. Many food marketers prepare special offers and ads for holidays. For example, Beatrice Foods runs special Thanksgiving and Christmas ads for Reddi-whip in November and December, months that account for 30 percent of all sales of whipped cream.

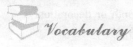 *Vocabulary*

1. characteristic [ˌkæriktə'ristik]
    n. a distinguishing quality, attribute, or trait
    特性，特色

2. identify [ai'dentifai]
    vt. to prove or recognize as being a certain person or thing; determine the identity of
    认出,识别,确定

3. foundation [faun'deiʃən]
    n. that on which something is founded; basis
    建立，设立，创办,创建

4. efficient [i'fiʃənt]
    adj. functioning or producing effectively and with the least waste of effort; competent
    能力的，效率高的

5. tailor ['teilə]
    vt. to adapt so as to make suitable for something specific
    调整,使适应

6. segment ['segmənt]
    n. one of several parts or sections into which an object is divided; portion
    部分, 份, 片, 段

7. segmentation [ˌsegmən'teiʃne]
    n. the act or an instance of dividing into segments
    分割,分隔

8. variable ['vɛəriəbl]
    n. an expression that can be assigned any of a set of values; a symbol, esp. x, y, or z, representing an unspecified member of a class of objects, numbers, etc.
    可变因素,变量

9. combination [ˌkɔmbi'neiʃən]
    n. the act of combining or state of being com-

bined

合作，结合，组合

10. geographic [dʒiə'græfik]   *adj.* of or relating to the science of geography

地理学的；地理的

11. demographic [ˌdemə'græfik]   *adj.* of or relating to demography

人口统计学的

12. psychographic [ˌpsaikəu'græfik]   *adj.* of psychograph

心理记录的

13. mitten ['mitən]   *n.* a glove having one section for the thumb and a single section for the other fingers

连指手套；露指手套

14. scarf [skɑːf]   *n.* a rectangular, triangular, or long narrow piece of cloth worn around the head, neck, or shoulders for warmth or decoration

围巾；披肩；领巾

15. assess [ə'ses]   *vt.* to judge the worth, importance, etc.; evaluate

估价，评定，核定

16. cosmetic [kɔz'metik]   *n.* any preparation applied to the body, esp. the face, with the intention of beautifying it

化妆品

17. retrieve [ri'triːv]   *vt.* get or fetch back again; recover

寻回，恢复，挽回

18. minority [mai'nɔːrəti]   *n.* a group that is different racially, politically, etc., from a larger group of which it is a part

少数，小部分

19. qualitative ['kwɔlitətiv]   *adj.* involving or relating to distinctions based on quality or qualities

定性的，性质（上）的；质量的

20. juggler ['dʒʌglə]   *n.* a person who fraudulently manipulates facts or figures

玩杂耍的人

21. additional [ə'diʃənəl]   *adj.* added or supplementary

增加的，额外的，另外的

Phrase and Expression

1. cope with   与……相适应，对付，应对
2. focus on   以……为焦点；集中于
3. in combination with   与……结合（联合）

4. call for   要求,需要

5. sales efforts   推销工作,销售活动

6. fall into   分成,变成,落入

7. put...aside   把……放在一边;撇开,不予理会

8. work out   锻炼,训练

9. think nothing of   不把……放在心里,轻视

10. account for   解释,说明

Notes for Text

1. A target market is a set of buyers sharing common needs or characteristics that a company decides to serve.

译文:目标市场是指特定的消费者群体。他们有共同的需求和特征,是公司决定要为之服务的对象。本句中 a set of buyers 带有两个定语,一个是 sharing common needs or characteristics 现在分词短语作定语,一个是 that a company decides to serve 定语从句。句中 set 意为"一伙,一群人"。例:I warned her to keep away from that bad set. 我警告过她不要接近那帮坏蛋。

2. A company identifies a target market in order to organize its tasks and cope with the particular demands of the marketplace.

译文:公司确定目标市场,旨在组织工作任务,应对市场的特定要求。短语 cope with 意为"与……相适应;对付;应对"。例:I can't cope with such a pile of work this week. 我本周处理不了这么一大堆工作。

3. Target marketing forms the foundation of a modern marketing strategy because doing it well helps a company be more efficient and effective by focusing on a certain segment of its market that it can best satisfy.

译文:目标市场营销是现代市场营销策略的基础。公司专注于属于它的那份市场份额,最大限度地满足市场,这样把目标市场做好了,公司业务就会更加有效和高效。本句中 doing it well 充当原因状语从句的主语,that it can best satisfy 是一个定语从句,修饰 a certain segment of its market。句中 efficient and effective 意为"有效及高效"。

4. Targeting also benefits consumers because a company can reach specific groups of consumers with offers carefully tailored to satisfy their needs.

译文:市场目标的确定也会让消费者从中受益。因为企业要通过为顾客精心推出各种商品供应,满足他们的各种需求,才可以拥有特定的消费群体。本句中 carefully tailored to satisfy their needs 为过去分词短语作定语修饰 offers,offer 作名词时意为"(待售物品的)供应",tailor 意为"修改,使合适"。例:The clinic tailors its treatment to individual needs. 那个诊所的治疗方法适合个别需要。

5. A company needs to research different segmentation variables alone, and in combination with others, to find its target market.

译文：公司需要对不同的细分变量进行单独调研，然后结合其他变量综合考虑，以便找到自己的目标市场。短语 in combination with 意为"与……结合（联合）"。例：This drug can be safely used in combination with other medicines. 这种药可以安全地与其他药物同时服用。

6. Many companies today are localizing their products—as well as their advertising, promotion, and sales efforts—to fit the needs of individual cities, regions, and neighborhoods.

译文：今天，许多公司正在将他们的产品、广告、促销和销售工作本地化，以适应个别城市、地区和街区的需要。这是一个简单句。动词不定式短语 to fit the needs of individual cities, regions, and neighborhoods 充当目的状语。短语 fit the need of 意为"满足……的需求"；as well as 意为"和……一样；和；也；以及"。例：He went to the party as well as his sister. 他和他妹妹都出席了晚会。He was kind as well as sensible. 他既懂道理又善良。

7. Geographic segmentation calls for dividing the market into different geographic units, such as nations, regions, states, counties, cities, or neighborhoods.

译文：按地理因素细分，就是要将市场分为不同的地理单位，如国家、地区、州、县、市或街区。本句中 call for 后接动名词短语 dividing the market into different geographic units，在这里 call for 意为"要求"。例：The present situation calls for rapid action by the government. 当前的局势需要政府迅速采取措施。

8. Demographics is the most popular basis for segmenting customer groups because consumer needs, wants, and usage rates often closely reflect demographic variables.

译文：人口统计因素是细分消费者群体最常用的重要依据，这是因为消费者的需要、欲望和使用率经常跟人口统计学中的各种变量密切相关。这是一个主从复合句，because 引导一个原因状语从句。

9. This information is also the easiest and least expensive to retrieve because it is secondary data; that is, it comes from research that has already been conducted.

译文：这方面的信息来自以往的调研，因为是间接数据，因此这方面的检索也最容易、最便宜。本句中 that is 是插入语，意为"也就是说；即"，它后面的句子对前面的原因状语从句作出解释。

10. An example of successful demographic target marketing is that of cosmetic companies that have responded to the special needs of minority market segments by adding products specifically designed for black, Hispanic, or Asian women.

译文：化妆品公司就是根据人口统计因素确定目标市场营销的一个成功例子，他们已经对少数群体的特殊需要作出反馈,增加了专门为黑人、西班牙裔或亚洲妇女设计的产品。本句中 that 指代前面出现的同一名词词组,即 successful demographic target marketing。

11. Individuals in the same demographic group may fall into very different psychographic segments.

译文:具有同一人口统计特征的消费者个体还可以按照心理因素的不同来进一步细分市场。短语 fall into 意为"分成,变成,落入"。例:The lecture series falls naturally into three parts. 该系列讲座可自然分三部分。

12. ...she refuses to put her pleasures aside. She's old enough to know what she wants, and young enough to get it.

译文:她拒绝放弃对快乐的追求。她已经长大成人,懂得什么是想要的,同时,她还很年轻,还可得到它。这里 refuse 后跟动词不定式 to put her pleasures aside 充当它的宾语。短语 put...aside 意为"把……放在一边;撇开;不予理会"。例:He put aside his work to spend more time with his son. 他把工作暂时搁下,以便有更多时间陪儿子。And 后是一个省略句,省略了 she's。

13. She wears out more exercise shoes, swallows more vitamins, drinks more diet soda, and works out more often than do consumers in other groups.

译文:她所穿的运动鞋、吃的维生素、喝的汽水饮料、身体接受的体能训练往往要多于其他消费者群体。本句是一个主从复合句,than 引导一个比较状语从句,more often than 后的句型为倒装句,主要使句子前后协调。在 than 引起的比较状语从句中,主谓可以倒装。do 指代主句中的几个并列的谓语动词短语。

14. Demographics and psychographics can provide many clues, but it is often helpful to consider additional factors as well.

译文:人口统计因素和心理因素可以提供很多线索,但是考虑其他因素经常会有所帮助。本句是一个并列句,but 是并列连词,在 but 后的并列子句中 it 充当形式主语,动词不定式短语 to consider additional factors as well 是真正的主语。

15. For example, a woman who shops only at discount stores for clothing may nonetheless think nothing of spending $100 on a bathing suit at a specialty shop for her Caribbean vacation.

译文:例如,对于一个只在服装折扣店购物的妇女来说,为她的加勒比海度假之旅到服装专卖店花上 100 美元买一件游泳衣也算不了什么。短语 think nothing of 意为"不把……放在心里,轻视"。例:They think nothing of piling on our homework or giving surprise quizzes. 他们给我们留一大堆作业,或搞突击测试,对此他们觉得没有什么。

16. For example, Beatrice Foods runs special Thanksgiving and Christmas ads for Reddi-whip in November and December, months that account for 30 percent of all sales of whipped cream.

译文：例如，比哥特丽斯食品公司在 11 月和 12 月份为鲜奶油 Reddi-whip 推出感恩节和圣诞节特别广告，这两个月的销售占全年鲜奶油所有销售收入的百分之三十。本句是一个复合句，that 引导一个定语从句修饰 months，months 充当 November and December 的同位语。短语 account for 意为"解释，对……负责"。例：He has been asked to account for his conduct. 他被要求解释他的行为。

Exercise

I. Text comprehension questions.

1. What is the purpose for a company to identify a target market?

2. What role does target marketing play in modern marketing strategy? Why?

3. How can a company reach specific groups of consumers?

4. What variables can be used in segmenting consumer markets?

5. Which segmentation involves qualitative aspects of consumer buying patterns according to the passage?

II. Decide whether each of the following statements is true (T) or false (F) or not mentioned (NM) in the text.

1. A target market is a place where buyers and sellers decide to go.

2. There is no alternative way to segment a market.

3. Many companies are localizing their products, advertising and sales efforts according to the variables of geographic segmentation.

4. The information of psychographic characteristics is easy to retrieve.

5. Demographic characteristics can help a company to assess the size of a market segment and reach it efficiently.

6. "*Redbook* jugglers" makes an ideal target for marketers of sweet foods and cosmic products.

7. A woman who shops only at discount stores for clothing may nonetheless think much of spending $100 on a bathing suit at a specialty shop for her Caribbean vacation.

8. Individuals act similarly depending on their situation or the occasion for using the product.

III. Choose the best answer to each question with the information from the text.

1. What does a company need to do in order to find its target market?

A. To study different factors alone.

B. To study the different segmentation variables alone and take them into consideration with each others.

C. To consider different variables all together.

D. To study a market segment.

2. What segmentation calls for dividing the market into different geographic units, such as nations, regions, states, counties, cities, or neighborhoods?

A. Geographic.   B. Demographic.   C. Psychographic.   D. Behavioral.

3. Why must demographic characteristics be known even when a market segment is first defined using other factors, such as psychographic or geographic segmentation?

A. To depend on the situation.   B. To assess the size of the target market.

C. To organize the task.   D. To evaluate the qualitative aspects.

4. What do "*Redbook* jugglers" refer to?

A. 13 to 19-year-old girls.

B. 20 to 25-year-old boys.

C. 25 to 44-year-old women who balances home, family, and career.

D. 35 to 50-year-old women who must juggle family, husband, and job.

5. What variables are believed to be the best starting points for building market segments?

A. Nationality.   B. Personality.   C. Behavior.   D. Education.

IV. Choose the word or phrase that is closest in meaning to the underlined one.

1. He was too far away to be able to <u>identify</u> faces.

A. show   B. recognize   C. understand   D. make

2. The account offered by the bank will be <u>tailored</u> exactly to your needs.

A. adopted   B. adapted   C. satisfied   D. cut

3. The insurer will also have to pay the <u>additional</u> costs of the trial.

A. supplementary   B. complementary   C. plenty   D. addictive

4. The men were trying to <u>retrieve</u> weapons left when the army abandoned the island.

A. fire   B. recover   C. turn   D. repair

5. The factory supplies electrical <u>components</u> for cars.

A. sections   B. regions   C. parts   D. individuals

6. The company controls this <u>segment</u> of the market.

A. zone   B. region   C. area   D. section

7. We need someone really <u>efficient</u> who can organize the office and make it run smoothly.

A. effective   B. clever   C. knowledgeable   D. competent

8. He said they were <u>conducting</u> a campaign against democrats across the country.

A. carrying out   B. laying   C. guiding   D. leading

9. There was a <u>promotion</u> in the supermarket and they were giving away free glasses of wine.

A. raise   B. improvement   C. advertising   D. increase

10. Euclid's axioms form the <u>foundation</u> of his system of geometry.

A. establishment   B. base   C. element   D. basement

11. Meanwhile, I am arranging for Mr. Smith, one of our inspectors, to call and <u>assess</u> the damage.

A. examine   B. decide   C. test   D. judge

12. Genes determine the <u>characteristics</u> of every living thing.

A. personalities   B. qualities   C. traits   D. letters

V. Fill in the blanks with the phrases and expressions from the text. Change forms where necessary.

> work out   put aside   account for   fall into   tailor … to
> in combination with   call for   cope with

1. She _____ regularly to keep fit.

2. You have to _____ losing such a large sum of money.

3. We can _____ the program _____ the patient's needs.

4. Our ancestors have to _____ cold, hunger as well as attack from wild animal.

5. The company _____ extreme difficulties due to the economic depression.

6. He _____ his work to spend more time with his son.

7. More work does not necessarily _____ more men.

8. The firm is working on a new product _____ several overseas partners.

VI. Match the words with their definitions.

1. successful, and working in the way that was intended

2. a quality or feature of something or someone that is typical of them and easy to recognize

3. working or operating quickly and effectively in an organized way

4. a part of a population that is different in race, religion, or culture from most of the population
minority

5. relating to the nature or standard of something, rather than to its quantity

6. the dividing of something into parts which are loosely connected

7. extra, and often more than expected

8. to recognize something and understand exactly what it is

9. something that may be different in different situations, so that you cannot be sure what will happen

10. to carefully consider a situation, person, or problem in order to make a judgment

(   ) variable   (   ) efficient   (   ) characteristic

(   ) assess   (   ) identify   (   ) qualitative

(   ) minority   (   ) additional   (   ) effective   (   ) segmentation

VII. Translate the following sentences into English.

1. 财务负责人必须说明交给他的钱是怎样用的。(account for)

_____

2. 尽管她没有经验,但她能巧妙地克服这些困难。(cope with)

_____

3. 统治者决定不向其他国家求援。(call for)

_____

4. 正如他们必须抛弃成见,我们也必须准备接受他们的诚意。(put aside)

_____

5. 他的书分成四章。(fall into)

_____

VIII. Oral exercises.

Students in groups of two will make conversations about marketing. In the conversation practice, some sentence patterns will be used. In this unit, students will use the following two sentence patterns

Don't take it for granted that...   别认为……理所当然

You are supposed to...   你应该……

Please follow example (1) and complete the following dialogue exercises. Student A and B will

exchange roles upon completion.

For example（1）：

> Student A：Don't take it for granted that targeting benefits only companies.
>
> Student B：Yes, there is a misunderstanding about it. Thank you for your advice.
>
> Student A：Don't take it for granted that marketing is just（advertising, defining a target market, reaching a specific group of customers）.
>
> Student B：Yes, there is a misunderstanding about it. Thank you for your advice.

Please follow example（2）and complete the following dialogue exercises. Student A and B will exchange roles upon completion.

For example（2）：

> Student A：What are you supposed to do in order to segment a market?
>
> Student B：Let me think about it.
>
> Student A：What are you supposed to do in order to（assess the size of the target market, localize your products, balance home, family, and career）?
>
> Student B：I have to think about it.

IX. Writing skills. Please look at the pictures, the words and phrases coming from the pictures in relation to marketing below. And then write 3 – 5 sentences to describe each of the pictures.

The expressions in the brackets may help you to start your writing.

(There is/are . . . in the picture; In the middle of the picture; Then let's look at the next picture; This picture is about . . . ; The person on the right. . . ; From the picture, you can see. . . ; The central focus of this picture is. . . ; In the top left corner /bottom right corner of the picture, a man/woman/boy/girl. . . ; From her/his facial expression, I can assume that. . . ; From the. . . , I can tell that. . . ; Perhaps this man is about to. . .)

Picture 1 (door to door sales, introduce, recommend, young salesman, old woman)

_____

_____

_____

Picture 2 (telemarketing, cold-calling, perspective customers, salesgirls and salesmen)

_____

_____

_____

Picture 3 (marketing mix, four elements, product ,price, place, promotion)

_____

_____

_____

Picture 4 (promo staff meeting , be satisfied with, sales records, sales manager, staff)

_____

_____

_____

X. PPT presentation. Two students in a group will work together to prepare 5 – 8 pages of PPT slides to be presented in class. The topic for this unit is about making a market plan for a product.

Further Reading One: Historical Eras of Marketing

Modern marketing began in the early 1900s. In the twentieth century, the marketing process progressed through three distinct eras—production, sales, and marketing. In the 1920s, firms operated under the premise（前提）that production was a seller's market. Product choices were nearly non-existent（不存在）because firm managers believed that a superior product would sell itself. This philosophy was possible because the demand for products outlasted（比……持久）supply. During this era, firm success was measured totally in terms of production. The second era of marketing, ushered（开创）in during 1950s, is known as the sales era. During this era, product supply exceeded demand. Thus, firms assumed that consumers would resist buying goods and services deemed nonessential. To overcome this consumer resistance, sellers had to employ creative advertising and skillful personal selling in order to get consumers to buy. The marketing era emerged after firm managers realized that a better strategy was needed to attract and keep customers because allowing products to sell themselves was not effective. Rather, the marketing concept philosophy was adopted by many firms in an attempt to meet the specific needs of customers. Proponents（支持者）of the marketing concept argued that in order for firms to achieve their goals, they had to satisfy the needs and wants of consumers.

Exercise

I. Choose the best answer to each question with the information from the text.

1. When did modern marketing begin?

A. In the 1990s.　　　B. In the 1900s.　　　C. In the late 1900s.　　D. In the early 1900s.

2. Why was the philosophy possible in the 1920s that production was a seller's market?

A. Because product choices didn't exist.

B. Because the demand for products outlasted supply.

C. Because product choices did exist.

D. Because supply outlasted the demand for products.

3. What is the second era of marketing known as?

A. The marketing era.　　　　　　　　B. The production era.

C. The sales era.　　　　　　　　　　D. The advertising era.

4. How did sellers overcome the consumer resistant in order to get consumers to buy?

A. Sellers improved the qualities of products.

B. Sellers increased the quantities of products.

C. Sellers employed creative advertising and skillful personal selling.

D. Sellers followed the trends of the market.

5. What is the philosophy of the marketing era?

A. In order for firms to achieve their goals, they had to satisfy the needs and wants of consumers.

B. To attract and keep customers.

C. Firm success was measured totally in terms of production.

D. A superior product would sell itself.

II. Decide whether each of the following statements is true (T) or false (F).

1. In the 2000s, the marketing process progressed through three distinct eras—production, sales, and marketing.

2. In the production era, firm managers believed that a superior product would sell itself.

3. During the sales era, product supply exceeded demand.

4. The marketing era emerged after firm managers realized that marketing are necessary to attract and keep customers.

5. The advertising concept philosophy was adopted by many firms in the marketing era.

Further Reading Two: Marketing in the Overall Business

There are four areas of operation within all firms: accounting, finance, management, and marketing. Each of these four areas performs specific functions. The accounting department is responsible for keeping track of income and expenditures(支出). The primary responsibility of the finance department is maintaining and tracking assets(财产). The management department is responsible for creating and implementing(使生效)procedural policies of the firm. The marketing department is responsible for generating revenue(收益)through the exchange process. As a means of generating revenue, marketing objectives are established in alignment with(与……成一直线)the overall objectives of the firm.

Aligning the marketing activities with the objectives of the firm is completed through the process of marketing management. The marketing management process involves developing objectives that promote the long-term competitive advantage of a firm. The first step in the marketing management process is to develop the firm's overall strategic plan. The second step is to establish marketing strategies that support the firm's overall strategic objectives. Lastly, a marketing plan is developed for each product. Each product plan contains an executive summary, an explanation of the current marketing situation, a list of threats and opportunities, proposed sales objectives, possible marketing strategies, action programs, and budget proposals.

The marketing management process includes analyzing marketing opportunities, selecting target markets, developing the marketing mix(市场营销组合), and managing the marketing effort. In order to analyze marketing opportunities, firms scan current environmental conditions in order to determine potential opportunities. The aim of the marketing effort is to satisfy the needs and wants of consumers. Thus, it is necessary for marketing managers to determine the particular needs and wants of potential customers. Various quantitative and qualitative techniques of marketing research are used to collect data about potential customers, who are then segmented into markets.

Exercise

I. Choose the best answer to each question with the information from the text.

1. Which department is responsible for creating and implementing procedural policies of the firms?

　A. The accounting department.　　　B. The marketing department.

　C. The finance department.　　　　D. The management department.

2. What does the marketing management process involve?

　A. Maintaining and tracking assets.

　B. Developing objectives that promote the long-term competitive advantage of a firm.

　C. Creating and implementing procedural policies of the firm.

　D. Generating revenue through the exchange process.

3. What is the purpose of the second step of the marketing management process?

　A. To establish marketing strategies that support the firm's overall strategic objectives.

　B. To develop the firm's overall strategic plan.

　C. To collect data about potential customers.

　D. To generate revenue.

4. Which of the following isn't included in the marketing management process?

　A. Selecting target markets.　　　　B. Keeping track of income and expenditures.

　C. Managing the marketing effort.　　D. Developing the marketing mix.

5. What do firms need to do in order to determine potential marketing opportunities?

　A. To determine the particular needs and wants of potential customers.

　B. To scan current environmental conditions.

　C. To satisfy the needs and wants of consumers.

　D. To collect data about customers.

II. Decide whether each of the following statements is true（T）or false（F）.

1. There are four areas of operation within all firms: accounting, finance, marketing management, and advertising.

2. The primary responsibility of the accounting department is maintaining and tracking assets.

3. Aligning the marketing activities with the objectives of the firm is completed through the process of marketing management.

4. The core of the marketing effort is to satisfy the needs and wants of consumers.

5. It is necessary for marketing managers to use various quantitative and qualitative techniques of marketing research to determine the particular needs and wants of potential customers.

Further Reading Three: Markets

The concept of exchange leads to the concept of a market. A market is the set of actual and po-

tential(潜在的)buyers of a product. These buyers share a particular need or want that can be satisfied through exchange. Thus, the size of a market depends on the number of people who exhibit the need, have resources to engage in exchange, and are willing to offer these resources in exchange for what they want.

Originally the term market stood for the place where buyers and sellers gathered to exchange their goods, such as a village square. Economists use the term to refer to a collection of buyers and sellers who transact(做交易)in a particular product class, as in the housing market or the grain market. Marketers, however, see the sellers as constituting an industry and the buyers as constituting a market. Modern economics operates on the principle of division of labour, where each person specializes in producing something, receives payment, and buys needed things with money. Thus, modern economies abound in(大量存在)markets. Producers go to resource markets (raw material markets, labour markets, money markets), buy resources, turn them into goods and services, and sell them to intermediaries, who sell them to consumers. The consumers sell their labour, for which they receive income to pay for the goods and services they buy. The government is another market that plays several roles. It buys goods from resource, producer and intermediary markets(中介市场); it pays them; it taxes these markets (including consumer markets); and it returns needed public services. Thus each nation's economy and the whole world economy consist of complex interacting sets of markets that are linked through exchange processes.

In advanced societies, markets need not be physical locations where buyers and sellers interact. With modern communications and transportation, a merchant can easily advertise a product on a late evening television programme, take orders from thousands of customers over the phone, and mail the goods to the buyers on the following day without having had any physical contact with them.

Business people use the term market to cover various groupings of customers. They talk about need markets (such as health seekers); product markets (such as teens or the baby boomers); and geographic markets (such as Western Europe or the United States). Or they extend the concept to cover non-customer groupings. For example, a labour market consists of people who offer their work in return for wages or products. Various institutions, such as employment agencies and job-counseling(职业咨询) firms, will grow up around a labour market to help it function better. The money market is another important market that emerges to meet the needs of people so that they can borrow, lend, save and protect money. The donor market has emerged to meet the financial needs of non-profit organizations.

Exercise

I. Choose the best answer to each question with the information from the text.

1. What leads to the concept of market according to the passage?

A. The set of actual and potential buyers of a product.

B. The concept of exchange.

C. The place where buyers and sellers gathered to exchange their goods.

D. A collection of buyers and sellers who transact in a particular product class.

2. What principle does modern economics operate on?

A. Division of labour.　　　　　　　　B. Meeting the needs of consumers.

C. Advertising strategies.　　　　　　D. Marketing strategies.

3. What roles does government market play?

A. It buys goods from resource, producer and intermediary markets; it pays them.

B. It taxes these markets (including consumer markets).

C. It returns needed public services.

D. A, B and C.

4. How does a merchant advertise a product with modern communications and transportation?

A. On a late evening television programme.　　B. Over the phone.

C. Mail the goods to the buyers.　　　　　　D. A, B or C.

5. Whose needs does the donor market emerge to meet?

A. The needs of people who can borrow, lend, save and protect money.

B. The financial needs of non-profit organizations.

C. The needs of health seekers.

D. The needs of labours.

II. Decide whether each of the following statements is true (T) or false (F).

1. The concept of a market leads to the concept of exchange.

2. Marketers see the buyers as constituting an industry and the sellers as constituting a market.

3. Resource markets include raw material markets, labour markets, money markets.

4. Complex interacting sets of markets are linked through exchange processes.

5. In advanced societies, markets need not be physical locations where buyers and sellers interact.

Unit Four   Marketing Mix

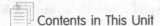 Contents in This Unit

1. Two pre-reading discussion questions.
2. A text on marketing mix.
3. New words and expressions.
4. Explanatory notes for the text.
5. Some exercises to build up your skills both in English and business.
6. A PPT hands-on assignment to give you spaces for creation.
7. Further readings on marketing.

Marketing Mix

Pre-reading Discussions for the Text

Please discuss these questions in pairs. You may talk over the topics either in English or in Chinese according to your teacher's instruction.

1. If you are the manufacturer of a certain product, how will you set the price of your products? You may write down some key words and phrases.

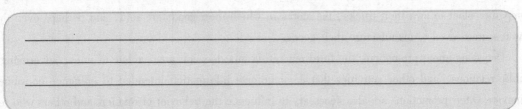

2. What kind of activities can you do to promote your selling? You may write 'down the key words and phrases before you talk.

Text: The Four Ps

The different elements of a company's marketing mix can be divided into four basic decision areas—known as the "four Ps": product, place, promotion, and price—which marketing managers can use to devise an overall marketing strategy for a product or group of goods. These four decision groups represent all of the variables that a company can control. But those decisions must be made within the context of outside variables that are not entirely under the control of the company, such as competition, economic and technological changes, the political and legal environment, and cultural and social factors.

Marketing decisions related to the product (or service) involve creating the right product for the selected target group. This typically encompasses research and data analysis, as well as the use of tools such as focus groups, to determine how well the product meets the wants and needs of the target group. Numerous determinants factor into the final choice of a product and its presentation. A completely new product, for example, will entail much higher promotional costs to raise consumer awareness, whereas a product that is simply an improved version of an existing item likely will make use of its predecessor's image.

A pivotal consideration in product planning and development is branding, whereby the good or service is positioned in the market according to its brand name. Other important elements of the complex product planning and management process may include selection of features, warranty, related product lines, and post-sale service levels.

Considerations about place, the second major decision group, relate to actually getting the good or service to the target market at the right time and in the proper quantity. Strategies related to place may utilize middlemen and facilitators with expertise in joining buyers and sellers, and they may also encompass various distribution channels, including retail, wholesale, catalog, and others. Marketing managers must also devise a means of transporting the goods to the selected sales channels, and they may need to maintain an inventory of items to meet demand. Decisions related to place typically play an important role in determining the degree of vertical integration in a company, or how many activities in the distribution chain are owned and operated by the manufacturer. For example, some larger companies elect to own their trucks, the stores in which their goods are sold, and perhaps even the raw resources used to manufacture their goods.

Decisions about promotion, the third marketing mix decision area, relate to sales, advertising, public relations, and other activities that communicate information intended to influence consumer behavior. Often promotions are also necessary to influence the behavior of retailers and others who resell or distribute the product. Three major types of promotion typically integrated into a market strategy are personal selling, mass selling, and sales promotions. Personal selling, which refers to face-to-face or telephone sales, usually provides immediate feedback for the company about the product and instills greater confidence in customers. Mass selling encompasses advertising on mass media, such as television, radio, direct mail, and newspapers, and is beneficial because of its broad scope. A relatively new means of promotion involves the Internet, which combines features of mass media with a unique opportunity for interactive communication with customers. Publicity entails the use of free media, such as feature articles about a company or product in a magazine or related interviews on television talk shows, to spread the word to the target audience. Finally, sales promotion efforts include free samples, coupons, contests, rebates, and other miscellaneous marketing tactics.

Determination of price, the fourth major activity related to target marketing, entails the use of discounts and long-term pricing goals, as well as the consideration of demographic and geographic influences. The price of a product or service generally must at least meet some minimum level that will cover a company's cost of producing and delivering its offering. Also a firm would logically price a product at the level that would maximize profits. The price that a company selects for its products, however, will vary according to its long-term marketing strategy. For example, a company may underprice its product in the hopes of increasing market share and ensuring its competitive presence, or simply to generate a desired level of cash flow. Another producer may price a good extremely high in the hopes of eventually conveying to the consumer that it is a premium product. Another reason a firm might offer a product at a very high price is to discount the good slowly in an effort to maximize the dollars available from consumers willing to pay different prices for the good. In any case, price is used as a tool to achieve comprehensive marketing goals.

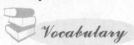
Vocabulary

1. promotion [prə'məuʃən]   *n.* advertising; publicity
   宣传,促销

2. devise [di'vaiz]   *v.* to work out, contrive or plan something in one's mind
   制定,设计

3. overall ['əuvəɔːl]   *adj.* including or covering everything
   全面的

4. variable ['vɛəriəbl]   *n.* something that is subject to variation
   变量

5. context ['kɔntekst]   *n.* the conditions and circumstances that are rele-

vant to an event, fact, etc.

环境

6. encompass [in'kʌmpəs]　　*v.* to include entirely or comprehensively

包括

7. determinant [di'tə:minənt]　　*n.* a factor, circumstance, etc., that influences or determines

决定因素

8. presentation [prezən'teiʃən]　　*n.* a show or display; the act of presenting something to sight or view

发布会

9. entail [in'teil]　　*v.* to bring about or impose by necessity

使……必要

10. promotional [prə'məuʃənl]　　*adj.* of or relating to serving as publicity

促销的

11. predecessor ['pri:disesə]　　*n.* something that precedes something else

前身

12. pivotal ['pivətəl]　　*adj.* being of crucial importance

关键的

13. warranty ['wɔrənti]　　*n.* a written assurance that some product or service will be provided or will meet certain specifications

保证

14. utilize ['ju:tilaiz]　　*v.* to make practical or worthwhile use of

利用

15. facilitator [fə'siliteitə]　　*n.* an organizer and provider of services for a meeting or other event

服务商

16. expertise [ekspə:'ti:z]　　*n.* special skill

专门知识或技能

17. retail ['ri:teil]　　*n.* the sale of goods individually or in small quantities to consumers

零售

18. wholesale ['həulseil]　　*n.* the selling of goods to merchants; usually in large quántities for resale to consumer

批发

19. catalog ['kætəlɔg]　　*n.* a complete list of things

目录册

20. inventory ['invəntəri]　　*n.* a detailed list of articles, goods, property, etc.

存货清单

21. vertical ['və:tikəl]   *adj.* at right angles to the horizon
                                     垂直的

22. integration [ˌinti'greiʃən]   *n.* the act of combining or adding parts to make a
                                     unified whole
                                     一体化

23. elect [i'lekt]   *v.* to select; choose
                                     选择

24. feedback ['fi:dbæk]   *n.* information in response to an inquiry, experi-
                                     ment, etc.
                                     反馈

25. instill [in'stil]   *v.* impart gradually
                                     逐渐使某人获得

26. beneficial [ˌbeni'fiʃəl]   *adj.* causing a good result; advantageous
                                     有益的

27. interactive [ˌintər'æktiv]   *adj.* capable of acting or influencing each other
                                     相互影响的

28. publicity [pʌb'lisəti]   *n.* information used to draw public attention to
                                     products
                                     宣传

29. coupon ['ku:pɔn]   *n.* a detachable part of a ticket or advertisement
                                     entitling the holder to a discount, free gift,
                                     etc.
                                     (购物)优惠券

30. rebate ['ri:beit]   *n.* a refund of some fraction of the amount paid
                                     折扣

31. miscellaneous [misi'leinjəs]   *adj.* composed of or containing a variety of
                                     things; mixed; varied
                                     各种各样的

32. discount ['diskaunt]   *n.* a deduction from the full amount of a price as
                                     in return for prompt payment
                                     折扣

33. demographic [demə'græfik]   *adj.* of or relating to demography
                                     人口统计学的

34. geographic [dʒiə'græfik]   *adj.* of or relating to the science of geography
                                     地理的

35. underprice [ˌʌndə'prais]   *v.* sell at artificially low prices
                                     以低价与……竞争

Phrase and Expression

1. marketing mix 销售组合
2. under the control of 在……控制下
3. target group 目标群体
4. focus group 中心小组，小组讨论
5. as well as 也
6. wants and needs 需求
7. make use of 使用
8. relate to 涉及
9. play an important role in 起重要作用
10. vertical integration 垂直管理
11. distribution chain 销售过程
12. integrate into 与……成为一体
13. cash flow 现金周转

Notes for Text

1. The different elements of a company's marketing mix can be divided into four basic decision areas—known as the "four Ps": product, place, promotion, and price—which marketing managers can use to devise an overall marketing strategy for a product or group of goods.

译文：企业营销组合中不同的要素，可以概括为四个基本决策域，即著名的 4Ps：产品，地点（渠道），促销和价格。市场营销经理可以利用 4Ps 营销理论制定一个产品或系列产品的整体营销策略。句中 known as 意为"以……著称"。例：Jingdezhen is known as the capital of porcelain. 景德镇被誉为瓷都。

2. But those decisions must be made within the context of outside variables that are not entirely under the control of the company.

译文：但是这些决策是在企业尚不能完全控制的外部变量环境下所确定的。短语 under the control of 意为"在……控制下"。例：This university is under the direct control of the Ministry of Education. 这所大学直属教育部管辖。

3. Marketing decisions related to the product (or service) involve creating the right product for the selected target group.

译文：与产品（或服务）相关的营销决策涉及为所选择的目标群体生产合适的产品。句中 related to the product 为过去分词短语作定语，修饰主语 marketing decisions。

4. This typically encompasses research and data analysis, as well as the use of tools such as fo-

cus groups, to determine how well the product meets the wants and needs of the target group.

译文：为此就要进行研究和数据分析，或采用中心小组讨论的方式来确定该产品如何满足目标群体的需求和欲望。短语 as well as 意为"此外，也……"，wants and needs 意为"需求"，target group 意为"目标群体"。

5. A completely new product, for example, will entail much higher promotional costs to raise consumer awareness, whereas a product that is simply an improved version of an existing item likely will make use of its predecessor's image.

译文：例如，一个全新的产品将需要更多的宣传费用，以期提高消费者意识，而对现有产品的改良品很有可能会利用其已有的形象。句中 whereas（用以比较或对比两个事实）意为"但是，然而，尽管"。例：He earns 8,000 a year, whereas she gets at least 20,000. 他一年挣八千元，而她却能赚二万元。

6. A pivotal consideration in product planning and development is branding, whereby the good or service is positioned in the market according to its brand name.

译文：产品规划和发展的关键因素是品牌。由此，产品或服务将根据其品牌名称在市场上定位。句中 whereby 在此作为副词，意为"借以，凭借"。例：Reinsurance is a device whereby insurers can do the risk sharing and risk transferring. 再保险是保险人分担危险、转嫁危险的一种方法。

7. Considerations about place, the second major decision group, relate to actually getting the good or service to the target market at the right time and in the proper quantity.

译文：地点（渠道）作为第二大决策域，与在适当的时间向目标市场投放一定数量的商品或服务相关。The second major decision group 是 place 的同位语；relate to 意为"与……相关"。例：These regulations only relate to people under the age of twenty one. 这些规定只针对21岁以下的人。

8. Marketing managers must also devise a means of transporting the goods to the selected sales channels, and they may need to maintain an inventory of items to meet demand.

译文：营销经理人还应制定一套运送货物到其选择的销售渠道的方式，而同时也需要维持一定的项目存货以满足客户需求。短语 a means of 意为"……的方式，……的手段"。inventory 意为"详细目录，存货清单，（商店的）存货，库存"。

9. Decisions related to place typically play an important role in determining the degree of vertical integration in a company, or how many activities in the distribution chain are owned and operated by the manufacturer.

译文：与地点相关的决策通常在决定一个公司纵向一体化程度上或者在明确分销链中有多少行为是由生产商拥有和经营这个问题上起着重要作用。句中 vertical integration 意为"垂直统一管理，纵向一体化"；distribution chain 意为"销售过程；分销链"。

10. some larger companies elect to own their trucks, the stores in which their goods are sold, and perhaps even the raw resources used to manufacture their goods.

译文：一些大型的公司选择拥有自己的卡车，在他们自己的商店销售商品，甚至拥有生产其产品的原材料。句中 raw resources 意为"原材料"。

11. Often promotions are also necessary to influence the behavior of retailers and others who resell or distribute the product.

译文：促销往往会影响到零售商和其他分销商的行为。

12. Three major types of promotion typically integrated into a market strategy are personal selling, mass selling, and sales promotions.

译文：融入市场策略的三种主要促销手段为个人销售、集体销售和促销行为。短语 integrate into 意为"与……成为一体"。

13. Personal selling, which refers to face-to-face or telephone sales, usually provides immediate feedback for the company about the product and instills greater confidence in customers.

译文：个人销售，即面对面的销售或者电话销售，通常为生产该产品的公司提供直接的反馈，并为客户注入更大的信心。句中 face-to-face 意为"面对面的"。

14. A relatively new means of promotion involves the Internet, which combines features of mass media with a unique opportunity for interactive communication with customers.

译文：相对较新的促销手段有因特网，它将大众媒体的功能同与客户之间互动交流的独特机会结合起来。句中 which 引导的宾语从句修饰 Internet；interactive communication 意为"互动、交流"。

15. ... a company may underprice its product in the hopes of increasing market share and ensuring its competitive presence, or simply to generate a desired level of cash flow.

译文：一家公司可能降低产品价位来增加市场份额，以确保其在激烈的竞争中生存，或者只是为了产生预期的现金周转。underprice 意为"以低价与……竞争"；cash flow 意为"现金周转"。

Exercise

I. Text comprehension questions.

1. What are the four basic decision areas of a company's marketing mix?

2. What is the pivotal consideration in product planning and development?

3. What is the function of decisions related to place?

4. Why does the Internet become the new means of promotion?

5. How does a company price a product?

II. Decide whether each of the following statements is true (T) or false (F) or not mentioned (NM) in the text.

1. The four decisions must be made within the context of outside variables that are under the control of the company.

2. Only a few determinants factor into the final choice of a product and its presentation.

3. A product that is simply an improved version of an existing item can make use of its predecessor's image.

4. Considerations about place relate to actually getting the good or service to the target market at

the right time and in the proper quantity.

    5. It is unnecessary to influence the behavior of retailers and others who resell or distribute the product.

    6. Personal selling includes the advertising on the television, radio, and newspaper.

    7. It is important to consider the demographic and geographic reasons when you price a product.

    8. A company may price its product extremely high to generate a desired level of cash flow.

III. Choose the best answer to each question with the information from the text.

1. Which of the following variables are not entirely under the control of the company?

A. Economic and technological changes.   B. Legal and political environment.

C. Cultural and social reasons.   D. A, B and C.

2. How to create the right product for the target group?

A. To make a research, data analysis and use the focus groups as a tool to meet the wants and needs of the customers.

B. To find the right middlemen and facilitators to enlarge the sales channels.

C. To underprice the product to ensure the market's competitive presence.

D. To use proper communication activities to influence consumer behavior.

3. Which one is FALSE about the decisions related to place?

A. It plays an important role in determining the degree of vertical integration in a company.

B. It relates to actually getting the good or service to the target market at the right time and in the proper quantity.

C. Its distribution channels include retail, advertising, publicity and catalog.

D. Strategies related to place may utilize middlemen and facilitators with expertise in joining buyers and sellers.

4. What are the three major types of promotion?

A. Sales, advertising and public relations.

B. Personal selling, mass selling, and sales promotions.

C. Television, radio and direct mail.

D. Interviews, magazines and internet.

5. Which one is FALSE about price?

A. It entails the use of discounts and short-term pricing goals, as well as the consideration of demographic and geographic influences.

B. The price should cover a company's cost of producing and delivering its offering.

C. The price a firm selects for its products should maximize its profits.

D. The price may vary according to the marketing strategy.

IV. Choose the word or phrase that is closest in meaning to the underlined one.

1. She must <u>devise</u> a new way for earning money during the summer vacation.

A. plan   B. develop   C. deal   D. destroy

2. The courses for science mainly <u>encompass</u> mathematics, physics, chemistry and biology.

A. encourage   B. include   C. encounter   D. exclude

3. There are some pivotal problems about the urbanization in the process of western development in China.

A. polar   B. premium   C. primitive   D. crucial

4. You must utilize all available resources to achieve your business goals.

A. convert   B. devote   C. use   D. commit

5. Cost is not the only or even the primary determinant in pricing a product.

A. influence   B. occasion   C. determination   D. factor

6. It is profitable to establish commercial brands and integrate social resources.

A. calculate   B. merge   C. disintegrate   D. consolidate

7. His boss is giving him feedback about his work.

A. answer   B. response   C. activity   D. submission

8. These policies instill strong feelings of loyalty in P&G employees.

A. impress   B. introduce   C. contribute   D. transfuse

9. Our hope is to establish mutual and beneficial trading relations between us.

A. fruitless   B. futile   C. favorable   D. harmful

10. I always try to be interactive with the city and meet people.

A. mutual   B. integral   C. integrated   D. intellective

11. All miscellaneous consumer goods are home produced.

A. general   B. varied   C. mixed   D. miracle

12. This gives purchasers the assurance that they will receive a premium product delivering long-term value and consistent quality.

A. usual   B. inferior   C. superior   D. elegant

V. Fill in the blanks with the phrases and expressions from the text. Change forms where necessary.

> be known as under the control of as well as make use of relate to
> play an important role in integrate into be necessary to

1. Take the reform of the pricing system for an example, the prices of most commodities are ___ market economy.

2. How does e-business strategy _____ strategy on the corporate level?

3. Radio, television, newspapers and magazines are _____ the mass media.

4. These products are ornamental, creative _____ practical.

5. They _____ advertisement to plug the new product.

6. You should _____ your dreams _____ your real life rather than consider them unattainable.

7. Additional finance _____ to meet expanding needs both at home and abroad.

8. The horticulture industry _____ preserving and enhancing the beauty and productivity of the environment.

VI. Match the words with their definitions.

1. an organizer and provider of services for a meeting or other event

2. the selling of goods to merchants; usually in large quantities for resale to consumer

3. a factor, circumstance, etc., that influences or determines

4. a detachable part of a ticket or advertisement entitling the holder to a discount, free gift

5. something that is subject to variation

6. a refund of some fraction of the amount paid

7. sell at artificially low prices

8. a written assurance that some product or service will be provided or will meet certain specifications

9. the sale of goods individually or in small quantities to consumers

10. a show or display; the act of presenting something to sight or view

(   ) determinant   (   ) variable   (   ) warranty

(   ) presentation   (   ) facilitator   (   ) wholesale

(   ) coupon   (   ) rebate   (   ) underprice   (   ) retail

VII. Translate the following sentences into English.

1. 一个产品应该满足顾客的需求。(wants and needs)

_____

2. 我认为正确的分销渠道有利于产品的销售。(be beneficial to)

_____

3. 我们应该利用各种方式提供售后服务。(make use of)

_____

4. 在给产品定价钱前考虑一些地理和人口因素是有必要的。(be necessary to)

_____

5. 在任何情况下,我们都不能忽视促销的效果。(in any case)

_____

VIII. Oral exercises.

Students in groups of two will make conversations about four Ps. In the conversation practice, some sentence patterns will be used. In this unit, students will use the following two sentence patterns:

It is reported that... 据说……/据报道……

Please don't hesitate to... 请随时……

Please follow example (1) and complete the following dialogue exercises. Student A and B will

exchange roles upon completion.

For example (1):

Student A: It is reported that cigarette smokers have lower IQs than non-smokers.

Student B: Yes, I agree with you.

Student A: It is reported that marketing decisions about (product involve creating the right product for the target group, place relate to getting the service to the target market, promotion relate to sales, advertising, public relations, and other activities that communicate information intended to influence consumer behavior).

Student B: Yes, these decisions are very useful in marketing.

Please follow example (2) and complete the following dialogue exercises. Student A and B will exchange roles upon completion.

For example (2):

Student A: Please don't hesitate to come to me if you need my help.

Student B: Thanks a lot. That's very kind of you.

Student A: Please don't hesitate to (use a market strategy to promote sales, vary the price of the products according to the marketing strategy, use a price tool to achieve comprehensive marketing goals).

Student B: That is absolutely right.

IX. Writing skills. Please look at the pictures, the words and phrases coming from the pictures in relation to marketing below. And then write 3 – 5 sentences to describe each of the pictures.

The expressions in the brackets may help you to start your writing.

(There is/are... in the picture; In the middle of the picture; The sign indicate...; Then let's look at the top left picture; This picture is about...; From the picture, you can see...; In this place, you can buy; The top right picture is about...; In the bottom left corner of the picture, an elephant is holding a board...; From that, I can assume that...; From the bottom right corner of the picture..., I can tell that...; Perhaps this picture is about to...)

Picture 1 (mall of America, stars, place for shopping)

Picture 2 (sales promotion, people, time, communication with customer)

Picture 3 (an elephant, low price guarantee)

Picture 4 (dolphin, best products, entails discounts, market)

X. PPT presentation. Two students in a group will work together to prepare 2 – 3 pages of PPT slides to be presented in class. The topic for this unit is about how to promote milk in the supermarket.

Further Reading One: Marketing

Many people think that marketing means " selling" or " advertising". It's true that these are parts of marketing. But marketing is much more than selling and advertising. To illustrate some of the other important things that are included in marketing, think about all the bicycles being peddled (沿街叫卖;兜售) with varying degrees of energy by bike riders around the world. Most of us don't make our own bicycles. Instead, they are made by firms like Schwinn, Performance, Huffy, and Murray.

Most bikes do the same thing—get the riders from one place to another. But a bike rider can choose from a wide assortment (各种各样) of models. They are designed in different sizes and with or without gears (齿轮). Off-road (越野的) bikes have large knobby (多节的) tires. Kids and older people may want more wheels—to make balancing easier. Some bikes need baskets or even trailers (拖车) for cargo(货物). You can buy a basic bike for less than \$50. Or you can spend more than \$2,500 for a custom frame.

This variety of styles and features complicates (使……复杂化) the production and sale of bicycles. The following list shows some of the things a firm should do before and after it decides to produce and sell a bike.

(1)Analyze the needs of people who might buy a bike and decide if they want more or different models.

(2)Predict what types of bikes—handlebar (把手) styles, type of wheels, brakes(刹车), and materials—different customers will want and decide which of these people the firm will try to satisfy.

(3)Estimate how many of these people will want to buy bicycles, and when.

(4)Determine where in the world these bike riders will be and how to get the firm's bikes to them.

(5)Estimate (估计) what price they are willing to pay for their bikes and if the firm can make a profit selling at that price.

(6)Decide which kinds of promotion should be used to tell potential customers about the firm's bikes.

(7)Estimate how many competing companies will be making bikes, what kind, and at what prices.

(8)Figure out how to provide warranty service if a customer has a problem after buying a bike.

The above activities are not part of production—actually making goods or performing services. Rather, they are part of a larger process—called marketing—that provides needed direction for pro-

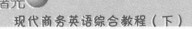
duction and helps make sure that the right goods and services are produced and find their way to consumers. Therefore, it is obvious that marketing plays an essential role in providing consumers with need-satisfying goods and services and, more generally, in creating customer satisfaction.

I. Choose the best answer to each question with the information from the text.

1. Why does the author mention the sales of bicycles in the text?

A. To illustrate other important things in marketing.

B. To tell the consumers the different features and styles of the bicycles.

C. To provide the direction for production of bicycles.

D. To create customer satisfaction with need-satisfying services.

2. Which one is FALSE about the marketing activities that a firm should do before and after it decides to product and sell its product?

A. Analyze the needs of people if they want more or different models.

B. Estimate how many people will want to buy the product and when.

C. Decide to make as more profits as possible.

D. Figure out how to provide warranty service in case a customer has a problem.

3. Which one is NOT TRUE about the functions of different types of bicycles?

A. To get the riders from one place to another.

B. To simplify the production and sale of bicycles.

C. To make balancing easier for kids and older people.

D. To make it easier to take a cargo.

4. What does the word custom mean in the last sentence of the second paragraph?

A. Specializing in the making or selling of made-to-order goods.

B. A habitual practice of a person.

C. The governmental agency to collect duties.

D. A duty or tax imposed on imported or exported goods.

5. Which of following is TRUE about marketing?

A. It provides need direction for production.

B. It helps make sure that the right goods and services are produced.

C. It helps the consumers to find the right goods and services.

D. All of the above.

II. Decide whether each of the following statements is true (T) or false (F).

1. Marketing means selling and advertising.

2. The variety of styles and features simplifies the production and sale of bicycles.

3. A firm should estimate what price the consumers are willing to pay for the bikes and if the firm can make a profit selling at that price.

4. Marketing provides needed direction for production and helps make sure that the right goods and services are produced and find their way to consumers.

5. Marketing plays an essential role in providing consumers with need-satisfying goods and services and, more generally, in creating customer satisfaction.

Further Reading Two: Marketing Study

As a consumer, you pay for the cost of marketing activities. In advanced economies, marketing costs about 50 cents of each consumer dollar. For some goods and services, the percentage (百分比) is much higher. Marketing affects almost every aspect of your daily life. All the goods and services you buy, the stores where you shop, and the radio and TV programs paid for by advertising are there because of marketing. Even your job résumé (简历) is part of a marketing campaign (活动) to sell yourself to some employer! Some courses are interesting when you take them but never relevant (相关联的) again once they're over. Not so with marketing—you'll be a consumer dealing with marketing for the rest of your life.

Another reason for studying marketing is that it offers many exciting and rewarding career opportunities in different areas of marketing. Even if you're aiming for a non-marketing job, knowing something about marketing will help you do your own job better. Further, marketing is important to the success of every organization. The same basic principles used to sell soap are used to sell ideas, politicians, mass transportation, health care services, conservation, museums, and even college.

An even more basic reason for studying marketing is that marketing plays a big part in economic growth and development. One key reason is that marketing encourages research and innovation (创新)—the development and spread of new ideas, goods, and services. As firms offer new and better ways of satisfying consumer needs, customers have more choices among products and this fosters (促进) competition for consumers' money. This competition drives down prices. Moreover, when firms develop products that really satisfy customers, fuller employment and higher incomes can result. The combination of these forces means that marketing has a big impact (影响) on consumers' standard of living—and it is important to the future of all nations.

Exercise

I. Choose the best answer to each question with the information from the text.

1. Which of the following activities are parts of marketing?

A. The radio and TV programs paid for by advertising.

B. The job résumé.

C. The goods and services you buy.

D. All of the above.

2. Which of the following statement is TRUE?

A. Some courses are not interesting when you take them but still relevant when they are over.

B. As a consumer, you will be dealing with marketing for the rest of your life.

C. In every nation, marketing costs about fifty cents of each consumer.

D. As a consumer, you don't need to pay for the cost of marketing activities.

3. Why does marketing play a big part in economic growth and development?

A. It encourages promotion to drive down prices.

B. It fosters competition for consumers' money and makes prices higher.

C. It will leads into fuller employment and higher incomes if the products really satisfy customers.

D. It has a big impact on consumers' life style.

4. What are the reasons for studying marketing?

A. It affects almost every aspect of your daily life.

B. It offers many exciting and rewarding career opportunities.

C. It plays a big part in economic growth and development.

D. A, B, and C.

5. Why is marketing important to the success of every organization?

A. Because the same basic principles used to sell one product can be used in other areas.

B. Because knowing something about marketing is irrelevant to your own job.

C. Because marketing can spread new ideas and services.

D. Because it can satisfy the needs of consumers.

II. Decide whether each of the following statement is true (T) or false (F).

1. Marketing affects almost every aspect of your daily life.

2. Your job résumé is part of a marketing campaign to sell yourself to some employer.

3. If you are having a non-marketing job, it is irrelevant to know something about marketing.

4. Marketing encourages research and innovation which helps to develop and spread the new ideas, goods and services.

5. Marketing fosters competition for consumers' money and makes the prices higher.

Unit Five   Promotion Activities

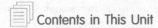Contents in This Unit

1. Two pre-reading discussion questions.
2. A text on promotion activities.
3. New words and expressions.
4. Explanatory notes for the text.
5. Some exercises to build up your skills
   both in English and business.
6. A PPT hands-on assignment to give you
   space for creation.
7. Further readings on advertising.

Pre-reading Discussions for the Text

Please discuss these questions in pairs. You may talk over the topics either in English or in Chinese according to your teacher's instruction.

1. Have you had any experience in selling in any industry? Can you share it with us your personal experience? You may write down the key words and phrases before you talk.

---

2. In order to increase sales, do you use some sales tactics? If yes, what kinds of sales tactics do you use? How do these sales tactics help you increase your sales? You may write down the key words and phrases before you talk.

Text : Special Promotional Activities

Companies use a variety of sales promotion tactics to increase sales, including advertising specialties, cash refund offers/rebates, contests and sweepstakes, coupons, patronage rewards, point-of-purchase displays, premiums, price packs/cents-off deals, samples, and trade shows.

Advertising specialties. Companies frequently create and give away everyday items with their names and logos printed on the items such as bottle/can openers, caps, coffee mugs, key rings, and pencils. Companies prefer to use inexpensive hand-outs that will yield constant free advertising when used by the recipient.

Cash refund offers/rebates. A cash refund or rebate is similar to a coupon except that the price reduction comes after the product is already purchased. In order to receive the cash refund/rebate, the consumer must send in a "proof of purchase" with the company offer in order to obtain the refund. Rebates are often an excellent form of sales promotion for a company to use because a high percentage of consumers will not send in the forms for the refund.

Contests and sweepstakes. Many companies use contests and sweepstakes to increase the sales of a product. As a reward for participating, consumers might win cash, free products, or vacations. With a contest, participants are required to demonstrate a skill; for example, entrants might be asked to suggest a name for a new product, design a company logo, or even suggest a company name change. Contest entries are then reviewed by a panel of judges; the originator of the winning entry receives a prize, usually in the form of cash or a vacation. In contrast to the skill required with contests, a sweepstakes winner is determined by chance. For example, consumers maybe given a scratch card in a fast-food restaurant; if three-of-a-kind or another predetermined criterion is achieved, the consumer would be given a free hamburger or some other selected prize.

Coupons. Coupons are certificates that give consumers a price savings when they purchase a specified product. Coupons are frequently mailed, placed in newspapers, or dispensed at the point of purchase. In addition, some companies have coupons generated when an item is scanned at the register. Companies can promote both new and mature products through the use of coupons.

Patronage rewards. Awards provided by companies to promote and encourage the purchasing of their products are called patronage rewards. Airlines use this strategy by awarding frequent-flyer miles to consumers who use their services often. When a consumer has earned enough frequent-flyer miles, he or she can redeem a free ticket. Credit card companies also use patronage rewards by providing a list of free products a person can order based on the number dollars charged in a specified time period.

Point-of-purchase displays. Point-of-purchase promotions can include displays and demonstra-

tions that take place at the point of purchase. The cardboard cutouts of popular movie stars that are put next to merchandise are excellent examples of this method. One drawback to point-of-purchase displays is that stores do not have time to set up all the ones that are offered, so only a handful of them are used. Companies frequently offer assistance in assembling and removing promotional displays to encourage storeowners to use their point-of-purchase displays.

Premiums. Premiums are the goods offered free or at a low cost to encourage consumers to buy a particular product. Companies can also offer premiums in the form of reusable containers bearing names and logos in order to help promote other products. In addition, a company may also decide to use a self-liquidating premium. The costs associated with self-liquidating premiums are passed along to consumers through the cost of product.

Price packs/cents-off deals. Price packs provide consumers with a reduced price that is marked directly on the package by the manufacture. Companies can offer price packs in the format of two for the price of one or offer products such as a tube of toothpaste and a toothbrush in one package for a lower price than that of the two items purchased separately. Consumers generally react favorably to price packs because they are perceived as a real bargain.

Samples. Some companies offer free samples of their products. The rationale for offering a free product sample is to achieve immediate consumer introduction to the product. Companies have several ways to introduce potential consumers to product samples. Commonly used delivery methods include mailing the product, passing the product out in stores, or door-to-door delivery of the product. The largest drawback of free samples is their high cost. However, it is expected that the associated sales will offset the initial cost of the free samples.

Trade shows. Most industries hold conventions and trade shows each year to show off new technology, assess consumer trends, and review other issues important to the industry. Trade shows provide firms that sell to a particular industry an excellent opportunity to promote new products, make new contacts, renew existing business relationships, maintain or build a reputation, and distribute promotional materials.

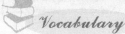

Vocabulary

1. tactic [ˈtæktik]   *n.* a plan for attaining a particular goal
                             方法,策略

2. refund [riˈfʌnd]   *n.* return of money to a purchaser or the amount
                             so returned
                             返还现金

3. sweepstake ['swiːpsteik]   *n.* a lottery in which the prize consists of the money paid by the participants
抽奖

4. patronage ['pætrənidʒ]   *n.* customers or patrons considered as a group; clientele
顾客,常客

5. premium ['priːmiəm]   *n.* an offer of something free or at a specially reduced price as an inducement to buy a commodity or service
赠品

6. logo ['lɔgəu]   *n.* a company emblem or device
公司标志

7. mug [mʌg]   *n.* a drinking vessel with a handle
圆筒形有柄大杯

8. handout ['hændaut]   *n.* a folder or leaflet circulated free of charge
免费散发的印刷品

9. recipient [ri'sipiənt]   *n.* a person who gets something
接受者

10. reduction [ri'dʌkʃən]   *n.* the amount by which something is reduced
降价

11. participate [pɑː'tisipeit]   *v.* take part
参与

12. entrant ['entrənt]   *n.* a person who enters a competition or contest
参赛人

13. originator [ə'ridʒəneitə]   *n.* someone who creates new things
创始人

14. predetermine [ˌpriːdi'təːmin]   *v.* to determine beforehand
预先确定

15. criterion [krai'tiəriən]   *n.* a standard by which something can be judged or decided
标准

16. dispense [dis'pens]   *v.* to give out
分发

17. generate ['dʒenəreit]   *v.* to produce or bring into being; create
产生

18. register ['redʒistə]   *n.* a device that automatically records a quantity or number
记录器

19. redeem [ri'diːm]   *v.* to turn in (coupons, for example) and receive

something in exchange
偿还

20. cutout ['kʌtaut]　　　　　*n.* a photograph from which the background has been cut away
剪贴画

21. merchandise ['mə:tʃəndaiz]　*n.* commercial goods; commodities
商品

22. assistance [ə'sistəns]　　　*n.* help; support
帮助

23. assemble [ə'sembl]　　　　*v.* collect in one place
汇编,组装

24. perceive [pə'si:v]　　　　　*v.* recognize or observe
认为,感知

25. rationale [,ræʃiə'nɑ:l]　　　*n.* fundamental reasons; the basis
根本原因

26. offset ['ɔfset]　　　　　　　*v.* to counterbalance or compensate for
补偿

27. assess [ə'ses]　　　　　　　*v.* to judge the worth, importance, etc.; evaluate
评估

28. reputation [,repju'teiʃən]　　*n.* the state of being held in high esteem and honor
荣誉

Phrase and Expression

1. point-of-purchase display　买点展示;购买点陈列
2. cents-off deal　降价销售
3. give away　赠送
4. be similar to　与……相似
5. except that　除了
6. a panel of　一个小组委员会
7. in contrast to　与……相反
8. three-of-a-kind　三张相同的牌
9. at the point of　在……时
10. frequent-flyer　飞机常客
11. pass out　分发

Notes for Text

1. Companies frequently create and give away everyday items with their names and logos printed

on the items such as...

译文：公司经常生产一些带有它们名称和标志的日用品，如开瓶器、瓶盖、咖啡杯、钥匙圈和铅笔，并把它们作为礼品赠送。句中 give away 意为"赠送"，everyday items 此处译为"日常用品"。

2. Companies prefer to use inexpensive handouts that will yield constant free advertising when used by the recipient.

译文：公司喜欢使用价格低廉的宣传单，这样当接受者使用时就会产生一种长久的免费的广告效应。此句中 that 引导的定语从句修饰 handouts，when 引导的是一个时间状语，该从句省略了主语，其完整形式应为"when these handouts are used by the recipient"。

3. A cash refund or rebate is similar to a coupon except that the price reduction comes after the product is already purchased.

译文：这种促销方式类似于优惠券，只是现金返还只有在购买产品后才会有。句中 except that 意为"除了"，此句解释了现金返还和优惠券的区别。

4. Contest entries are then reviewed by a panel of judges; the originator of the winning entry receives a prize, usually in the form of cash or a vacation.

译文：所有参赛者将由一组评审团评议，获奖作品的创作者将获取奖品，通常是以现金或者是假期的形式。这是由两个简单句组合而成的并列句。

5. In contrast to the skill required with contests, a sweepstakes winner is determined by chance.

译文：与竞赛所要求的技能不同，抽奖的获胜者是由机遇决定的。in contrast to 意为"与……相反"；be determined by 意为"由……决定"。例：His salary was determined by his rank and seniority. 他的工资取决于他的等级和资历。

6. For example, consumers maybe given a scratch card in a fast-food restaurant; if three-of-a-kind or another predetermined criterion is achieved, the consumer would be given a free hamburger or some other selected prize.

译文：例如，消费者可以拿到一些餐馆的刮奖卡，如果连续三次抽的牌都一样或者达到另一个预定的标准，消费者将得到一个免费的汉堡或者其他可选奖品。句中 scratch card 意为"刮奖卡"；predetermined 意为"预先确定的"。例：at a predetermined time 在预定的时间。

7. Coupons are certificates that give consumers a price savings when they purchase a specified product.

译文：优惠券即是为消费者购买某种特定产品时提供价格优惠的证明。that 引导了定语

从句修饰 certificates。

8. Coupons are frequently mailed, placed in newspapers, or dispensed at the point of purchase.

译文：优惠券经常通过邮寄、在报纸中夹带或者在购买该产品时赠予。句中 dispense 意为"分发"；at the point of 意为"在……时"。

9. In addition, some companies have coupons generated when an item is scanned at the register.

译文：此外，一些公司会在产品在柜台扫描时就提供优惠券。句中 in addition 意为"此外"；at the register 意为"在柜台"。

10. Airlines use this strategy by awarding frequent-flyer miles to consumers who use their services often.

译文：航空公司使用这种策略为其常客提供频飞航空积分里程回馈。句中 frequent-flyer 意为"常客"。例：Gathering frequent-flyer miles is one of the perks of business travel. 积累飞行里程是商务旅行的额外补贴之一。

11. Premiums are the goods offered free or at a low cost to encourage consumers to buy a particular product.

译文：赠品就是免费提供的某种商品或者是以低价来鼓励消费者购买某种特定的产品。句中 goods 意为"商品"，offered free or at a low cost 作后置定语修饰 goods。

12. The costs associated with self-liquidating premiums are passed along to consumers through the cost of product.

译文：而这笔与自付优惠相关的费用则通过产品的价格转嫁到消费者身上。句中 self-liquidating premium 意为"自偿赠品"，即消费者在购买产品后，再支付些许代价取得厂商提供的其他商品。

13. Consumers generally react favorably to price packs because they are perceived as a real bargain.

译文：消费者一般对折价包装产品反应良好，因为它们被认为是物美价廉的产品。句中 perceive 意为"认为，感知"。例：to perceive a change in the market 感知市场的变化。

14. The rationale for offering a free product sample is to achieve immediate consumer introduction to the product.

译文：提供免费样品的理由是直接向消费者介绍某种产品。to achieve... 是不定式短语作表语；rationale 意为"合理性；理由"。注意与 rational 的区别，rational knowledge 意为"理性知识"。

15. It is expected that the associated sales will offset the initial cost of the free samples.

译文：据预计，其相关的销售额将抵消免费样品的初始成本。句中 associated sales 意为"相关的销售额"；offset 意为"抵消"，弥补；offset the loss 意为"弥补损失"。

Exercise

Ⅰ. Text comprehension questions.

1. Can you list a variety of sales promotional tactics?

2. What is the difference between cash refund and coupon?

3. What is the definition of coupon?

4. In which industries are patronage awards quite frequently used?

5. What is the drawback of point-of-purchase display?

Ⅱ. Decide whether each of the following statements is true（T）or false（F）or not mentioned（NM）in the text.

1. Companies prefer to use expensive handouts that will yield free advertising when used by recipient.

2. Customers don't need to send in a proof of purchase to obtain the refund.

3. A sweepstakes winner is determined by their skills rather than chance.

4. Companies can promote both new and mature products through the use of coupons.

5. Companies frequently offer assistance in assembling and removing promotional displays to encourage storeowners to use their point-of-purchase displays.

6. The costs associated with self-liquidating premiums are passed along to consumers and manufacturers.

7. Consumers generally react unfavorably to price packs because they are of poor quality.

8. The reason for offering a free product sample is to achieve immediate consumer introduction to the product.

III. Choose the best answer to each question with the information from the text.

1. How can the consumers receive the cash refund?

A. They can receive it immediately after their purchase.

B. The cash refund will automatically transact to their credit card.

C. They have to send in a proof of purchase with the company offer.

D. They have to wait until the company's notice.

2. What are the rewards for contests and sweepstakes?

A. Cash.　　　　　B. Free products.　　　C. Vacations.　　　　D. All of the above.

3. Which of the following statements is TRUE about coupons?

A. Coupons are certificates that give consumers a price savings when they purchase a specified product.

B. Coupons are certificates that offer consumers with free products.

C. Consumers may use coupons to purchase different kinds of products.

D. Consumers can get coupons from the store displays.

4. What are the special features of point-of-purchase display?

A. Discount and free samples.　　　　　B. Displays and demonstrations.

C. Price packs and premiums.　　　　　D. Conventions and trade shows.

5. Why do some companies offer free samples of their products?

A. To build the reputation for the products.

B. To assess whether the products will meet the consumers' demand.

C. To achieve immediate consumer introduction to the product.

D. To maintain business relationship with their consumers.

IV. Choose the word or phrase that is closest in meaning to the underlined one.

1. Where this <u>tactic</u> was applied, victory was achieved.

A. maneuver　　　B. plot　　　　　C. plan　　　　　D. intrigue

2. We will supply you with a class <u>handout</u> at the beginning of each class.

A. donation　　　B. brochure　　　C. announcement　　D. charity

3. The <u>recipient</u> of the prize will have their names printed on the newspaper.

A. successor   B. reciprocal   C. recipe   D. receiver

4. Practice is the sole criterion for testing truth.

A. critic   B. standard   C. pattern   D. paradigm

5. Let us dispense these food and clothes as charity.

A. grant   B. dispel   C. distribute   D. administer

6. My boss screamed at me to generate more sales.

A. create   B. reveal   C. cause   D. demonstrate

7. Their merchandise is of high quality; therefore, supermarkets buy it in the gross.

A. advertisement   B. trade   C. merchant   D. commodity

8. Mary requested assistance from her friends.

A. opposition   B. resistance   C. support   D. appearance

9. He raised his prices to offset the increased cost of materials.

A. reduce   B. reward   C. compensate   D. onset

10. This store has an excellent reputation for fair dealing.

A. fame   B. distinction   C. rank   D. status

11. You should assess your potential power sources and use them to your advantage.

A. assemble   B. evaluate   C. criticize   D. section

12. They perceived that they were unwelcome and left.

A. penetrated   B. compassed   C. distinguished   D. realized

Ⅴ. Fill in the blanks with the phrases and expressions from the text. Change forms where necessary.

> give away   be similar to   except that   in contrast to   pass out   at the point of

1. _____ resignation, he revealed the truth of the fact.

2. I would have bought the car, _____ it was too expensive.

3. The gaiety and lightness of his work were _____ his own sad nature.

4. He wants to _____ all his modern possessions and return to nature.

5. People sometimes _____ their business cards as if they were dealing at a poker game which is impolite and unprofessional.

6. These two buildings _____ each other in many aspects.

Ⅵ. Match the words with their definitions.

1. return of money to a purchaser or the amount so returned

2. a lottery in which the prize consists of the money paid by the participants

3. a detachable part of a ticket or advertisement entitling the holder to a discount, free gift, etc.

4. customers or patrons considered as a group

5. a company emblem or device

6. the amount by which something is reduced

7. a standard by which something can be judged or decided

8. fundamental reasons; the basis

9. to determine beforehand

10. a person who enters a competition or contest

(   ) entrant   (   ) logo   (   ) patronage

(   ) rational   (   ) reduction   (   ) refund

(   ) criterion   (   ) coupon   (   ) sweepstake   (   ) predetermine

VII. Translate the following sentences into English.

1. 我们在展销会上发了 4 000 个塑料袋。(give away)

_____

_____

2. 商品交易会举办者免费为顾客提供样品来吸引顾客购买商品。(pass out)

_____

_____

3. 这个计划总的来说想得倒不错, 就是不经济。(except that)

_____

_____

4. 预计 2010 年销售总额将达到 2 000 万。(it is expected)

_____

_____

5. 在他购买此类产品时, 看到有很多广告特价品。(at the point of)

_____

_____

VIII. Oral exercises.

Students in groups of two will make conversations about promotion activities. In the conversation practice, some sentence patterns will be used. In this unit, students will use the following two sentence patterns:

As a matter of fact...   实际上……

In general...   一般而言, ……

Please follow example (1) and complete the following dialogue exercises. Student A and B will exchange roles upon completion.

For example (1):

Student A：<u>As a matter of fact,</u> I think a couple of candidates would make great replacements for you!

Student B：I hope so.

Student A：<u>As a matter of fact,</u> sales promotion tactics include (advertising specialties, cash refund offers, contests and sweepstakes, coupons, patronage rewards, point-of-purchase displays, premiums, price packs, samples, and trade shows).

Student B：Yes, these are quite useful in sales promotion.

Please follow example (2) and complete the following dialogue exercises. Student A and B will exchange roles upon completion.

For example (2)：

Student A：<u>In general,</u> this activity is full of originality, but I think it is hard to carry out.

Student B：I agree with you(or, I don't agree with you).

Student A：<u>In general,</u> companies use (a variety of sales promotion tactics, some inexpensive handouts to yield free advertising, contests and sweepstakes to increase the sales of a product, coupons to give consumers a price savings, a cash refund as a form of sales promotion).

Student B：I agree with you(or, I don't agree with you).

IX. Writing skills. Please look at the pictures, the words and phrases coming from the pictures in relation to promotional activities below. And then write 3 − 5 sentences to describe each of the pictures.

The expressions in the brackets may help you to start your writing.

(There is/are ... in the picture; In the middle of the picture; Then let's look at the next picture; This picture is about ... ; The person on the right... ; From the picture, you can see... ; The central focus of this picture is... ; In the top left corner /bottom right corner of the picture, a man/woman/boy/girl... ; From her/his facial expression, I can assume that... ; From the... , I can tell that... ; Perhaps this man is about to...)

Picture 1 (billboard, advertisement, promotion, highway)

Picture 2 (truck, painting of CocaCola, promotion)

Picture 3 (bright and yellow M, logo, Mc Donald's, hamburger)

X. PPT presentation. Two students in a group will work together to prepare 2 – 3 pages of PPT slides to be presented in class. The topic for this unit is to use one of the promotional tactics to increase your sales for your company.

Further Reading One: Types of Advertising

Regardless of the medium(媒介,方法) used, advertisements fall into one of these three cate-

gories.

Brand advertising(品牌广告)promotes a specific brand, such as *People* magazine, Amtrak rail service, and Ricoh copiers. A variation on brand advertising, product advertising promotes a general good or service, such as milk or dental services.

Advocacy advertising(倡导广告) promotes a particular cause, viewpoint, or candidate. The Sierra Club actively promotes a policy of population stabilization(稳定性)for the United States and internationally because they believe that population growth is a major cause of degradation(恶化)in the environment. Financial institutions(机构), such as credit unions and banks, advertise the idea that private home ownership leads to happiness, pride, and a more fulfilling life. Others focus on even more specialized concepts: the Aruba Gastronomic Association promotes Aruba's reputation as an island for culinary(烹饪的) excellence.

Institutional advertising(厂商广告)promotes a firm's long-term image. Hoechst runs a continuing series of ads to acquaint (使熟悉) the public with its name, its industries, and its long-term vision: "Creating Value Through Technology." Their colorful ads cleverly capitalize on the firm's unusual name (pronounced "Herkst") and announce its leadership in diverse life sciences and other industries, such as crop protection, vaccines(疫苗) for animal health, drugs for allergies(过敏症) and cancer, and industrial gases and gas supply systems.

Exercise

I. Choose the best answer to each question with the information from the text.

1. Which of the following types of advertising is NOT mentioned in the text?

A. Brand advertising.   B. Advocacy advertising.

C. Institutional advertising.   D. Celebrity advertising.

2. Among all the following brand names, which one is a kind of brand advertising?

A. Ricoh copier.   B. Aruba Gastronomic Association.

C. Hoechst.   D. Sierra Club.

3. What is the function of advocacy advertising?

A. It promotes a firm's long-term image.

B. It helps to promote a general good or service.

C. It promotes a particular cause, viewpoint, or candidate.

D. It tries to protect crops and animal health.

4. What are the functions of the Sierra Club?

A. It advertises the idea that private home ownership leads to happiness, pride, and a more fulfilling life.

B. It promotes a policy of population stabilization for the world.

C. It promotes its reputation for culinary excellence.

D. It announces its leadership in different industries.

5. How does Hoechst acquaint the public with its name, its industries, and its long-term vision?

A. It has its unusual name and announces its leadership in diverse life sciences.

B. It promises its potential customer with a more fulfilling life.

C. It produces drugs for allergies and cancer.

D. It runs a continuing series of advertisements.

II. Decide whether each of the following statements is true (T) or false (F).

1. Regardless of the medium used, advertisements fall into three categories.

2. Sierra Club believes that economical growth is a major cause of degradation in the environment.

3. Banks usually advertise the idea that private home ownership leads to a more fulfilling life.

4. Institutional advertising promotes a firm's long-term image.

5. Hoechst's long-term vision is to create value through innovation.

Further Reading Two: Advertising Strategies

An advertising strategy (战略) is a campaign developed to communicate ideas about products and services to potential (潜在的) consumers in the hopes of convincing them to buy those products and services. This strategy, when built in a rational (合理的) and intelligent manner, will reflect other business considerations (overall budget, brand recognition (赏识) efforts) and objectives (public image enhancement(提高), market share growth) as well. As *The Portable MBA in Marketing* authors Alexander Hiam and Charles D. Schewe stated, a business's advertising strategy "determines the character of the company's public face." Even though a small business has limited capital and is unable to devote as much money to advertising as a large corporation, it can still develop a highly effective advertising campaign. The key is creative and flexible(灵活的) planning, based on an indepth knowledge of the target consumer and the avenues(途径,手段) that can be utilized to reach that consumer.

Today, most advertising strategies focus on achieving three general goals: promote awareness of a business and its product or services; stimulate sales directly and "attract competitors' customers"; and establish or modify a business' image. In other words, advertising seeks to inform, persuade, and remind the consumer. With these aims in mind, most businesses follow a general process which ties advertising into the other promotional efforts and overall marketing objectives of the business.

I. Choose the best answer to each question with the information from the text.

1. What is the definition of advertising strategy?

A. It is a campaign developed to communicate ideas about products and services to potential consumers in the hopes of convincing them to buy those products and services.

B. It is the delivery of the message that certain products or services are less expensive than others.

C. It is a tactic to convey that your products have more beneficial characteristics than your competitors'.

D. It is to set your products' positive image for your potential consumers.

2. What is the main objective of advertising strategy?

A. To reduce the cost budget.

B. To make its brand known to most consumers.

C. To enhance its public image and market share.

D. To maximize its profits.

3. Who are the authors of *The Portable MBA in Marketing*?

A. Barbara S. Shea and Jennifer Haupt.   B. Alexander Hiam and Charles D. Schewe.

C. William Cohen and Gerald Hills.   D. Courtland L. Bovee and William F. Arens.

4. How can a small business develop a highly effective advertising campaign?

A. It should pay more attention to its market share growth.

B. It should reduce its overall budget.

C. It should devote as much money as a large corporation to advertising.

D. It should be creative and flexible in planning and have a thorough understanding about its target consumers.

5. Which of the following is NOT the goal of advertising strategy?

A. Promote awareness of a business and its products or services.

B. Stimulate sales and attract competitors' customers.

C. Establish or modify a business' image.

D. Attain the company's long-term achievements.

II. Decide whether each of the following statement is true (T) or false (F).

1. A business' advertising strategy determines the character of the company's public face.

2. Even though a small business has limited capital, it should devote as much money to advertising as a large corporation.

3. A small business should be creative and flexible in advertising planning.

4. One of the goals of advertising is to stimulate sales and attract competitors' customers.

5. Advertising seeks to persuade, remind, and mislead the consumers.

Unit Six   Brand Strategy

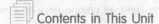

Contents in This Unit

1. Two pre-reading discussion questions.
2. A text on brand strategy.
3. New words and expressions.
4. Explanatory notes for the text.
5. Some exercises to build up your skills both in English and business.
6. A PPT hands-on assignment to give you space for creation.
7. Further readings on brand strategy.

Pre-reading Discussions for the Text

Please discuss these questions in pairs. You may talk over the topics either in English or in Chinese according to your teacher's instruction.

1. Can you list some famous brand names in any industry as far as you know? Why are they so attractive to you? You may write down some of the key words and phrases before you talk.

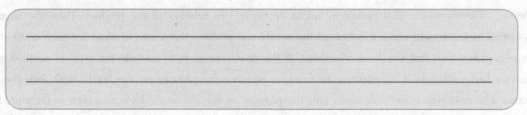

2. If you are an employee in a small business and you are asked to suggest a brand name for it, how can you choose a good brand name for it? You may write down the key words and phrases before you talk.

Text: Brand Strategy

Brand names are very important for small businesses, as they provide potential customers with information about the product and help them form an immediate impression about the company. A well-chosen brand name can set a small business's product apart from those of competitors and communicate a message regarding the firm's marketing position or corporate personality. When preparing to enter a market with a product or service, an entrepreneur must decide whether to establish a brand and, if so, what name to use.

Experts claim that successful branding is most likely when the product is easy to identify, provides the best value for the price, is widely available, and has strong enough demand to make the branding effort profitable. Branding is also recommended in situations where obtaining favorable display space or locations on store shelves will significantly influence sales of the product. Finally, a successful branding effort requires economies of scale, meaning that costs should decrease and profits should increase as more units of the product are made.

After deciding to establish a brand, a small business faces the task of selecting a brand name. An entrepreneur might decide to consult an advertising agency, design house, or marketing firm that specializes in naming, or to come up with a name on their own. A good brand name should be short and simple; easy to spell, pronounce, and remember; pronounceable in only one way; suggestive of the product's benefits; adaptable to packaging and labeling needs or to any advertising medium; not offensive or negative; not likely to become dated; and legally available for use.

In order to create a brand name for a product without the help of experts, a small business owner should begin by examining names already in use in the market and evaluating their effectiveness. The next step is to identify three to five attributes that make the product special and should help influence buyers to choose it over the competition. It may also be helpful to identify three to five company personality traits—such as friendly, innovative, or economical—that customers might appreciate in relation to the product. Then the small business owner should make a list of all the words and phrases that come to mind for each attribute or personality trait that has been identified. If the brand name is to include the type of product or service being offered, it is important to consider whether the phrases on the list fit well with these terms. The next step is to think about how the phrases on the list would look on a sign or on a product package, including possible visual images and typefaces that could be used to enhance their appearance.

Next, the entrepreneur should narrow down the list with the help of a few friends. It may be helpful to say the possible names aloud, thinking about how they would sound if they were used by a

receptionist answering a telephone or by a customer requesting a product from a store. It is also important to consider whether the names will stand the test of time as the business grows, or whether they include an in-joke that may become dated. Once the list has been narrowed down to between ten and fifteen candidates, then the possibilities should be tested for impact on at least thirty strangers, perhaps through a focus group or survey. The opinions of people who may be potential customers should be given the most weight.

Finally, once the top few choices have been identified, the entrepreneur can find out whether they are available for use—or are already being used by another business—by conducting a trademark search. This search can be performed by advertising or marketing firms, or by some attorneys, for a fee. Alternatively, the small business owner can simply send in a formal request for a trademark and wait to see whether it is approved. The request must be sent to the state patent and trademark office, and also to the federal office if the business will be conducting interstate commerce. In order for a trademark to be approved, it must be available and distinctive, and it must depart from a mere description of the product.

 *Vocabulary*

1. well-chosen ['wel'tʃəuzn]	*adj.* carefully selected to produce a desired effect 精选的;适当的
2. personality [,pə:sə'næləti]	*n.* the distinctive character of a person that makes him socially attractive 人格
3. entrepreneur [,ɔntrəprə'nə:]	*n.* the owner or manager of a business enterprise who attempts to make profits 企业家
4. profitable ['prɔfitəbl]	*adj.* productive of profit 有益的,有好处的
5. favorable ['feivərəbl]	*adj.* advantageous 有利的
6. scale [skeil]	*n.* a relative level or degree 规模
7. pronounceable [prə'naunsəbl]	*adj.* capable of being uttered or pronounced 可发音的
8. suggestive [sə'dʒestiv]	*adj.* tending to suggest or imply 引起联想的
9. adaptable [ə'dæptəbl]	*adj.* capable of adapting 有适应能力的
10. offensive [ə'fensiv]	*adj.* unpleasant or disgusting, as to the senses 令人不快的
11. dated ['deitid]	*adj.* unfashionable; outmoded

过时的

12. evaluate [i'væljueit]   *v.* to judge or assess the worth of; appraise
评价，估计

13. attribute [ə'tribju:t]   *n.* a property, quality, or feature belonging to or representative of a person or thing
特性

14. trait [treit]   *n.* a characteristic feature or quality distinguishing a particular person or thing
显著的特点

15. innovative ['inəuveitiv]   *adj.* using or showing new methods, ideas, etc.
有创意的

16. economical [ˌi:kə'nɔmikəl]   *adj.* not wasteful of time, effort, resources, etc.
实惠的

17. appreciate [ə'pri:ʃieit]   *v.* value highly
欣赏

18. typeface ['taipfeis]   *n.* a specific size and style of type
字体

19. enhance [in'hɑ:ns]   *v.* make better or more attractive
提高

20. receptionist [ri'sepʃənist]   *n.* a secretary whose main duty is to answer the telephone and receive visitors
接待员

21. in-joke ['inˌdʒəuk]   *n.* a joke that is appreciated only by members of some particular group of people
（圈内人才领会的）小范围或内部笑话

22. impact ['impækt]   *n.* the power of making a strong, immediate impression
影响力

23. weight [weit]   *n.* importance, influence, or consequence
影响力；重要性

24. attorney [ə'tə:ni]   *n.* a lawyer qualified to represent clients in legal proceedings
代理律师

25. patent ['peitənt]   *n.* a government grant to an inventor assuring him the sole right to make, use, and sell his invention for a limited period
专利权

26. interstate [ˌintə'steit]   *n.* between or involving two or more of the states of the US

州际的

27. distinctive [dis'tiŋktiv]　　　*adj.* serving or tending to distinguish

区别性的

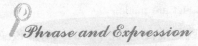

Phrase and Expression

1. apart from　与……脱离，与……区别
2. specialize in　专攻，精通
3. come up with　想出，提出
4. personality traits　个性品质
5. in relation to　与……相关
6. narrow down　使……缩小
7. a focus group　（销售）讨论组
8. state patent　国家专利局

Notes for Text

1. Brand names are very important for small businesses, as they provide potential customers with information about...

译文：品牌名称对小企业来说是非常重要的，因为它们给潜在的客户群提供了……的信息。本句内含原因状语从句，由 as 引导。

2. A well-chosen brand name can set a small business's product apart from those of competitors and communicate a message regarding the firm's marketing position or corporate personality.

译文：一个经过精挑细选的品牌名称可以将一个小企业的产品与其竞争对手的产品区别开来，同时可以传递有关该公司的市场定位及其法人人格等信息。短语 apart from 意为"与……区别"。例：The products should not be set apart from the demands of the market. 不能把产品与市场需要区别开来。

3. When preparing to enter a market with a product or service, an entrepreneur must decide whether to establish a brand and, if so, what name to use.

译文：当一个企业家准备将一种产品或服务推向市场，他必须决定是否建立一个品牌，如果要的话，该使用什么名称。when preparing... 这一从句中省略了主语与谓语 an entrepreneur was。If so, 也是一个省略句，so 指代前文出现的 decide to establish a brand, 其完整形式是 if an entrepreneur decides to establish a brand, and then he must decide what name to use。

4. Branding is also recommended in situations where obtaining favorable display space or locations on store shelves will significantly influence sales of the product.

译文：品牌在以下这些情况下也被广泛推荐使用，如在商店货架上获取有利的陈列空间

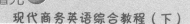
或者展示台,这将大大影响产品的销售。句中 where 引导一个状语从句,修饰 situations。

5. Finally, a successful branding effort requires economies of scale, meaning that costs should decrease and profits should increase as more units of the product are made.

译文:最后,一个成功的品牌推广需要规模经济,也就是说,在扩大生产的同时应该减少成本,以获取更高利润。句中 economies of scale 意为"规模经济",as 在此处引导从句,表示"随着"的意思。

6. An entrepreneur might decide to consult an advertising agency, design house, or marketing firm that specializes in naming, or to come up with a name on their own.

译文:企业家可能决定咨询那些擅长于命名的广告公司、设计公司或者营销公司,或者干脆自己命名。句中 that 引导定语从句修饰前面的 agency, design house, or marketing firm. specialize in 意为"擅长,专营"。例: We specialize in the export of table-cloths. 短语 come up with 意为"想出"。例:come up with a good idea,想出一个好主意。

7. It may also be helpful to identify three to five company personality traits — such as friendly, innovative, or economical—that customers might appreciate in relation to the product.

译文:同时,确定三至五个公司的个性品质——如友好的,创新的,或者经济实惠的,也是有益的,这是因为顾客可能欣赏与产品相关的某些个性特质。It 在此处是形式主语,该句子的真正主语是 to identify three to five company personality traits, such as friendly, innovative, or economical 是插入语,是对 company personality traits 的解释;in relation to 意为"与……相关"。

8. The next step is to think about how the phrases on the list would look on a sign or on a product package, including possible visual images and typefaces that could be used to enhance their appearance.

译文:下一步是考虑名单上的名称做成标识或者在产品包装上会是怎样的,包括可能用来提高它们形象的视觉图像和字体。句中 product package 意为"产品包装";that 引导的定语从句修饰前文的 images and typefaces。

9. Next, the entrepreneur should narrow down the list with the help of a few friends.

译文:接下来,企业主应该在朋友的帮助下缩小清单的范围。句中 narrow down 意为"使……缩小"。例:Narrow down the target market. 缩小你的目标市场。短语 with the help of 意为"在……的帮助下"。例:We can reduce the production costs with the help of the computer. 我们可以利用计算机降低生产成本。

10. It is also important to consider whether the names will stand the test of time as the business grows, or whether they include an in-joke that may become dated.

译文：随着业务的增长，考虑这些名称能否经得起时间的考验，它们是否还包含了内部笑话，是否容易过时等也同样是很重要的。句中 stand the test of time 意为"经得起时间的考验"；as 在此处意为"随着"，表示伴随状态；in-joke 意为"（圈内人才领会的）小范围笑话，内部笑话"。

11. The opinions of people who may be potential customers should be given the most weight.

译文：对那些可能成为潜在客户群的意见应该予以足够的重视。句中 who 引导的主语从句修饰 people，强调潜在客户群的意见；give the most weight 意为"予以重视"。

12. The request must be sent to the state patent and trademark office, and also to the federal office if the business will be conducting interstate commerce.

译文：该申请必须要送到国家专利局和商标事务所，如果企业将进行州际贸易的话，该申请还要递交到联邦办公室。句中 state patent 意为"国家专利局"，trademark office 意为"商标事务所"；interstate commerce 意为"州际贸易"。

I. Text comprehension questions.

1. Why are brand names important for small businesses?

2. What are the special features of successful branding?

3. What kinds of organizations can an entrepreneur consult?

4. How can a small business owner select a brand name?

5. How can the entrepreneur find out whether the names are available for use?

_____

_____

II. Decide whether each of the following statements is true（T）or false（F）or not mentioned（NM）in the text.

1. A well-chosen brand name can communicate a message about the firm's marketing position.

2. Economies of scale means that both costs and profits should increase as more products are made.

3. After deciding to establish a brand, an entrepreneur has to consult an advertising agency to think about the name.

4. A good brand name should be short and simple and suggestive of the product's benefits and sometimes can exaggerate its function to increase the sales.

5. It is important to identify some attributes and personality traits of the products.

6. The proper visual images and typefaces can enhance the products' appearance.

7. Conducting a trademark search can only be performed by some attorneys.

8. It is not necessary for a small business to send in a formal request to the federal office.

III. Choose the best answer to each question with the information from the text.

1. How to set a small business's product apart from those of competitors?

A. To choose a good brand name.

B. To broadcast from TV and Internet.

C. To promote its product in the supermarket.

D. To sell its product in a cheaper price.

2. What are the characteristics of a good brand name?

A. It should be easy to spell, pronounce, and remember.

B. It should be short and simple.

C. It should be adaptable to packaging and labeling needs.

D. All of the above.

3. Which one the following statement is NOT mentioned about the ways of selecting a brand name in the text?

A. The entrepreneur should examine the names in use in the market and evaluate its effectiveness.

B. The entrepreneur should try to find the special attributes about their products.

C. The entrepreneur should send free samples to customers and test their reactions to the products.

D. The entrepreneur should think about their products' visual images on a sign or a product

package.

4. How can small business owners test the impact of the brand name?

A. They can make a survey on whether the potential customers will accept their brand name.

B. They can find some strangers to see their reactions to the brand name.

C. They can organize a focus group to discuss about their brand name.

D. All of the above.

5. In order to get approved of a trademark, which organizations should a small business owner send the request to?

A. State Patent and Trademark Office.　　B. State Patent and Attorney Associations.

C. Federal Office and Tax Bureau.　　D. Trademark Office and Federal Office.

IV. Choose the word or phrase that is closest in meaning to the underlined one.

1. There is prospect of a very <u>profitable</u> market for your product in my country.

A. productive　　　B. advisable　　　C. desirable　　　D. aiding

2. His mode of doing business is <u>offensive</u> to me.

A. hateful　　　B. disgusting　　　C. unpleasant　　　D. defensive

3. The age of knowledge economy demands interdisciplinary talents with <u>innovative</u> consciousness and abilities.

A. radical　　　B. progressive　　　C. subversive　　　D. novel

4. As company performance improves, the <u>entrepreneur</u> obtains more control rights.

A. gentleman　　　B. millionaire　　　C. investor　　　D. tycoon

5. These years, there would be more <u>favorable</u> Credit Policy for the Grand Exploitation of the West in China.

A. convenient　　　B. helpful　　　C. sympathetic　　　D. promising

6. The company will <u>evaluate</u> your application form including your resume.

A. assess　　　B. appreciate　　　C. reckon　　　D. ascertain

7. Humility is an elusive <u>attribute</u>, which often seems to evade definition.

A. quantity　　　B. contribute　　　C. quality　　　D. specialty

8. For most people in the village, it is more <u>economical</u> to travel by car.

A. expensive　　　B. luxurious　　　C. frugal　　　D. wasteful

9. The manager should lead our local distributor to <u>enhance</u> our business coverage.

A. magnify　　　B. promote　　　C. reduce　　　D. minify

10. A trademark is a kind of <u>distinctive</u> name to identify the products of a company.

A. aesthetic　　　B. prejudicial　　　C. ordinary　　　D. particular

11. A personality <u>trait</u> includes the qualities of both introversion and extroversion.

A. peculiarity　　　B. nature　　　C. novelty　　　D. enthusiasm

12. The customers always <u>appreciate</u> efficient service.

A. praise　　　B. cherish　　　C. recognize　　　D. detect

V. Fill in the blanks with the phrases and expressions from the text. Change forms where necessary.

> apart from   come up with   specialize in   in relation to   narrow down

1. The executive board of the IOC will _____ the candidate cities again before a final decision is made.

2. He _____ a good idea for the product promotion which helped the company earn a lot of money.

3. There can be no knowledge _____ practice.

4. We _____ automotive parts and supplies only.

5. Your remarks seem strange _____ what I heard you said previously.

VI. Match the words with their definitions.

1. carefully selected to produce a desired effect

2. the owner or manager of a business enterprise who attempts to make profits

3. unpleasant or disgusting, as to the senses

4. to judge or assess the worth of; appraise

5. a property, quality, or feature belonging to or representative of a person or thing

6. a secretary whose main duty is to answer the telephone and receive visitors

7. a joke that is appreciated only by members of some particular group of people

8. a lawyer qualified to represent clients in legal proceedings

9. a government grant to an inventor assuring him the sole right to make, use, and sell his invention for a limited period

10. between or involving two or more of the states of the US

( ) offensive   ( ) evaluate   ( ) receptionist

( ) in-joke   ( ) attorney   ( ) patent

( ) well-chosen   ( ) interstate   ( ) entrepreneur   ( ) attribute

VII. Translate the following sentences into English.

1. 一个好的品牌名称将使你从竞争对手中脱颖而出。(apart from)

_____

2. 我们公司专门进出口国外产品。(specialize in)

_____

3. 他想出一个推广产品的好方法。(come up with)

_____

4. 最后只剩下三至五个特性可供选择，看哪个更适合品牌名称。(narrow down)

_____

5. 企业家要对市场上与该产品相关的名称作一下调查。(in relation to)

_____

VIII. Oral exercises.

Students in groups of two will make conversations about brand strategy. In the conversation practice, some sentence patterns will be used. In this unit, students will use the following two sentence patterns:

I insist on (doing) ...   我坚持……

We must do something to...   我们必须采取行动以……

Please follow example (1) and complete the following dialogue exercises. Student A and B will exchange roles upon completion.

For example (1) :

Student A: How about changing your company's name into a more innovative one?

Student B: No, I insist on the original one since our products have already had a large share in the market.

Student A: Do you think a good brand name would set your products apart from your competitors' ?

Student B: Yes. So I insist on (examining names already in use in the market, evaluating their effectiveness, identifying some attributes to make our products special, thinking about how the name would sound to the receptionists, etc.).

Please follow example (2) and complete the following dialogue exercises. Student A and B will exchange roles upon completion.

For example (2) :

Student A: We must do something to collect some useful information before we decided to get into the market.

Student B: That is reasonable.

Student A: We must do something to (set a small business' product apart from those of competitors, communicate a message regarding the firm's marketing position or corporate personality, enhance the products' appearance on a sign or a product package, narrow down the names on the list to a few candidates, etc.).

Student B: That is sensible.

IX. Writing skills. Please look at the pictures, the words and phrases coming from the pictures in relation to brand names below. And then write 3 – 5 sentences to describe each of the pictures.

The expressions in the brackets may help you to start your writing.

> (*There is/are . . . in the picture; The top left picture is about. . . ; The one on the right is the brand name of. . . ; In the bottom left corner of the picture, the green animal is. . . ; And the bottom right corner of the picture is about. . .*)

Picture 1 (German brand, sportswear company, typical feature, three parallel bars)

Picture 2 (American brand, sports related equipment, logo, just do it)

Picture 3 (green crocodile logo, headquarter, tennis wear)

Picture 4 (carbonated soft drink, internationally, beverage, Coke, registered trademark, dominance of the world soft-drink market)

X. PPT presentation. Two students in a group will work together to prepare 2 –3 pages of PPT slides to be presented in class. The topic for this unit is about how to create a brand name for a car, or accessories, or cosmetics, or sportswear, etc.

Further Reading One: Products and Services

People satisfy their needs and wants with products. A product is anything that can be offered to a market to satisfy a need or want. Usually, the word product suggests a physical object, such as a car, a television set or a bar of soap. However, the concept of product is not limited to physical objects—anything capable of satisfying a need can be called a product. In addition to tangible (有形的) goods, products include services, which are activities or benefits offered for sale that are essentially intangible and do not result in the ownership of anything. Examples are banking, airline, hotel and household appliance(家用电器) repair services. Broadly defined, products also include other entities such as persons, places, organizations, activities and ideas. Consumers decide which entertainers (艺人) to watch on television, which political party to vote for, which places to visit on holiday, which organizations to support through contributions and which ideas to adopt. Thus the term product covers physical goods, services and a variety of other vehicles that can satisfy consumers' needs and wants. If at times the term product does not seem to fit, we could substitute(替换) other terms such as satisfier, resource or offer.

Many sellers make the mistake of paying more attention to the physical products they offer than to the benefits produced by these products. They see themselves as selling a product rather than providing a solution to a need. The importance of physical goods lies not so much in owning them as in the benefits they provide. We don't buy food to look at, but because it cooks our food. A manufacturer of drill bits(钻头) may think that the customer needs a drill bit, but what the customer really needs is a hole. These sellers may suffer from marketing myopia. They are so taken with their products that they focus only on existing wants and lost sight of underlying customer needs. They forget that a physical product is only a tool to solve a consumer problem. These sellers have trouble if a new product comes along that serves the need better or less expensively. The customer with the same need will want the new product.

Exercise

I. Choose the best answer to each question with the information from the text.

1. Which of the following statement about product is TRUE?

A. It just refers to some tangible things that can be offered to a market and satisfy a need or want.

B. Anything capable of satisfying consumers' needs and wants can be called a product.

C. Products don't include the organizations, political party, activities and ideas.

D. A product merely means the consumers' ownership of something.

2. What is the importance of physical goods?

A. It lies in customers' ownership of them.

B. It lies in its beautiful visual images.

C. It lies in the benefits they provide to the customers.

D. It lies in the sense of security that the products bring to the customers.

3. Which of the following products or services are NOT intangible goods?

A. Household appliance repair services.　　B. Hotel reservation.

C. Airline services.　　D. Vehicles.

4. What's your understanding about marketing myopia?

A. It means the entrepreneur's short sighted and inward looking approach to marketing.

B. It means the entrepreneur's looking forward to meeting the demands of customers.

C. It means the customers' ignorance of the underlying needs.

D. It means the customers' reluctance to cope with the market trends.

5. How can sellers help customers solve their problems?

A. They should only focus on the customers' existing wants.

B. They should pay attention to the customers' underlying needs.

C. They should import more new products for customers to choose.

D. They should sell the products less expensively so that most customers can afford it.

II. Decide whether each of the following statements is true (T) or false (F).

1. The concept of product is limited to physical objects such as a car, a television set or a bar of soap.

2. We can use other terms such as satisfier, resource or offer to substitute the word product.

3. Many sellers see themselves as selling a product rather than providing a solution to a need.

4. A successful product should not only focus on existing wants but also pay attention to the underlying customer needs.

5. Most customers would like to use new products to solve their troubles.

Further Reading Two: Names and Identities

Large companies frequently invest a great deal of time and money into choosing the name for a major new product, often hiring the services of an outside firm that specializes in naming. The naming process considers such factors as

Is the name easy to pronounce on hearing and on sight?

Is it easy to remember?

Does the name invoke (引起) any negative or unfavorable associations(联想) (e. g. , it has more than one meaning or rhymes (同韵词) with an unflattering word (不讨好人的))?

Are the name's connotations (内涵意义) consistent with the intended (计划的) product (e. g. awhimsical (滑稽离奇) looking product should probably not have a formal sounding name)? What does the name mean or sound like in foreign markets where the product may be sold?

Some naming experts deliberately avoid descriptive (说明的) names that restate what the product or service is. Instead, they advise crafting (精心制作) a highly original name. An example would be naming an Internet access service National Internet Networks (descriptive) versus GeoNetworking (individualistic). Proponents (拥护者) of unique brand names note that they are less susceptible (可能……的) to imitation by competitors and may provide a more expansive umbrella for future extensions. In the hypothetical (假设的) Internet service example, National Internet Networks not only sounds generic(普通的), but the name also may not lend itself well to international expansion or to branching into non-Internet data services.

Using an interesting or unique name doesn't guarantee, however, that a brand will have a strong identity and resonate (共鸣) with its target customers. To achieve these goals, the marketer must patiently and consistently employ the brand name in advertising and other marketing endeavors (努力) to further the image or concept behind the product, not just as a label for it. Thus, if the image behind GeoNetworking is one of an expert service to assist small to medium businesses with breaking into international electronic commerce, then the notion of GeoNetworking as a dependable, knowledgeable, and worldwide resource must be emphasized in the company's communications with its customers. Advertising should showcase(展示) these traits and avoid presenting contradictory messages that are convenient for the current ad campaign (e. g. a humorous animated commercial) but do nothing to provide identity to the GeoNetworking brand.

I. Choose the best answer to each question with the information from the text.

1. How do large companies choose the name for its new products?

A. They will invest a great deal of time in it.

B. They will spend a lot of money on it.

C. They will hire the services of an outside firm that specializes in naming.

D. All of the above.

2. What factors should the naming experts consider in the naming process?

A. Pronunciation.   B. Associations.   C. Connotations.   D. All of the above.

3. Why do naming experts advise crafting a highly original name?

A. Because it is connotative.   B. Because it is descriptive.

C. Because it is individualistic.   D. Because it can flatter its potential customers.

4. How can a brand have a strong identity and resonate with its target customers?

A. It should have an interesting or unique name.

B. It should advertise patiently and consistently.

C. It should have a whimsical looking and a favorable sounding name.

D. It should consider its future extensions

5. Why is the brand name GeoNetworking better than National Internet Networks according to the author's opinion?

A. GeoNetworking sounds more individualistic.

B. GeoNetworking delivers company's communications with its potential customers and provides a more expansive choice for future extensions.

C. National Internet Networks can imply the further image or concept behind it.

D. National Internet Networks can lend itself well to international expansion and break into non-Internet data services.

II. Decide whether each of the following statement is true (T) or false (F).

1. Large companies frequently invest a great deal of time and money into choosing the name for a major new product.

2. Some naming experts deliberately avoid descriptive names because they are not original.

3. The unique brand names are quite easy to be imitated by their competitors.

4. Using an interesting name will guarantee that a brand will have a strong identity and resonate with its target customers.

5. The marketer must consistently employ the brand name in advertising to further the image and its concept behind the product.

Unit Seven   Business and Managerial Ethics

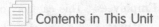

Contents in This Unit

1. Two pre-reading discussion questions.
2. A text on business and managerial ethics.
3. New words and expressions.
4. Explanatory notes for the text.
5. Some exercises to build up your skills both in English and business.
6. A PPT hands-on assignment to give you space for creation.
7. Further readings on business and managerial ethics.

Pre-reading Discussions for the Text

Please discuss these questions in pairs. You may talk over the topics either in English or in Chinese according to your teacher's instruction.

1. Do you hear any stories about business ethics? If yes, tell us the story . You may write down some key words and phrases before you talk.

_____

_____

_____

2. Do you want to be an ethical businessman? Discuss how to do this with your classmates. You may write down the key words and phrases before you talk.

_____

_____

_____

Text: Business and Managerial Ethics

Managerial ethics are the standards of behavior that guide individual managers in their work. Although your ethics can affect your work in any number of ways, it's helpful to classify them in terms of three broad categories.

Behavior Toward Employees This category covers such matters as hiring and firing, wages and working conditions, and privacy and respect. Ethical and legal guidelines suggest that hiring and firing decisions should be based solely on ability to perform a job. A manager who discriminates against African Americans in hiring exhibits both unethical and illegal behavior. But what about the manager who hires a friend or relative when someone else might be more qualified? Such decisions may not be illegal; but they may be objectionable on ethical grounds.

Wages and working conditions, though regulated by law, are also areas for controversy. If there is a manager who pays a worker less than he deserves because the manager knows that the employee can't afford to quit his job, some people will see the behavior as unethical, while others will see it as smart business, so cases such as these are hard enough to judge.

Behavior Toward the Organization Ethical issues also arise from employee behavior toward employers, especially in such areas as conflict of interest, confidentiality, and honesty. A conflict of interest occurs when an activity may benefit the individual to the detriment of his or her employer. Most companies have policies that forbid buyers from accepting gifts from suppliers. Businesses in highly competitive industries—software and fashion apparel, for example—have safeguards against designers selling company secrets to competitors. Relatively common problems in the general area of honesty include such behavior as stealing supplies, padding expense accounts, and using a business phone to make personal long-distance calls. Most employees are honest, but most organizations are nevertheless vigilant. Enron is a good example of employees' unethical behavior toward an organization. Top managers not only misused corporate assets, but they often committed the company to risky ventures in order to further personal interests.

Behavior Toward Other Economic Agents Ethics also comes into play in the relationship between the firm and its employees with so-called primary agents of interests—mainly customers, competitors, stockholders, suppliers, dealers, and unions. In dealing with such agents, there is room for ethical ambiguity in just about every activity—advertising, financial disclosure, ordering and purchasing, bargaining and negotiation, and other business relationships.

For example, businesses in the pharmaceutical industry are under criticism because of the ris-

ing prices of drugs. They argue that high prices cover the costs of research and development programs to develop new drugs. The solution to such problems seems obvious: find the right balance between reasonable pricing and price gouging (responding to increased demand with overly steep price increases). But like so many questions involving ethics, there are significant differences of opinion about the proper balance.

Another recent area of concern is financial reporting, especially by high-tech forms like WorldCom. Some of these companies have been very aggressive in presenting their financial positions in a positive light, and in a few cases, they have overstated earnings projections in order to entice more investment. Certainly, again, there's Enron.

■ Senior officials continued to mislead investors into thinking that the firm was solvent long after they knew that it was in serious trouble.

■ The company violated numerous state regulations during the California energy crisis, causing thousands of consumers' hardships and inconvenience.

■ Many of its partnerships with other firms violated terms of full disclosure and honesty, resulting in losses for other firms and their employees.

Another problem is global variations in business practices. In many countries, bribes are a normal part of doing business. U. S. law, however, forbids bribes, even if rivals from other countries are paying them. A U. S. power-generating company recently lost a $320 million contract in the Middle East because it refused to pay bribes that a Japanese firm used to get the job.

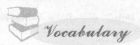

Vocabulary

1. ethics ['eθiks]
    n. moral principles that govern a person's behavior or the conducting of an activity
    道德准则,行为准则

2. category ['kætigəri]
    n. a group of people or things with particular features in common
    种类,类别

3. solely ['səulli]
    adv. only; not involving anyone or anything else
    单独地,唯一地;仅仅

4. objectionable [əb'dʒekʃənəbl]
    adj. arousing distaste or opposition
    有异议的

5. regulate ['reg.juleit]
    vt. to control sth. by means of rules
    管理,控制

6. controversy ['kɔntrəvəːsi]
    n. public disagreement or heated discussion
    争议;纠纷

7. deserve [di'zə:v]　　　　　　　*vt.* to have earned or to be given something because of the way you have behaved or the qualities you have
应受,应得,值得

8. issue ['isju:]　　　　　　　　*n.* an important topic that people are discussing or arguing about
问题,议题,争议

9. interest['intrist]　　　　　　　*n.* a share in a business or company and its profits
利益,私利

10. confidentiality[,kɔnfi,denʃi'æləti]　　*n.* the state or condition of being secret or private
机密

11. occur [ə'kə:]　　　　　　　　*vi.* to happen
发生,出现

13. detriment ['detrimənt]　　　　*n.* the state of being harmed or damaged
损害,不利

14. apparel[ə'pærəl]　　　　　　*n.* clothes or clothing
衣着,服饰

15. pad [pæd]　　　　　　　　*vt.* to dishonestly add items to bills to obtain more money
虚报(账目)

16. nevertheless [,nevəðə'les]　　*adv.* despite sth. that you have just mentioned
然而

17. vigilant ['vidʒilənt]　　　　　*adj.* very careful to notice any signs of danger or trouble
警觉的,警惕的

18. asset ['æset]　　　　　　　　*n.* a thing of value, especially property, that a person or company owns, which can be used or sold to debts
资产

19. ambiguity [,æmbi'gju:iti]　　*n.* the states of being difficult to understand or explain because of involving many different aspects
含糊不清,不明确

20. disclosure [dis'kləuʒə]　　　*n.* the action of making new or secret information known
揭露,披露,公开

21. pharmaceutical [,fɑːmə'sjuːtikəl]　*adj.* connected with making and selling drugs and medicines

制药的

22. aggressive [əˈgresiv]	*adj.*	full of enterprise and initiative 积极进取的,活跃的
23. solvent [ˈsɔlvənt]	*adj.*	having enough money to pay your debts; not in debt 有偿付能力的,无债务的
24. violate [ˈvaiəleit]	*vt.*	to go against or refuse to obey a law, an agreement, etc. 违背,违犯,违反
25. bribe [braib]	*n.*	a sum of money or sth. valuable that you give or offer to sb. to persuade them to help you, especially by doing sth. dishonest 贿赂
26. rival [ˈraivəl]	*n.*	a person, company, or thing that competes with another in sport, business, etc. 竞争对手
27. contract [ˈkɔntrækt]	*n.*	an official written agreement 合同,契约

 *Phrase and Expression*

1. in terms of   就……而言;根据
2. be based on   取决于;以……为基础
3. discriminate against   歧视
4. on ... grounds   以……为由
5. arise from   由……引起、产生
6. forbid sb. from doing   禁止某人做某事
7. commit... to...   把……交付给,委托于
8. come into play   开始活动,投入使用,起作用
9. so-called   所谓的
10. respond to   反应,应对
11. in a positive light   从积极的角度

Notes for Text

1. A manager who discriminates against African Americans in hiring exhibits both unethical and illegal behavior.

译文:一位在雇佣时歧视美国黑人的管理者表现出的行为既不道德也不合法。who... in hiring 是限定性定语从句,修饰主语 manager;exhibit 意为"展示、表现"。

2. Such decisions may not be illegal; but they may be objectionable on ethical grounds.

译文：这样的用人决定也许并不违法，但是会遭到以道德为由的反对。短语 on...grounds 意为"以……为由"。例：The playground was closed down on safety grounds. 操场因安全原因而被关闭了。

3. Wages and working conditions, though regulated by law, are also areas for controversy.

译文：虽然有法律的制约，工资和工作环境也是民事纠纷的主要方面。句中 though...by law 引导让步状语从句，在此为插入语。

4. If there is a manager who pays a worker less than he deserves because the manager knows that the employee can't afford to quit his job, some people will see the behavior as unethical, while others will see it as smart business, so cases such as these are hard enough to judge.

译文：如果管理者因为知道员工害怕丢掉工作而不敢辞职，而向该员工支付少于其应得的工资，有人将此行为视为不道德，而也有人将其看做是一场精明的生意，所以像这样的案例通常很难作出论断。If...his job 是条件状语从句，主句为 some people will see...business。在条件状语从句中，who pays...his job 是定语从句，修饰主语 a manager；than he deserves 是该定语从句所带的比较状语从句；because 又是该定语从句中所带的原因状语从句。主句由 while 转折连词连接两个并列句；so...judge 是结果状语从句。

5. Enron is a good example of employees' unethical behavior toward an organization.

译文：在员工对企业组织实施不道德行为方面，安然公司是一个绝佳的反面教材。Enron 即安然公司，曾是一家位于美国得克萨斯州休斯敦市的能源类公司，是世界上最大的电力、天然气公司之一。拥有上千亿资产的该公司于 2002 年在几周内破产。从那时起，"安然"已经成为公司欺诈以及堕落的象征。

6. Ethics also comes into play in the relationship between the firm and its employees with so-called primary agents of interests—mainly customers, competitors, stockholders, suppliers, dealers, and unions.

译文：在公司与其员工之间的关系方面，伦理道德也起着作用，这些员工是所谓的主要利益代理人，通常是客户、竞争者、股东、供应商、证券经纪人以及工会。句中 come into play 意为"起作用；产生效果"。例：The new rules have already come into play. 新规则已经开始生效。All your faculties have come into play in your work. 在你的工作中，你的全部才能已起到了作用。

7. Another recent area of concern is financial reporting, especially by high-tech forms like WorldCom.

译文：近来令人关注的还有财务报告，尤其是像 WorldCom 这样的高新技术公司作出的。WorldCom 即世通公司，是一家美国的通信公司，于 2003 年破产。目前公司已更名 MCI 有限公

司,总部位于弗吉尼亚州。世通公司经历了美国电信业半个世纪以来的风风雨雨:它曾推动了美国反垄断的立法过程,这导致了 AT&T 的被分拆;它对 MCI 的收购以及后爆出的会计丑闻反映了 20 世纪 90 年末互联网泡沫中电信业的躁动不安。

8. The company violated numerous state regulations during the California energy crisis, causing thousands of consumers'hardships and inconvenience.

译文:在加州能源危机期间,该公司违反大量州政府条例,给成千上万的客户带来苦难与不便。California energy crisis 即"加州能源危机",又称"美国西部能源危机",指的是 2000 年至 2001 年间加州的电力短缺。

Exercise

Ⅰ. Text comprehension questions.

1. What are the matters involved in the first category called "Behavior towards Employees"?

2. What are the unethical behaviors toward employers in conflict of honesty?

3. Who are the primary agents of interests?

4. What can we learn about the financial reporting according to the author?

5. What is the attitude to the bribe in America?

Ⅱ. **Decide whether each of the following statements is true（T）or false（F）or not mentioned in the text（NM）.**

1. It is suggested ethically and legally that hiring and firing decisions should be based only on ability to work.

2. If a manager hires a friend or relative instead of someone who is more qualified, his behavior is considered as illegal.

3. Different people have different opinions on unethical behaviors.

4. A conflict of interest occurs when an activity may bring the benefit to the individual and his or her employer.

5. Most organizations don't consider making personal long-distance calls with a business phone as a problem of honesty.

6. Most employees are dishonest so the organization keeps a close eye on them.

7. We know the pharmaceutical industry has their reasons for the problem and we understand that.

8. A U.S. company is not allowed to bribe unless it knows its competitors are paying them.

Ⅲ. **Choose the best answer to each question with the information from the text.**

1. Which of the following aspects is not covered by the standards of behavior according to the definition of managerial ethics?

A. The manager makes a decision to hire or fire an employee.

B. The organization is worried about its employees' unfaithful behaviors.

C. The employee has opportunity to self-improve by studying abroad.

D. The organization lies to its investors, customers for its reasons.

2. What do we think of his behavior if a manager discriminates against African American in making hiring decisions?

A. His behavior is unethical but legal.

B. His behavior is illegal but ethical.

C. His behavior is far away from legal and ethical.

D. His behavior is neither illegal nor unethical.

3. Which one is FALSE about the controversy on wage and working condition?

A. Wages and working conditions are main controversies because they are unprotected by law.

B. Some think less payment than the worker deserves is not ethical.

C. Some think less payment than the worker deserves is reasonable.

D. One of the reasons for controversy is that the employee can do nothing if he quits his job.

4. Which of the following statements could be regarded as price gouging?

A. The price of fresh food is much higher than that is close to the expiration date.

B. The price of a CD is much higher than that of a tape.

C. The price of a gauze mask was much higher than usual time during the spread of influenza A-H1N1.

D. The price of the hard-cover dictionary is much higher than that of the paper-cover one.

5. Which one is TRUE about the bribery?

A. It is very common in many nations.

B. It is forbidden by law in America.

C. American businessmen would rather lost a contract than bribe the opponent.

D. All the above.

IV. Choose the word or phrase that is closest in meaning to the underlined one.

1. She resigned over an issue of personal ethics.

A. rules   B. morals   C. principles   D. bottom lines

2. I think we can classify this as an emergency situation.

A. categorize   B. divide   C. dismiss   D. separate

3. We can't rely solely on the television for news.

A. merely   B. individually   C. lonely   D. significantly

4. We must learn to discriminate right from wrong.

A. differentiate B. tell   C. separate   D. different

5. They regulate their temperature by making a variety of internal adjustments.

A. reset   B. correct   C. modify   D. adjust

6. His views have excited a lively controversy among fellow scientists.

A. rejection   B. forbiddance   C. control   D. disagreement

7. Most manufacturing occurred in relatively small plants.

A. showed   B. happened   C. appeared   D. presented

8. Not only the professionals but also the amateurs will benefit from the new training facilities.

A. derive   B. acquire   C. profit   D. reward

9. He has to learn how to remain vigilant through these long nights.

A. calm   B. watchful   C. careful   D. nervous

10. It's far too risky to generalize from one set of results.

A. unsafe   B. uncertain   C. unknown   D. unfamiliar

11. The bargain prices are expected to entice customers away from other stores.

A. involve   B. seduce   C. tempt   D. introduce

12. They violated the terms of a ceasefire.

A. disobey   B. disagree   C. dishonor   D. disprove

V. Fill in the blanks with the phrases and expressions from the text. Change forms where necessary.

respond to	come into play	arise from	in terms of	be based on

1. It was the worst plane crash _____ casualties.

2. His illness _____ malnutrition.

3. Companies should _____ this kind of situation in an honest and open way.

4. The movie _____ a real-life incident.

5. The main factors that _____ should never be ignored.

VI. Match the words with their definitions.

1. trouble or problems, especially concerning what you need or would like yourself

2. a situation in which people, groups or countries are involved in a serious disagreement or argument

3. the money that you invest, or the thing that you invest in

4. rules or instructions that are given by an official organization telling you how to do sth.

5. large or important enough to have an effect or to be noticed

6. to decide whether sb. is guilty or innocent in a court

7. a relationship between two people, organizations, etc.

8. a statement showing disapproval

9. formal discussion between people who are trying to reach an agreement

10. contrary to or forbidden by law, especially criminal law

( ) illegal   ( ) conflict   ( ) guidelines

( ) criticism   ( ) investment   ( ) judge

( ) partnership   ( ) negotiation   ( ) inconvenience   ( ) significant

VII. Translate the following sentences into English.

1. 这就是所谓的生产标准化吗？（so-called）

_____

2. 他禁止孩子们再提这件事情。（forbid ... from ...）

_____

3. 政府迫于压力撤销了那项提议。（respond to）

_____

4. 就艺术宝藏而言，意大利是世界最富有的国家之一。（in terms of）

_____

5. 事故可能因疏忽而引起。（arise from）

_____

VIII. Oral exercises.

Students in groups of two will make conversations about business and managerial ethics. In the conversation practice, some sentence patterns will be used. In this unit, students will use the following two sentence patterns：

It depends on whether...   这取决于……是否……

In that case,... 既然那样,……

Please follow example (1) and complete the following dialogue exercises. Student A and B will exchange roles upon completion.

For example (1):

> Student A: <u>It depends on whether</u> the chairman is efficient.
> Student B: Yes, I agree with you.
> Student A: <u>It depends on whether</u> (your ethics can affect your work, someone else might be more qualified, the manager knows that the employee can't afford to quit his job, a conflict of interest occurs).
> Student B: Yes, I agree with you.

Please follow example (2) and complete the following dialogue exercises. Student A and B will exchange roles upon completion.

For example (2):

> Student A: <u>In that case</u>, you may do whatever you want.
> Student B: Yes, you're right.
> Student A: <u>In that case</u>, (such decisions may not be illegal, the employee can't afford to quit his job, a conflict of interest occurs, most organizations are nevertheless vigilant, there is room for ethical ambiguity, businesses in the pharmaceutical industry are under criticism).
> Student B: Yes, you're right.

IX. Writing skills. Please look at the pictures, the words and phrases coming from the pictures about business and managerial ethics below. And then write 3 – 5 sentences to describe each of the pictures.

The expressions in the brackets may help you to start your writing.

(There is/are ... in the picture; In the middle of the picture; Then let's look at the next picture; This picture is about ...; The person on the right...; From the picture, you can see...; The central focus of this picture is...; In the top left corner /bottom right corner of the picture, a man/woman/boy/girl...; From her/his facial expression, I can assume that...; From the..., I can tell that...; Perhaps this man is about to...)

Picture 1（Chinese Ethics, successful management, modern management）

Picture 2（bribery, prohibit, ethical and legal）

Picture 3（office, make private calls, violate, confidentiality and loyalty）

Picture 4（equality, respect, cooperation, honesty, integrity）

X．PPT presentation. Two students in a group will work together to prepare 5 – 8 pages of PPT slides to be presented in class. The topic for this unit is about presenting an unethical business case.

Further Reading One:Ethics in Business

Ethics in business, or business ethics as it is often called, is the application of the discipline (规章制度), principles, and theories of ethics to the organizational context(环境). Business ethics have been defined as "principles and standards that guide behavior in the world of business". Business ethics is also a descriptive(描述性的) term for the field of academic(学术的) study in which many scholars conduct research and in which undergraduate(本科生) and graduate students are exposed(影响,暴露) to ethics theory and practice, usually through the case method of analysis.

Ethical behavior in business is critical. When business firms are charged with infractions(违犯), and when employees of those firms come under legal investigation(调查), there is a concern raised about moral behavior in business. Hence, the level of mutual(相互的,共同的) trust, which is the foundation of our free-market economy, is threatened.

Although ethics in business has been an issue for academics, practitioners(实践者), and governmental regulators(管理者) for decades(十年), some believe that unethical, immoral, and/or illegal behavior is widespread in the business world. Numerous scandals(丑行) in the late 1990s and early 2000s seemed to add credence(可靠,确实) to the criticism of business ethics. Corporate executives(主管) of WorldCom, a giant in the telecommunications field, admitted fraud(骗局) and misrepresentation in financial statements. WorldCom's former CEO went on trial(审判) for alleged(被指控的) crimes related to this accounting ethics scandal.

A similar scandal engulfed(陷入) Enron in the late 1990s and its former CEO, Ken Lay, also faced trial. Other notable ethical lapses were publicized involving ImClone, a biotechnological(生物科技) firm; Arthur Andersen, one of the largest and oldest public accounting(会计) firms; and Healthsouth, a large healthcare(医疗保健) firm located in the southeast United States. These companies eventually suffered public humiliation(耻辱), huge financial losses, and in some cases, bankruptcy(破产) or dissolution. The ethical and legal problems resulted in some corporate officials going to prison, many employees losing their jobs, and thousands of stockholders losing some or all of their savings invested in the firms' stock.

Exercise

I. Choose the best answer to each question with the information from the text.

1. Which of the following is NOT included in business ethics?

A. Discipline.   B. Principles.

C. Theories.   D. The organizational context.

2. Which one is NOT TRUE about the mutual trust?

A. It's the base of free-market economy.

B. It means the companies trust their employees and vice versa.

C. It is regarded as moral problems if either of the forms and the employees has any problem in ethics.

D. The employees have problems in trust and the firms don't.

3. Which one of the following statements is TRUE?

A. Some believes that there isn't any unethical behavior in business world.

B. There is no unethical behavior until the late 1990s.

C. The unethical behaviors are very common in business world.

D. The big firms can be trusted.

4. Which company manages in keeping out of unethical problems?

A. Ken Lay.　　　　B. ImClone.　　　　C. Healthsouth.　　　　D. Arthur Andersen.

5. What are the consequences for the firms involving in unethical problems?

A. Public humiliation.　　　　　　　　B. Financial losses.

C. Bankruptcy.　　　　　　　　　　　　D. All of the above.

II. Decide whether each of the following statement is true（T）or false（F）.

1. Business ethics are principles, standards, and also a academic term.

2. Only the firm would be questioned about its moral image if its employees have unethical problems.

3. Ten years' efforts cannot stop those immoral behaviors appearing in business world.

4. WorldCom was involved with the fraud on money.

5. All of the three sides, the firm officials, the employees and the stockholders, lose much if they are unethical and illegal when doing business.

Further Reading Two: Professions

A distinguishing(识别性) mark of professions such as medicine and accounting is acceptance of their responsibilities to the public. The AICPA Code of Professional Conduct(美国会计师协会职业行为道德标准) describes the accounting profession's public as consisting of "clients, credit grantors, governments, employers, investors, the business and financial community, and others who rely on the objectivity(客观性) and integrity(完整性) of CPAs to maintain the orderly functioning of commerce". Many, but not all, CPAs work in firms that provide accounting, auditing(审计), and other services to the general public; these CPAs are said to be in public practice. Regardless of where CPAs work, the AICPA Code applies to their professional conduct, although there are some special provisions(条款) for those in public practice. Internal auditors, management accountants, and financial managers most commonly are employees of the organizations to which they provide these services; but, as professionals, they, too, must also be mindful of their obligations(义务) to the public.

The responsibilities placed on accounting professionals by the three ethics codes and the related

professional standards have many similarities. All three require professional competence, confidentiality(机密性), integrity, and objectivity. Accounting professionals should only undertake tasks that they can complete with professional competence, and they must carry out their responsibilities with sufficient(充分的) care and diligence(勤奋), usually referred to as due professional care or due care. The codes of ethics of the AICPA, IMA, and IIA all require that confidential information known to accounting professionals not be disclosed to outsiders. The most significant exception to the confidentiality rules is that accounting professionals' work papers are subject to subpoena(传唤) by a court; nothing analogous(相似的) to attorney-client privilege exists.

Exercise

I. Choose the best answer to each question with the information from the text.

1. Which one of the following statements is TRUE?

A. Professions mean the acceptance of their responsibilities.

B. Accounting profession's public refers to the individuals whose works are accounts.

C. CPAs only work for the public.

D. Financial manager is mindful of the public over the organizations.

2. What does "credit grantors" mean?

A. The people who sell credit cards.

B. The people who lend money.

C. The people who provide credits.

D. The people who seek credit.

3. Which one is the code of ethics of the AICPA, IMA, and IIA?

A. Confidential information should be closed to both professionals and outsiders.

B. Confidential information should be disclosed to both professionals and outsiders.

C. Confidential information should be closed to professionals but not to outsiders.

D. Confidential information should be disclosed to professionals but not to outsiders.

4. What does "due" mean?

A. Required.   B. Deserved.   C. Ruled.   D. Covered.

5. What title can you give to this article?

A. Ethical Behaviors.   B. Ethical Responsibilities.

C. Ethical Professionals.   D. Ethical Publics.

II. Decide whether each of the following statement is true (T) or false (F).

1. Managers in publishing companies, for example, frequently contract with freelance editors to copyedit new manuscripts that they intend to publish.

2. Outsourcing can sometimes allow managers to make use of human resource at a lower cost.

3. Outsourcing has not only advantages but disadvantages.

4. Outsourcing can give managers increased feasibility, especially when accurately forecasting human resource needs is difficult, and human resource needs fluctuate over time.

5. The organization does not have to provide benefits to workers.

Unit Eight   Gender and Race in Business

Contents in This Unit

1. Two pre-reading discussion questions.
2. A text on women in history.
3. New words and expressions.
4. Explanatory notes for the text.
5. Some exercises to build up your skills both in English and business.
6. A PPT hands-on assignment to give you space for creation.
7. Further readings on gender and race in business.

Pre-reading Discussions for the Text

Please discuss these questions in pairs. You may talk over the topics either in English or in Chinese according to your teacher's instruction.

1. Do you have any stories about women entrepreneurs? If yes, tell us the story. You may write down some key words and phrases before you talk.

---

2. What do you think of women's contribution to business? Discuss this with your classmates. You may write down the key words and phrases before you talk.

Text: Women in History

In 17th and 18th-century America, women worked at home with their husbands to contribute to the family's economic support. Employment opportunities for women were scarce. In this essentially self supporting rural lifestyle, centers of commerce emerged as small towns and cities. Working out of necessity, women became shopkeepers, artisans, and merchants. The most frequent reason for working was widowhood. Examples of working women in colonial America are often associated with the clothing trade. Women printers, however, illustrate a particularly significant departure from textile-based employment. Women entrepreneurs such as

Elizabeth Cady Stanton

Elizabeth Timothy and Cornelia Smith Bradford operated as independent printers and bookbinders in South Carolina and Boston, respectively, in 18th-century America. The employment of women in the printing trades was well-regarded and common at the time. Frequently, a woman would inherit her husband's printing business at the time of his death. As proprietors and purveyors of the printed word, women printers enjoyed a small but significant minority role in colonial America. The impending war with England created a demand for goods made in America, thus opening business opportunities to women engaged in the production of cloth and food. Even as women worked, however, they still worked out of necessity. The prevailing societal attitude projected the ideal woman as family oriented, not business oriented.

Two women strikers picketing during the shirtwaist strike of 1909

Post revolutionary America found women engaged in the business of working at home. Piecework or take-home work formed roots during this time that continue to modern day. In conjunction with increased industrialization, textile mills in the northeastern states sought women out as a source of cheap labor and the organized movement of women into the workforce first appeared. Combined with the endeavors of early women's rights activists such as Elizabeth Cady Stanton (1815 – 1902), the idea of women in the workplace began to gain approval. As cities grew and transportation improved, work and business increased, and homework or piecework decreased. The influx of immigration from 1840 on increased the labor force. Society began to embrace the idea of the ideal woman and diminished the expectation for a woman's contribution to family financial health. Instead, men assumed the burden of sole provider while women stayed at home more and more frequently. With the advent of the Civil War, this model changed.

Clerical and teaching opportunities opened to women during the Civil War. Nursing began to assume a professional component due to the casualties of the war. As a result of the great many deaths

in the Civil War, thousands of women were left to fend for themselves financially and economically. A conflict arose between the economic need for survival and the cultural expectations of family responsibility.

By the turn of the 19th century, women altered the cultural landscape by creating the idea of a new woman to replace the ideal women. Changing ideas of women included the central role of woman as partner to the economic well-being of the family and society as a whole. By 1900, more than 20 percent of women worked for a wage. The range and variety of employment in the 1900 census indicates that women held jobs in law, journalism, dentistry, medicine, engineering, mining, and other typical occupations. Women were counted in 295 of the 305 occupations listed on the census. The increasing industrialization of the United States resulted in a surge in factory work. More than one million women worked in factories in 1900. Most of these women were young, single, and foreign-born. They worked for low wages and knew no job security. Factories were unsafe and dirty. As a result, the businesswoman's first association with labor unionism appeared. In the Uprising of the 20,000 in 1909, women banded together and struck to protest working conditions and wages in the clothing industry.

Even as women worked in industry to fuel its growth, the outcome created new business opportunities for women in clerical jobs. Between 1900 and 1920, the number of women clerical workers grew from 187,000 to 1,421,000. Women entered professional and managerial jobs during this time as well. Health, education, and caring professions emerged to alleviate suffering caused by industrialization while simultaneously expanding professional opportunities for women. During World War I, women assumed many of the roles and jobs of men during their absence. After the war, however, women were expected to return to familial pursuits. Still considered a secondary labor force, women were encouraged to engage in volunteer and charity work. Many who chose to remain in the workforce took lower-paying jobs as men returned from military service.

During World War II, women again entered the workforce in great numbers. In response to a need for new workers and new production, six million women went to work during the war. Society's approval of this phenomenon was reflected in posters of Rosie the Riveter and other cultural signals. Magazines and movies and other media all reinforced a woman's patriotic duty to work. Again, however, at the end of the war, women were encouraged to leave the workplace and return to the family environment. While half the women in the workplace left between 1945 and 1946, by 1947 the employment rate of women had regained its wartime levels. And, by 1950, almost one third of all women worked outside the home.

From the end of World War II to present, women continued to gain a significant presence in the work world. In the 1960s, the women's movement articulated a number of issues that concerned women employees, including low pay, low status, and sexual discrimination. Gaining steam, women networked and organized and successfully lobbied for governmental protections such as the Equal Pay Act of 1963 and the Pregnancy Discrimination Act of 1978. Through a series of redress such as court decisions, laws, and affirmative action, women found new rights and opportunities in the workplace. During this time, married women and mothers continued to participate in employment outside the home in increasing numbers. Spurred by consumerism and the need to make more money to buy more things, married women composed almost two-thirds of the female labor force in the mid-1970s. And, as more women emerged as single parents, mothers also entered the workforce in increasing numbers as a matter of economic survival.

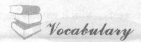

Vocabulary

1. opportunity [ˌɔpə'tjuːnəti]	*n.* a situation that makes it possible for you to do something that you want to do 机会,时机
2. scarce [skɛəs]	*adj.* not enough or only available in small quantities 稀有,缺乏
3. rural ['ruːrəl]	*adj.* connected with or like the countryside 乡村的
4. widowhood ['widəuhud]	*n.* the state or period of being a widow or widower 孀居,守寡
5. colonial [kə'ləunjəl]	*adj.* of or relating to the colonies 殖民的
6. illustrate ['iləstreit]	*vt.* to show that sth. is true or that a situation exists 表明,阐明,表示,显示
7. respectively [ri'spektivli]	*adv.* separately or distinctly 各自地,分别地
8. inherit [in'herit]	*vt.* to receive a position, property, etc. from a predecessor 继承(职位、财产等)
9. impending [im'pendiŋ]	*adj.* about to occur or happen 即将发生的,逼近的
10. oriented ['ɔːriəntid]	*adj.* having a particular interest in sth. ; targeted 有兴趣趋向的;定向的
11. activist ['æktivist]	*n.* a person who works to achieve political or social change, especially as a member of an organiza-

tion with particular aims

（政治活动的）积极分子，活动家

12. influx ['inflʌks]   *n.* an arrival or entry of large numbers of people or things

流入，涌入

13. assume [ə'sju:m]   *vt.* to think or accept that sth. is true without proof of it

假定，假设，臆断

14. casualty ['kæʒjuəlti]   *n.* a person killed or injured in a war or accident

伤亡者

15. conflict ['kɔnflikt]   *n.* a serious difference between two or more beliefs, ideas, or interests, which cannot be reconciled

（信念、意见、利益等之间不可调和的）严重分歧，冲突

16. alter ['ɔ:ltə]   *v.* to become different; to make sb./sth. different

改变，变样

17. census ['sensəs]   *n.* the process of officially counting sth., especially a country's population, and recording various facts

统计数，记录

18. uprising [ʌp'raiziŋ]   *n.* a situation in which a group of people join together in order to fight against the people who are in power

起义，暴动

19. protest ['prəutest]   *n.* a statement or action expressing disapproval of or objection to something

抗议；对……提出异议；反对

v. to make strong objection to something

抗议；反对

20. fuel [fjuəl]   *vt.* to provide with some kind of energy; stimulate; stir

增加能量；刺激；引起

21. military ['militəri]   *adj.* of or relating to the armed forces (esp. the army)

军事的，军人的

22. phenomenon [fi'nɔminən]   *n.* a fact or an event in nature or society, especially one that is not fully understood

现象，特别的事情

23. patriotic [ˌpetri'ɔtik] *adj.* having or expressing devotion to and vigorous support for one's country
爱国的,有爱国心的

24. articulate [ɑː'tikjulit] *vt.* to express or explain your thoughts or feelings clearly in words
清楚地表达

25. discrimination [diˌskrimi'neiʃən] *n.* the practice of treating sb. or a particular group in society less fairly than others
差别对待;歧视

26. redress [ri'dres] *n.* remedy or compensation for a wrong or grievance
补偿,补救

Phrase and Expression

1. out of necessity   出于需要
2. be associated with   与……有关
3. engage in   从事
4. even as   正如;正当
5. in conjunction with   与……共同;与……结合
6. combined with   与……联合;与……结合
7. fend for oneself   自己谋生,照料自己
8. result in   导致……(后果)
9. in response to   对……的答复;对……的反应
10. lobby for   为争取……而游说

Notes for Text

1. Working out of necessity, women became shopkeepers, artisans, and merchants.

译文:出于需要而工作的妇女当起了店主、工匠以及商人。本句中 Working out of necessity 为现在分词短语作原因状语;out of necessity 意为"迫不得已,出于需要"。例:This spirit will continue to live in the future out of sheer necessity. 这种精神今后必然会继续存在下去。

2. Women entrepreneurs such as Elizabeth Timothy and Cornelia Smith Bradford operated as independent printers and bookbinders in South Carolina and Boston, respectively, in 18th-century America.

译文:18 世纪的美国,像伊丽莎白·提摩西和科尼莉亚·史密斯·布雷德福这样的女性企业家分别在南卡罗莱纳州和波士顿,以独立印刷商和装订商的身份经营。句中 respectively 意为"分别地,各自地",作插入语。例:John and Peter work and study respectively. 约翰和彼得一个工作,一个学习。

3. Post revolutionary America found women engaged in the business of working at home.

译文：独立战争后期的美国女性开始从事居家劳动。句中 post 意为"之后的"。例：post doctorate 博士后学位；postgraduate institution 研究生院。

4. Combined with the endeavors of early women's rights activists such as Elizabeth Cady Stanton (1815 – 1902), the idea of women in the workplace began to gain approval.

译文：加之诸如伊丽莎白·卡迪·斯坦顿(1815—1902)这样的早期女权主义者的艰苦努力与尝试，女工这一概念开始得到承认。combined with... 是过去分词短语作状语。Elizabeth Cady Stanton 斯坦顿夫人，原名伊丽莎白·卡迪，美国社会改革者和女权运动领袖。曾在纽约为通过一部赋予已婚妇女财产权的法案而努力，1850 年曾参加争取妇女选举权运动，出版女权刊物《革命周刊》，1869 年当选全国妇女选举权协会首任主席。

5. Society began to embrace the idea of the ideal woman and diminished the expectation for a woman's contribution to family financial health.

译文：社会开始接受关于模范女性的理念，不再那么期待依靠妇女来改善家庭的经济状况。句中 embrace 意为"（欣然）接受/采纳"。例：She eagerly embraced the offer of a trip. 她热情地接受了旅行的建议。

6. As a result of the great many deaths in the Civil War, thousands of women were left to fend for themselves financially and economically.

译文：由于南北战争中大量的人员死亡，成千上万的女性只得孤身一人赚钱养家糊口。The Civil War (1861—1865) 美国南北战争，又称美国内战，美国北部诸州同南部发动叛乱的各奴隶制州之间的战争，是资本主义北部同奴隶制南部之间对抗性矛盾激化的结果。1860 年，奴隶制度的反对派共和党候选人林肯当选为美国总统。短语 fend for oneself 意为"照料自己；自己谋生"。例：The old couple have no one to do the washing and cleaning: they have to fend for themselves. 没人给这对老年夫妇洗衣服和打扫卫生，他们只得自己照料自己。

7. Even as women worked in industry to fuel its growth, the outcome created new business opportunities for women in clerical jobs.

译文：在工业行业工作的女性加快工业增长的同时，也为女性在文职方面创造了新的工作机会。短语 even as 意为"正当；正如"。例：Even as he spoke, she entered. 正在他讲话的时候，她进来了。It happened even as I expected. 事情正如我预料的那样发生了。句中 fuel 为动词，意为"激起；引发"。例：inflation fuelled by military spending，军费开支引发的通货膨胀。

8. Still considered a secondary labor force, women were encouraged to engage in volunteer and charity work.

译文：社会鼓励那些仍被看做是次要劳动力的女性从事志愿者或慈善工作。Still consid-

ered a secondary labor force 是过去分词短语作状语,修饰整个主句;engage in 意为"参与,从事"。例:He engaged in a long-winded dispute. 他参加了一场冗长的辩论。

9. In response to a need for new workers and new production, six million women went to work during the war.

译文:为了满足新工人和新产业的需求,六百万女性在战争期间参加工作。短语 in response to 意为"对……的答复;对……的反应"。例:These comments came in response to specific questions often asked by local newsmen. 这些评论是对当地记者时常提出的各种具体问题的回答。

10. Society's approval of this phenomenon was reflected in posters of Rosie the Riveter and other cultural signals.

译文:女子铆钉工的海报以及其他文化符号均反映了当时社会对这种现象的认同。Rosie the Riveter 女子铆钉工,是美国的文化象征,代表二战期间六百万进入制造业工厂工作的女性(这些工作传统上是由男性做的)。女子铆钉工的形象现在被当做女性主义以及女性经济力量的象征。美国开始接受女性穿裤子也被归功于女子铆钉工。女子铆钉工最有名的形象是一张由 J. Howard Miller 于 1943 年设计的海报,标题是"我们做得到!"。

11. Gaining steam, women networked and organized and successfully lobbied for governmental protections such as the Equal Pay Act of 1963 and the Pregnancy Discrimination Act of 1978.

译文:借助这样的势头,女性广泛联系,组织并通过游说,成功通过了一系列的政府保护政策,如 1963 年颁布的《同工同酬法案》和 1978 年颁布的《怀孕歧视法案》。现在分词状语从句,强调进行中。短语 gain steam 意为"借助势头,蓄势待发"。例:He is gaining steam to prepare for his coming big English examination. 他正在全力以赴准备即将到来的英语大考。

12. Through a series of redress such as court decisions, laws, and affirmative action, women found new rights and opportunities in the workplace.

译文:通过一系列的补救措施,比如法庭裁决、相关法律以及反歧视行动,女性获得了新的工作权利和机会。短语 affirmative action 意为"反歧视行动",在美国以努力改善妇女和少数民族族群成员的就业或教育机会为宗旨的一种积极行动。划时代的 1964 年《民权法》通过以后,由联邦政府着手计划,旨在消除以前种族歧视的影响。其政策和计划的设计在工作聘雇、学院入学许可、政府合同的裁定和其他社会福利的分配方面,都给予妇女和少数民族优先的待遇,主要的标准是民族、性别、种族、宗教、残障和年龄。

13. Spurred by consumerism and the need to make more money to buy more things, married women composed almost two-thirds of the female labor force in the mid-1970s.

译文:20 世纪 70 年代中期,在保护消费者利益运动和挣更多钱、购更多物的需求的推动

下,已婚女性占据了几乎女性劳动力三分之二的比例。Spurred by consumerism 是过去分词短语作状语;spur 意为"刺激,鼓舞,促进"。例:The shortage of labor acts as a powerful spur to more economical methods of production. 缺乏劳动力会强有力地激励使用更经济的生产方法。句中 consumerism 意为"消费主义（认为高消费对个人和社会有利的看法）"。

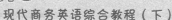

I. Text comprehension questions.

1. What was the situation about women employment in 17th and 18th-century America?

2. Why did women have to fend for themselves in the Civil War?

3. What did women protest while they banded together in the Uprising in 1909?

4. Why did six billion women go to work during the Second World War?

5. Why did married women become the majority of female labor force?

II. Decide whether each of the following statements is true (T) or false (F) or not mentioned (NM) in the text.

1. In the 18th century women who lived in rural places went to work because they were left alone.

2. It was very unusual for a woman to do the printing trades because her husband did the same business.

3. Men thought they were free from the burden of finance while women worked outside home more and more frequently.

4. More than one million women worked in offices in 1900. Most of them worked for high salary and knew well about job security.

5. In the early 1900s, the first labor union appeared.

6. Women entered new business such as clerical jobs as industry was growing increasingly.

7. Rosie the Riveter reflected the society's approval of encouraging women to get a job rather than staying at home.

8. From the end of World War II, women managed to gain a significant presence in the work world and still fought for women's rights.

Ⅲ. Choose the best answer to each question with the information from the text.

1. What kinds of jobs did women engage in during the 17th and 18th century?

A. Shopkeepers.   B. Artisans.   C. Merchants.   D. All the above.

2. Why did the businesswoman's first association with labor unionism appear in the early 19th century?

A. The war broke.

B. The industrialization increased.

C. Women wanted to make money on their own.

D. Women were eager to present themselves to the world.

3. Which of the following is FALSE about the women development in history?

A. Elizabeth Timothy and Cornelia Smith Bradford operated as independent printers and book-binders in South Carolina and Boston together.

B. Women engaged in the production of cloth and food when the war with England was coming.

C. With the advent of the Civil War, men did not assume the burden of sole provider any longer.

D. The census indicates that women held a majority in all the occupations.

4. Which item is FALSE about the ideal women?

A. They were neither family oriented nor business oriented.

B. They were either family oriented or business oriented.

C. They were rather family oriented than business oriented.

D. They were both family oriented and business oriented.

5. What's the writer's attitude to women in history?

A. Critical.   B. Approved.   C. Objective.   D. Opposed.

Ⅳ. Choose the word or phrase that is closest in meaning to the underlined one.

1. If this kind of fish becomes <u>scarce</u>, future generations may never taste it at all.

A. minimum   B. short   C. seldom   D. uncommon

2. Technological advance will bring about the decline of <u>rural</u> industries and an increase in urban populations at the same time.

A. country   B. urban   C. technical   D. suburban

3. Nothing <u>illustrates</u> his selfishness more clearly than his attitude to his wife.

A. suggests   B. shows   C. seems   D. finds

4. With a last <u>significant</u> look at her husband, Mrs. Hochstadt went to answer the door.

A. wonderful   B. considerable   C. important   D. meaningful

5. My brother and I ordered a hot dog and a pizza <u>respectively</u>.

A. personally   B. particularly   C. specifically   D. individually

6. Jim has been living in the lap of luxury since he <u>inherited</u> his father's money.

A. got   B. received   C. accepted   D. left

7. We were well aware of <u>impending</u> disaster.

A. coming   B. upcoming   C. threatening   D. nearing

8. An increasing housing shortage has been caused by a large <u>influx</u> of foreigners.

A. exodus   B. rush   C. invasion   D. intrusion

9. I <u>assume</u> everyone here is a sophomore.

A. suppose   B. suspect   C. presume   D. imagine

10. I wasn't surprised to learn that he'd served in the <u>military</u>.

A. army   B. air force   C. navy   D. militia

11. They <u>reinforce</u> that pressure with political tricks.

A. enrich   B. strengthen   C. support   D. toughen

12. I could not define or articulate the <u>dissatisfaction</u> I felt.

A. point   B. express   C. complain   D. speak

V. Fill in the blanks with the phrases and expressions from the text. Change forms where necessary.

> as well   engage in   as a whole   result in   in response to

1. This remarkable girl was sent to me _____ my request for a suitable secretary.

2. The temperature for the country _____ is relatively high.

3. He gave me advice, and money _____.

4. Such behavior may _____ the executive being asked to leave.

5. Even in prison, he continued to _____ criminal activities.

VI. Match the words with their definitions.

1. the process of coming to live permanently in a country that is not your own; the number of people who do this

2. agreeing with or consenting to a statement or request

3. considered in relation to trade, industry, and the creation of wealth

4. express an objection to what someone has said or done

5. relating to or occurring in a family or its members

6. the activity of buying and selling, especially on a large scale

7. having or expressing devotion to and vigorous support for one's country

8. to work in an office, especially routine documentation and administrative tasks

9. the voluntary giving of help, typically in the form of money, to those in need

10. the protection or promotion of the interests of consumers

(　　) economic　　　　(　　) commerce　　　　(　　) familial

(　　) immigration　　　(　　) consumerism　　　(　　) protest

(　　) clerical　　　　　(　　) charity　　　　　(　　) patriotic　　　(　　) affirmative

VII. Translate the following sentences into English.

1. 人们忙于工作来养活自己。(engage in)

_____

2. 安全带和安全气囊一起使用，效果更好。(in conjunction with)

_____

3. 我上学迟到是由于一场交通事故。(due to)

_____

4. 这笔生意整体来看是成功的。(as a whole)

_____

5. 一旦那些小海豹能独立生活，就必须把它们放回到海里去。(fend for oneself)

_____

_____

VIII. Oral exercises.

Students in groups of two will make conversations about gender and race in business. In the conversation practice, some sentence patterns will be used. In this unit, students will use the following two sentence patterns:

It doesn't make sense to... ……没有任何意义

It is possible / impossible to... ……是(不)可能的

Please follow example (1) and complete the following dialogue exercises. Student A and B will exchange roles upon completion.

For example (1):

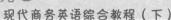
Student A: Do you think if it makes sense to buy the most up-to-date commodities?

Student B: No, it doesn't make sense to do so.

Student A: Do you think if it makes sense to (contribute to family's economic support, engaged in the production of cloth and food, leave the workplace and return to the family environment).

Student B: No, it doesn't make sense to do so.

Please follow example (2) and complete the following dialogue exercises. Student A and B will exchange roles upon completion.

For example (2):

Student A: It is possible for you to finish your assignment by dinner time, isn't it?

Student B: Sure, it is possible(or No, I'm afraid not).

Student A: It is possible to (gain a significant presence in the work world, create new business opportunities for women in clerical jobs, band together and strike to protest working conditions and wages).

Student B: Of course it is possible(or No, not always).

IX. Writing skills. Please look at the pictures, the words and phrases coming from the pictures about women in business below. And then write 3 – 5 sentences to describe each of the pictures.

The expressions in the brackets may help you to start your writing.

(There is/are . . . in the picture; In the middle of the picture; Then let's look at the next picture; This picture is about . . . ; The person on the right. . . ; From the picture, you can see. . . ; The central focus of this picture is. . . ; In the top left corner /bottom right corner of the picture, a man/woman/boy/girl. . . ; From her/his facial expression, I can assume that. . . ; From the. . . , I can tell that. . . ; Perhaps this man is about to. . .)

Picture 1 (inequality between men and women, career women)

_____

_____

_____

Picture 2 (leaders, self-respect, self-reliance, self-confidence, self-development)

_____

_____

_____

Picture 3 (outstanding women, Zhao Xiaolan, minister, United States Department of Labor)

_____

_____

_____

Picture 4 (success, harmony, well-being, joint efforts)

_____

_____

_____

X. PPT presentation. Two students in a group will work together to prepare 5 – 8 pages of PPT slides to be presented in class. The topic for this unit is about a position more suitable for women.

Further Reading One: Racial Conflicts

Unfortunately, examples of racial (种族的) conflicts and discrimination are found worldwide. There are black-versus-white conflicts in the United States, South Africa, Great Britain, and elsewhere, and Arab-, Indian-, or Pakistani-versus-black conflicts in Africa. Racial friction (摩擦) exists because of the guest workers in parts of Europe. There has been bloody conflict in Sri Lanka (斯里兰卡) between Tamils and Sinhalese. The list, of course, goes on.

Japan has come under increasing criticism for its laws denying Japanese citizenship to anyone not of the Japanese race. The largest alien group affected is the Koreans, many of whom were brought to Japan as workers when Japan occupied Korea. Now the second- and third-generation descendants (后代) of those Koreans, all of whom were born in Japan, with Japanese as their native tongue, are still considered aliens and not granted the rights and privileges of Japanese citizenship. The relatively few Vietnamese refugees (难民) permitted into Japan are beginning to feel the same racial discrimination.

Things may be changing for the better for Koreans in Japan, however, as they no longer must be fingerprinted (鉴别) as aliens, and some local authorities, though not yet the central government, now employ Koreans. More than 80 percent of these Koreans marry Japanese, and their children are automatically Japanese. Naturalization (同化, 入籍) is possible, and a growing number of Koreans are taking that route to Japanese citizenship. On the other hand, a diehard (顽固分子), mostly pro-North Korean minority (少数民族) clings to Korean ways, for example, by sending their children to Korean schools dressed in traditional Korean costume.

Exercise

I. Choose the best answer to each question with the information from the text.

1. Where can we find the examples of racial conflicts and discrimination?

A. The United States.   B. South Africa.   C. Great Britain.   D. Worldwide.

2. Which of the following statements is NOT TRUE about racial conflicts and discrimination?

A. Racial conflicts and discrimination can be found everywhere.

B. Sometimes, the conflicts can be bloody.

C. The largest alien group affected by Japanese criticism is the Chinese.

D. Most Koreans marry Japanese and their children are Japanese.

3. How does the pro-North Korean minority keep their Korean tradition?

A. To ask their children to learn Korean in school.

B. To ask their children to dress in traditional Korean costume.

C. To ask their children to learn tae kwon do.

D. Both A and B.

4. What does "alien" mean?

A. Belonging to a foreign country.   B. Unfamiliar and disturbing.

C. Supposedly from another world.   D. None of the above.

5. Which of the following statements is TRUE about Japanese attitude to racial conflicts and discrimination?

A. Japan was blamed for its laws against non-Japanese race.

B. Japan treats Japanese and non-Japanese races equally.

C. The second- and third-generation of Koreans can be granted the same rights and privileges as Japanese.

D. Vietnamese refugees are luckier than Koreans in Japan.

II. Decide whether each of the following statement is true（T）or false（F）.

1. Luckily, the racial conflicts and discriminations are all non-violent though they are found in all the countries and districts.

2. There are racial conflicts between the resident workers and guest workers somewhere in Europe.

3. Many Koreans were brought to Japan as refugees when Japan occupied Korea.

4. Even though Koreans marry Japanese, their children are still considered as aliens now.

5. Mostly pro-North Korean minority insist in living in Korean ways.

Further Reading Two: Working Women

Women work in the trades and labor jobs, in professional and managerial jobs, and in the service industry. Although women's work is as varied as the women themselves, these traditional categories of workplace employment serve as a useful framework(准则) to evaluate (评价) women in business. In trade and labor employment, women find themselves at particular odds with male-dominated occupational patterns. For example, blue-collar jobs are often associated with male-dominated unions. In professional and managerial jobs, women continue to enter business only to encounter a phenomenon called the glass ceiling. The glass ceiling documents the rise of women only to a certain point within a business and points to sex discrimination as the cause of this limited advancement. As a result of more equal access (进入) to higher education and professional programs, women continue to advance themselves within the professional and managerial fields. In the service sector, women dominate business at the lowest levels. Almost 45 percent of all working women are employed within the low-paying and low-status jobs of the service sector.

The service industry, so thoroughly dominated by the female labor force, represents another category of employment frequently called the pink-collar jobs. These pink-collar jobs are characterized by low pay and low status. Clerical positions are perhaps the most widely recognized of these positions in the business world. With the advent of the typewriter in the late 1800s, women came forward to apply for and receive employment as typists. While previous male clerical workers had seen these entry level jobs as an effective means to move up within the organization, female workers soon discovered that management relied on breaking down clerical tasks so that workers would be interchangeable（可交换的）. In 1990, 80 percent of all clerical workers were women and more than 25 percent of all working women found themselves in clerical jobs. Retail sales workers account for another large segment of the service sector employment. Since the early 1900s, retail sales clerks have been transformed to cashiers with the restructuring（重新编排）of retail from full-service to self-service format.

Exercise

I. Choose the best answer to each question with the information from the text.

1. What kind of work do women always take as their jobs?

A. Trades and labor.　　　　　　　　　B. Service.

B. Professional and managerial jobs.　　C. All the above.

2. Which one is NOT TRUE about pink-collar jobs?

A. Pink-collar jobs belong to the service industry.

B. The pay and the status of pink-collar jobs are not so good.

C. Pink-collar means the collar of a worker's uniform is pink.

D. Pink-collar jobs are dominated by women.

3. Which one is TRUE about the clerical jobs?

A. Women wanted to take typist as their jobs when the typewriters were used.

B. Women were asked to be typists because they typed faster than men did.

C. In 1990, there was no place for men in clerical jobs.

D. In 1990, 25 percent of all women found themselves in clerical jobs.

4. What does "glass ceiling" mean?

A. The ceiling is made of glass.

B. The ceiling which is as fragile as glass.

C. The imaginary barrier that stops women from getting the best jobs.

D. None of the above.

5. Which of the following jobs is NOT possible for women to get according to the author?

A. Secretary.　　　B. Cashier.　　　C. Nurse.　　　D. Manager.

II. Decide whether each of the following statement is true (T) or false (F).

1. Women work in service industry as well as in other occupations.

2. Women find there is a glass ceiling for them to see and know how to get higher position in work.

3. Pink-collar jobs refer to the jobs that require strength but the pay isn't high.

4. Women went to apply for typists as their jobs because men were not willing to do such jobs.

5. Retail sales clerks transformed to cashiers because the customers liked to pick and buy what they wanted on their own.

Unit Nine　The Stocks

 Contents in This Unit

1. Two pre-reading discussion questions.

2. A text on the stocks.

3. New words and expressions.

4. Explanatory notes for the text.

5. Some exercises to build up your skills both in English and business.

6. A PPT hands-on assignment to give you space for creation.

7. Further readings on the stocks.

Pre-reading Discussions for the Text

Please discuss these questions in pairs. You may talk over the topics either in English or in Chinese according to your teacher's instruction.

1. Have you or your family ever invested before? If yes, tell us the story. You may write down some key words and phrases before you talk.

_____

_____

_____

2. Do you think all investments are profitable? Discuss this with your classmates. You may write down the key words and phrases before you talk.

_____

_____

_____

Text: The Stocks

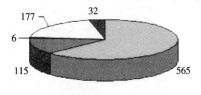

☐ Sole proprietorship
■ Limited partnership,
  unlimited
  general partnership
☐ Co-operative
☐ Limited liablity
  company
■ Company limited by
  shares

An entrepreneur with a good idea can do nothing without capital to act on that idea. As a start, the entrepreneur can use personal resources to form a sole proprietorship. In this form the entrepreneur and the business are indistinguishable, and the amount of capital is limited to the personal wealth and borrowing power of the entrepreneur. The entrepreneur is personally liable for all obligations. Forming a partnership with other parties solves some of the problems, adding the personal resources of one or more partners. This form of organization dilutes the claim and authority of the entrepreneur. Partnerships do not work well if large amounts of capital are required since potential investors with large amounts of capital are hard to find. Once found, they are reluctant to enter partnerships for three reasons. The first reason is that all partners are equally and totally responsible for the obligations of the partnership. This risk exposure may easily exceed the original investment. The second reason is that the partnership is a temporary alliance. Partners may withdraw at any time. Finally, partnership interests are not liquid. Liquidity is the ability to convert an asset to cash quickly and at a fair price. Potential investors are reluctant to enter partnerships because of the difficulties of disposing of the investment and realizing a return. Many of these problems are avoided by the corporate form of ownership.

In the corporate form, a business is set up as legal entity. This entity by itself has no net legal value, as recognized in the basic accounting equation: "Assets equals liabilities plus owners' equity." This creation of a legal person, however, separates the liabilities of the corporation from the liabilities of the owners. This results in "limited liability": should the firm fail, the obligations of the firm are not the obligations of the

owners. The value of owning the firm may go to zero, but the investors' loss is limited to their original investment. Limited liability greatly reduces investors' risk, so that investors are willing to consider more and riskier investments. This increased willingness to undertake new projects encourages innovation. Limited liability of investors has been an important factor encouraging economic growth. Another attraction of the corporate form is that ownership is subdivided into shares of stock. Shares may

be sold to many investors, resulting in higher liquidity, and this higher liquidity reduces investors' risk. The stockholder can exit the investment for another investment. In this way, the pool of potential investors becomes much larger. Given these advantages, it is not surprising that many business ventures choose the corporate form.

The corporate form does have some disadvantages. One disadvantage is double taxation of earnings. The earnings of sole proprietorships and partnerships are taxed once, as the earnings of the proprietor. The firm is a legal entity, however, and its earnings are taxed. Any distribution of the already once-taxed earnings is income of the investors, and the earnings are taxed a second time. Another disadvantage is that as ownership becomes wider, it becomes more diverse. Entrepreneurs  remaining as managers may be distracted more often by fellow owners and more formal requirements. A different style of management may be required. On the positive side, the corporate form facilitates separation of ownership and management. This separation is a mixed blessing—it allows professional management and the application of expertise, but raises the agency, or control, problem. The professional manager is an agent of the stockholders, not necessarily part of the ownership, and may have different goals and agenda. Finally, ownership may be diluted.

Securities issued by a corporation are classified as debt or as equity, which may be complicated under the corporate form. The main types of equity claims are common and preferred stock. These equity claims may take many forms. There are related claims, such as rights, warrants, and convertible securities. The securities also may be divided into those that are publicly traded, and those that are not. Although the underlying securities are in the same class, public trading implies a much wider ownership and liquidity, and often a much different set of problems. Securities of firms that have few shareholders look quite different from an investment viewpoint.

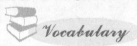 *Vocabulary*

1. entrepreneur [ˌɔntrəprə'nəː]	*n.* a person who makes money by starting or running businesses, especially when this involves taking financial risks 企业家
2. capital ['kæpitəl]	*n.* a large amount of money that is invested or used to start a business 资本,资金
3. indistinguishable [ˌindis'tiŋgwiʃəbl]	*adj.* not clear; not able to be clearly identified 难以识别的
4. obligation [ˌɔbli'geiʃən]	*n.* something which you must do because it is your duty, or because of law, etc. 义务,责任
5. partnership ['pɑːtnəʃip]	*n.* a business owned by two or more people who

share the profits
合伙企业

6. dilute [dai'ljuːt]　　　　　　*vt.* to make sth. weaker or less effective
　　　　　　　　　　　　　　　　削弱；降低

7. claim [kleim]　　　　　　　*n.* a right that sb. believes they have to sth. , es-
　　　　　　　　　　　　　　　　pecially property, land, etc.
　　　　　　　　　　　　　　　　权利，所有权

8. authority [ɔː'θɔrəti]　　　　*n.* the power or right to do sth.
　　　　　　　　　　　　　　　　权力，权威

9. reluctant [ri'lʌktənt]　　　　*adj.* hesitating before doing sth. because you do
　　　　　　　　　　　　　　　　not want to do it or because you are not sure
　　　　　　　　　　　　　　　　that it is the right thing to do
　　　　　　　　　　　　　　　　勉强，不情愿的

10. exposure [ik'spəuʒə]　　　　*n.* the state of having the true facts told after they
　　　　　　　　　　　　　　　　have been hidden because they are bad, im-
　　　　　　　　　　　　　　　　moral or illegal
　　　　　　　　　　　　　　　　暴露，揭发

11. withdraw [wið'drɔː]　　　　*vi.* to stop taking part in an activity or being a
　　　　　　　　　　　　　　　　member of an organization
　　　　　　　　　　　　　　　　撤回，退出

12. entity ['entiti]　　　　　　　*n.* a thing with distinct and independent exist-
　　　　　　　　　　　　　　　　ence
　　　　　　　　　　　　　　　　实体，本质

13. net [net]　　　　　　　　　*adj.* remaining after the deduction of tax or other
　　　　　　　　　　　　　　　　contributions
　　　　　　　　　　　　　　　　净的

14. creditor ['kreditə]　　　　　*n.* a person or company to whom money is owing
　　　　　　　　　　　　　　　　债权人

15. undertake [ˌʌndə'teik]　　　*vt.* to make yourself responsible for sth. and start
　　　　　　　　　　　　　　　　doing it
　　　　　　　　　　　　　　　　从事

16. subdivide [ˌsʌbdi'vaid]　　*vt.* to divide sth. into smaller parts
　　　　　　　　　　　　　　　　再分

17. share [ʃɛə]　　　　　　　　*n.* any of the units of equal value into which a
　　　　　　　　　　　　　　　　company is divided and sold to raise money
　　　　　　　　　　　　　　　　股份

18. venture ['ventʃə]　　　　　*n.* a business project or activity, especially one
　　　　　　　　　　　　　　　　that involves taking risks
　　　　　　　　　　　　　　　　商业活动；企业

19. taxation [tæk'seiʃən]   *n.* money that has to be paid as taxes
                                    税,税收

20. proprietor [prə'praiətə]   *n.* the owner of a business, or a holder of proper-
                                    ty
                                    所有者;业主

21. distribution [ˌdistri'bjuʃən] *n.* the system of transporting and delivering goods
                                    销售,销售量

22. positive ['pɔzətiv]   *adj.* thinking about what is good in a situation
                                    积极的,肯定的

23. facilitate [fə'siliteit]   *vt.* to make an action or a process possible or
                                    easier
                                    使变得容易,促进

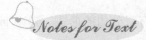

1. act on   对……起作用(有功效);按照……而行动

2. as a start   作为开端;首先

3. be reliable for   负有(法律)责任的;有义务的

4. accounting equation   会计等式

5. be willing to do sth.   愿意做某事

6. mixed blessing   好坏参半的事物

7. take form   形成,产生

Notes for Text

1. Forming a partnership with other parties solves some of the problems, adding the personal resources of one or more partners.

译文:和其他合伙人一起办合伙企业,注入一个或更多合伙人的个人资金是解决该问题的方法。Forming a partnership with other parties 是动名词短语作主句;adding. . . more partners 是现在分词形式作方式状语修饰整个句子。

2. Liquidity is the ability to convert an asset to cash quickly and at a fair price.

译文:变现能力是指以公道的价格把资产迅速转化为现金的一种能力。liquidity 意为"资产变现力;清偿力"(注:个人或公司在不付出较大成本或遭受较大损失的条件下所具有的将资产转换成现金的能力和程度,这关系到个人或公司清偿债务的能力)。

3. This entity by itself has no net legal value, as recognized in the basic accounting equation: "Assets equals liabilities plus owners' equity."

译文:就法人实体本身来说,它没有法定净值,但可用一个基本会计等式来说明:资产 =

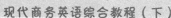

负债＋业主产权。句中 entity 意为"存在者;实体"（为税收上的目的而独立存在的组织或个人）,accounting equation 会计恒等式（注:这个恒等式不仅是会计处理经济业务的理论基础,同时也反映了所有企业拥有财产的对应关系。即企业现在拥有的全部财产,包括流动资产、固定资产、无形资产,它们的对应关系。从会计恒等式中就可以看出,等式右边的两项即负债,也就是欠别的钱;再一个就是业主产权,即就是属于企业自己的钱有多少,这是会计恒等式的真正意义）。

4. This results in "limited liability": should the firm fail, the obligations of the firm are not the obligations of the owners.

译文:"有限责任"就此产生:一旦公司倒闭,该公司的义务责任不再是所有者的义务责任。句中 limited liability 即有限责任（注:有限公司在其企业遭受损失时只承担以它投入企业的资本额为限的赔偿责任）。

5. Limited liability greatly reduces investors' risk, so that investors are willing to consider more and riskier investments. This increased willingness to undertake new projects encourages innovation.

译文:有限责任大大降低了投资者的风险,所以投资者们会主动考虑更多和更高风险的投资,既提高了开发新项目的主动性又鼓励创新。

6. Given these advantages, it is not surprising that many business ventures choose the corporate form.

译文:考虑到这么多优势,也难怪这么多的企业选择股份有限公司的形式。句中 given 意为"考虑到"。例: Given their inexperience, they've done a good job. 考虑到他们缺乏经验,这工作他们做得不错。

7. On the positive side, the corporate form facilitates separation of ownership and management.

译文:从积极的方面来看,股份有限公司的形式有助于所有权和管理权相分离。句中 positive 意为"积极的,肯定的"。例:Customer comments, both positive and negative, are recorded by staff. 对于顾客的意见,无论是肯定的还是否定的,都由职员予以记录。

8. This separation is a mixed blessing—it allows professional management and the application of expertise, but raises the agency, or control, problem.

译文:这种分离好坏参半——虽然专业管理和专业知识在这里有了用武之地,但会出现代理问题,或者说是控制问题。句中 mixed blessing 意为"好坏参半的事物"。例:These shoes are a mixed blessing. Although they look pretty, they hurt my feet. 这双鞋优缺点都有:样子好看,穿起来却脚疼。

9. The main types of equity claims are common and preferred stock.

译文：资产请求权有很多种形式，其主要形式是普通股和优先股。句中 preferred stock 意为"优先股"（注：对公司收益有优先于普通股权利的股票，它通常在发放普通股股利之前由董事会公布。优先股要保障按规定股利先于普通股发放）。

10. There are related claims, such as rights, warrants, and convertible securities.

译文：同时还有诸如认股权、认股证书以及可转换证券等相关权利。其中 rights 意为"认股权；权利"（注：企业为筹集资金发行新股时，原有股东拥有优先认股权）；warrant 意为"认股证书；购股证"（注：在投资经济学中，指持有人有权在规定的时期内按特定价格购买一定数量股票的一种证书）；convertible security 意为"可转换证券"（注：所有人可依据发行条件将其转换为原发行公司的其他证券，尤其是普通股的证券。可转换证券和由之转换得来的证券之间的比率通常在发行可转换证券时即已确定，并且保证不使证券贬值）。

11. Although the underlying securities are in the same class, public trading implies a much wider ownership and liquidity, and often a much different set of problems.

译文：虽然保证附属公司债券也属同一范畴，但是公开发行意味着更加广泛的所有权和资产变现力，同时还有一系列不同的问题。句中 underlying security 意为"保证附属公司债券；抵押担保"（注：由控股公司担保，并由附属公司发行的证券）。

I. Text comprehension questions.

1. How can an entrepreneur start a sole proprietorship?

2. How can we solve the problem that the entrepreneur is personally liable for all obligations?

3. What does limited liability mean?

4. Why are shares sold to many investors?

5. What are the main types of equity claims?

Ⅱ. **Decide whether each of the following statements is true（T）or false（F）or not mentioned（NM）in the text.**

1. An entrepreneur with lots of capital can achieve everything in his/her career.

2. Once found, potential investors are willing to enter partnerships.

3. The corporate form of ownership can avoid many of those problems a partnership has.

4. The basic accounting equation is "Assets equals liabilities minus owners' equity".

5. One of the advantages the corporate form does have is double taxation of earnings.

6. However, the firm is a legal entity, so its earnings are not taxed.

7. The securities can only be divided into those that are publicly traded, and those that are not.

8. The corporate form is recommended because it is complicated.

Ⅲ. **Choose the best answer to each question with the information from the text.**

1. Which of the following is NOT the reason why potential investors are reluctant to enter partnerships?

A. Partners may withdraw at any time.

B. All partners are equally and totally responsible for the obligations of the partnership.

C. Partnership interests are not liquid.

D. The entrepreneur is personally liable for all obligations.

2. Which statement is FALSE about the limited liability?

A. The obligations of the firm are not the obligations of the owners.

B. Investors' loss is limited to their original investment.

C. Limited liability greatly reduces investor risk.

D. Investors are reluctant to consider more and riskier investments.

3. Which item is TRUE about the disadvantages of the corporate form?

A. No taxation of earnings.　　　　　　B. The corporate form is complicated.

C. Ownership is becoming diverse.　　　D. Separation of ownership and management.

4. Which item refers to the main types of equity claims?

A. Common stock and public-traded stock.

B. Preferred stock and non-public-traded stock.

C. Common stock and preferred stock.

D. Public-traded stock and non-public-traded stock.

5. Which item doesn't belong to the related claims?

A. Convertible security.   B. Warrant.

C. Debt.   D. Rights.

IV. Choose the word or phrase that is closest in meaning to the underlined one.

1. The company has a capital of $500,000.

A. first city   B. urban   C. money   D. capital letter

2. The male of the species is almost indistinguishable from the female.

A. identical   B. unpredictable   C. dissimilar   D. inconvincible

3. People who earn under a certain amount are not liable to pay tax.

A. willing   B. responsible   C. likely   D. unaccountable

4. I enquired if this might not dilute the excellence of the university.

A. concentrate   B. widen   C. strengthen   D. weaken

5. The dispute has scared away potential investors.

A. impossible   B. possible   C. possibility   D. impossibility

6. She has the sole responsibility for bringing up the child.

A. mere   B. unique   C. all   D. united

7. The advertisements by the side of the road sometimes distract the attention of motorists.

A. disturb   B. call   C. disorder   D. attract

8. In spite of these positive signs, economists are not predicting a recovery.

A. negative   B. favorable   C. pessimistic   D. certain

9. Books are classified according to subject area.

A. divided   B. torn   C. separated   D. categorized

10. That puzzle is too complicated for the children.

A. easy   B. simple   C. difficult   D. complex

11. The common people in those days suffered a lot.

A. ordinary   B. unusual   C. private   D. noble

12. His silence implied consent.

A. hinted   B. suggested   C. included   D. means

V. Fill in the blanks with the phrases and expressions from the text. Change forms where necessary.

> be willing to   act on   be reliable for   take form   be classified

1. None of the banks _____ bear such a loss.

2. Why didn't you _____ her suggestion?

3. Complicated negotiations may _____ the _____ of a long series of counter-offers.

4. Eggs _____ according to size.

5. None of the witnesses _____ .

Ⅵ. Match the words with their definitions.

1. wealth in the form of money or other assets

2. the state of being forced to do sth. because it is your duty, or because of a law, etc.

3. a person or an organization that invests money in sth.

4. not permanent

5. the amount of profit that you get from sth.

6. remaining after the deduction of tax or other contributions

7. the action or process of innovating

8. a formal request to an authority

9. a way of thinking about a subject

10. the action of sharing something out among a number of recipients

(　　) obligation　　　(　　) temporary　　　(　　) distribution

(　　) net　　　　　　(　　) application　　　(　　) investor

(　　) innovation　　　(　　) viewpoint　　　(　　) capital　　　(　　) return

Ⅶ. Translate the following sentences into English.

1. 这台机器很耐用而且极其可靠。（be reliable）

_____

2. 我认为这应该归为紧急情况。（be classified as）

_____

3. 孩子们可能同时带来欢乐和烦恼。（mixed blessing）

_____

4. 随着雾慢慢散去，湖逐渐清晰起来。（take form）

_____

5. 你的国际贸易知识很令人惊讶。（be surprising）

_____

Ⅷ. Oral exercises.

Students in groups of two will make conversations about the stocks. In the conversation practice, some sentence patterns will be used. In this unit, students will use the following two sentence patterns:

I can't imagine...　　我无法想象……

I suggest（that）... 　我建议……

Please follow example（1）and complete the following dialogue exercises. Student A and B will exchange roles upon completion.

For example（1）：

Student A：I can't imagine that I will borrow money from him.

Student B：I can't either.

Student A：I can't imagine（an entrepreneur can do anything without capital, the machine can work long without maintenance, the business can perform without good management）.

Student B：Me neither.

Please follow example（2）and complete the following dialogue exercises. Student A and B will exchange roles upon completion.

For example（2）：

Student A：I suggest that we have lunch at the new restaurant.

Student B：As you wish.

Student A：I suggest that（these problems be solved today, the stockholder invest more money for the company, the style of management be improved）.

Student B：I think that is a good idea.

IX. Writing skills. Please look at the pictures, the words and phrases coming from the pictures below. And then write 3 – 5 sentences to describe each of the pictures.

The expressions in the brackets may help you to start your writing.

(There is/are . . . in the picture ; In the middle of the picture ; Then let's look at the next picture ; This picture is about . . . ; The person on the right. . . ; From the picture, you can see. . . ; The central focus of this picture is. . . ; In the top left corner /bottom right corner of the picture, a man/woman/boy/girl. . . ; From her/his facial expression, I can assume that. . . ; From the. . . , I can tell that. . . ; Perhaps this man is about to. . .)

Picture 1 (a bull market, a bear market, trend)

Picture 2 (clap hands, excited, celebrate, a bull market)

Picture 3 (sad, hopeless, decline, a bear market)

Picture 4 (stock exchange, trading, electronic, transaction)

X. PPT presentation. Two students in a group will work together to prepare 5 - 8 pages of PPT slides to be presented in class. The topic for this unit is about a listed company and its stock. To complete this hands-on task, you will have to visit some stock related Internet homepages.

Further Reading One: Market Capitalization

Market capitalization (市场资本总额) is defined as the total dollar value of a stock's outstanding shares and is computed by multiplying the number of outstanding shares by the current market price. Thus, market capitalization is a measure of corporate size. With approximately (大约) 8,500 stocks available to trade on U. S. stock exchanges, many traders judge (判断) a company by its size, which can be a determinant (决定性因素) in price and risk. In fact, there are four unofficial (非官方,非正式) size classifications for U. S. stocks: blue-chips(蓝筹股,绩优股), mid-caps(中盘股), small-caps(小盘股), and micro-caps(便士股票).

1. Blue-chip stocks. Blue chip is a term derived from poker, where blue chips in a card game hold the most value. Hence (因此), blue-chip stocks are those stocks that have the most market capitalization in the marketplace (more than $5 billion). Typically they enjoy solid value and good security, with a record of continuous dividend payments(股利支付) and other desirable investment attributes.

2. Mid-cap stocks. Mid-caps usually have a bigger growth potential than blue-chip stocks but they are not as heavily capitalized ($500 million to $5 billion).

3. Small-cap stocks. Small-caps can be potentially difficult to trade because they do not have the benefit of high liquidity (valued at $150 million to $500 million). However, these stocks, although quite risky, are usually relatively(相对的) inexpensive and big gains are possible.

4. Micro-cap stocks. Micro-caps, also known as penny stocks, are stocks priced at less than $2 per share with a market capitalization of less than $150 million.

Some traders like to trade riskier stocks because they have the potential for big price moves; others prefer the longer-term stability of blue-chip stocks. In general, deciding which stocks to trade depends on your time availability, stress threshold(起始点), and account size.

I. Choose the best answer to each question with the information from the text.

1. Which of the following statements is NOT TRUE about blue-chip stocks?

A. Blue chip is the term from poker games.　　B. Blue-chip stocks are most valuable.

C. Blue-chip stocks are good in security.　　D. Blue-chip stocks are always inexpensive.

2. Which one of the following is true about mid-cap stocks?

A. They have smaller growth potential than blue-chip stocks.

B. They have more capitalization than blue-chip stocks.

C. They have bigger growth potential and less capitalization than blue-chip stocks.

D. They have bigger growth potential and more capitalization than blue-chip stocks.

3. Which one of the following is NOT TRUE about small-cap stocks?

A. They are difficult to trade.　　　　　B. They do not have the benefit of high liquidity.

C. They are riskier but cheaper.　　　　D. They are cheap and big gains are impossible.

4. Which one is true about micro-cap stocks?

A. They have the smallest capitalization.　B. They are the cheapest.

C. They are not risky at all.　　　　　　D. They have the most value.

5. Which one is TRUE about the traders according to the author?

A. Some traders like riskier stocks because they are risk takers.

B. Some traders like blue-chip stocks because they don't want to take any risks.

C. Choosing which stock depends on traders' time.

D. Get ready for taking stress before choosing blue-chip stocks.

II. Decide whether each of the following statement is true（T）or false（F）.

1. Market capitalization means the total dollar value of a stock's shares.

2. Market capitalization measures corporate size.

3. Many traders judge a company by its capitalization.

4. Actually, the unofficial size classifications for U. S. stocks cannot be trusted.

5. Different traders choose their own stocks according to themselves.

Further Reading Two：Dividends

American companies may periodically（定期地）declare cash and/or dividends（股利）on a quarterly or yearly basis. Dividends are provided to the shareholders—otherwise referred to as stock-holders—as an income stream that they can rely on. This is quite similar to a bank paying interest on certificates of deposit（CDs）（存单）or savings accounts. There are a number of companies that boast that they have never missed a dividend or have always increased dividends.

Companies that distribute their income as dividends are usually in mature（成熟的）industries. You typically will not find fast-growing companies distributing dividends, as they may need the capital for future expansion and may feel they can reinvest（再投资）the funds at a higher rate of return than the stockholders. As a stock trader, you need to know how this process affects your long or short investment. Basically, a company's board of directors will decide whether to declare a dividend, which is paid out and distributed to shareholders on a date set by the company. Also, some companies will declare a special dividend from time to time. This dividend is paid out and distributed to shareholders on a date set by the company, referred to as a payable date.

In order to qualify for a dividend, you must be a shareholder on record as of the record date（the date you are "recorded" as the owner of the shares）of the dividend. You can also sell the stock as soon as the next day after the payable date and still receive the dividend.

A beginner may think this is a profitable way to buy and sell shares：Buy the shares a few days before the record date and sell them on the day after the payable date. However, before you run out and open a stock brokerage（手续费）account in order to implement this tactic, you may want to

consider that, in most cases, the stock prices will be trading lower on the day that the dividend is payable. That's because on the dividend payable date (i. e. the date on which you get paid the dividend), the stock should trade at its regular price minus the dividend.

Let's consider an example. If IBM declare a $1 per share dividend payable on June 30, and closed at $90 on June 29, then on June 30, IBM would open at $89. As a stock trader, it is important to be aware of dividends and how they can affect a stock. You can find stocks declaring dividends by looking in the newspaper financial pages or at various financial web sites.

I. Choose the best answer to each question with the information from the text.

1. Which of the following statements is TRUE about dividends?

A. They are declared on regular basis.

B. They are provided to the shareholders.

C. They are not different from the income stream.

D. All of the above.

2. Why won't you find fast-growing companies distributing dividends?

A. Because they don't have extra money for dividends sometimes.

B. Because they want future expansion and reinvest the funds.

C. Because they lied to investors on their dividends.

D. Because shareholders don't care whether they get dividends or not.

3. Who will decide whether to declare a dividend or not?

A. Shareholders.　　　B. Market.　　　　　C. Board of directors.　　D. Share traders.

4. Which statement is FALSE about the record date?

A. The record date is the date on which you are recorded as the owner of the shares.

B. Investors can sell the stock the next day after the payable date and still receive the dividend.

C. Beginners think they have found a profitable way to buy and sell shares.

D. None of the above.

5. How can you find stocks declaring dividends?

A. By reading newspapers or finding an agency.

B. By searching on the Internet or watching TV.

C. By searching on the Internet or finding an agency.

D. By reading newspapers financial pages or at various financial web sites.

II. Decide whether each of the following statement is true (T) or false (F).

1. American companies may declare cash and/or dividends irregularly.

2. There is almost no difference between dividends and bank paying interest.

3. It's not easy for you to find fast-growing companies distributing dividends.

4. Some companies will declare a special dividend periodically.

5. The stock should be traded at its regular price plus the dividend.

Unit Ten Business Recession

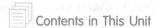 Contents in This Unit

1. Two pre-reading discussion question.
2. A text on business recessions.
3. New words and expressions.
4. Explanatory notes for the text.
5. Some exercises to build up your skills both in English and business.
6. A PPT hands-on assignment to give you space for creation.
7. Further readings on business recession.

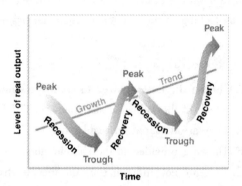

Pre-reading Discussions for the Text

Please discuss these questions in pairs. You may talk over the topics either in English or in Chinese according to your teacher's instruction.

1. Do you have any knowledge of recessions? If yes, discuss with your partner and name some big recessions or depressions happened in the world.

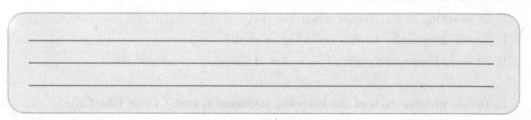

2. What do you think the causes and consequences of recessions are? You may write down the key words and phrases before you talk.

Text: Business Recessions

One of the most popular definitions of recessions is that they are periods when real gross national product (GNP) has declined for at least two consecutive quarters. In 1990, real GNP declined between the third and fourth quarters and again between the fourth quarter of 1990 and the first quarter of 1991. Hence, there is general agreement that a recession did occur.

Although the definition worked quite well in this instance, there are several problems with it. One is that it does not provide monthly dates of when recessions began or ended. For this purpose the National Bureau of Economic Research (NBER), whose chronology of recessions is widely accepted, uses monthly measures of production, employment, sales, and income, all expressed in real terms (after allowing for inflation). GNP figures are not available monthly. The NBER found that the latest recession, from business cycle peak to trough, ran from July 1990 to March 1991.

Another problem with the two-consecutive-quarters definition is that there can be serious declines in economic activity even without two consecutive quarters of negative growth. Suppose that in one period, real GNP declines 5 percent in the first quarter, rises 1 percent in the second, and declines 5 percent again in the third. In another period let's say real GNP declines 1 percent in each quarter. Obviously the first period shows a much more serious drop in GNP, but only the second period qualifies as a recession according to the definition.

These and other considerations have led the NBER to use a broader definition of recessions, which takes into account three dimensions of the decline in aggregate economic activity—its depth, duration, and diffusion across industries. These are known as the three Ds. One significant study by using three Ds approach indicates that recessions have been getting shorter and expansions longer. The average recession during the past fifty years lasted eleven months, whereas the average recession was more than twice that long in the nineteenth century. Expansions, on the other hand, now last about twice as long as they did in earlier times. A number of factors account for this trend. One is the growing importance of the service industries, such as trade and transportation, where employment is usually more stable than in manufacturing. As the more stable industries have grown in importance, this has made the whole economy more stable and less susceptible to prolonged and severe recessions. Also, the government has been playing a bigger role in moderating recessions, especially since the thirties. Unemployment insurance has helped to reduce the loss of income during recessions, and monetary policy has been used to reduce interest rates and make credit more accessible.

Recessions have a global as well as domestic dimension. Financial markets in many countries are closely watched in other countries, and many investors are making investments on an international scale. Exports and imports have become more important to business enterprises, and managements must now deal with global competition. As a result, periods of recession are likely to encompass many countries at about the same time. During recessions in the United States, a majority of the industrial countries in Europe and the Pacific are apt to show signs of recession also. This, in turn, has depressing effects on the United States by slowing the foreign demand for U. S. exports.

The upshot is that even though recessions are not as severe as they used to be, they have serious consequences in many directions. Some industries, some occupations, and some areas of the country are hit much harder than others. Hence, it pays to keep close watch on them with all the daily, weekly, monthly, and quarterly data that are available for that purpose.

 *Vocabulary*

1. recession [ri'seʃən]　　　　　*n.* a period when the economy is not good
经济不景气,经济衰退

2. definition [ˌdefi'niʃən]　　　*n.* a concise explanation of the meaning of a word or phrase or symbol
定义,释义

3. gross [grəus]　　　　　　　*adj.* excessively fat or bulky with no deductions for expenses, tax, etc.
总的

4. decline [di'klain]　　　　　*n.* to grow smaller, diminish
缩小,衰弱,降低

5. consecutive [kən'sekjutiv]　*adj.* (of a narrative, account, etc.) following a chronological sequence; following one another without interruption
连续的

6. provide [prə'vaid]　　　　　*v.* supply or furnish
提供

7. purpose ['pə:pəs]　　　　　*n.* the reason for which anything is done, created, or exists
目的; 意图

8. chronology [krə'nɔlədʒi]　　*n.* the arrangement of dates, events, etc. in order of occurrence
年表

9. available [ə'veiləbl]　　　　*adj.* obtainable or accessible; capable of being made use of, at hand
可用的,可得到的

10. peak [pi:k]　　　　　　　*n.* the period of greatest prosperity or productivity
顶点

11. trough ['trɔ:f]　　　　　　*n.* the lowest point or depressed stage of trade cycle

低谷,低谷期,萧条期

12. negative ['negətiv]   *adj.* lacking positive or affirmative qualities
    负的,消极的

13. qualify ['kwɔlifai]   *v.* to attribute a quality to; characterize
    把……称为……

14. consideration [kən,sidə'reiʃən]   *n.* a fact or circumstance to be taken into account
    when making a judgment or decision
    考虑因素,要考虑的事

15. dimension [di'menʃən]   *n.* aspect
    方面

16. aggregate ['ægrigeit]   *adj.* collective, corporate
    总数的,总计的

17. duration [djuə'reiʃən]   *n.* the length of time that something lasts or con-
    tinues
    持续时间

18. diffusion [di'fju:ʒən]   *n.* spread
    传播,扩散

19. significant [sig'nifikənt]   *adj.* important in effect or meaning
    重要的

20. approach [ə'prəutʃ]   *n.* the way or means of entering or leaving; access
    方法,途径

21. indicate ['indikeit]   *v.* to point out or show
    指出,表明

22. trend [trend]   *n.* general tendency or direction
    趋势,倾向

23. stable ['steibl]   *adj.* steady in position or balance
    稳定的

24. susceptible [sə'septəbl]   *adj.* liable to be affected by, prone
    易受影响的

25. prolong [prə'lɔŋ]   *v.* to lengthen in duration or space, extend
    拉长,延长

26. severe [si'viə]   *adj.* intensely or extremely bad or unpleasant in
    degree or quality
    严重的

27. moderate ['mɔdərət]   *v.* to become less extreme or intense
    使减轻(缓和),节制

28. insurance [in'ʃuərəns]   *n.* the act of providing financial protection for
    property, life, health, etc. against specified
    contingencies

保险

29. credit ['kredit]   *n.* money available for a client to borrow
信贷

30. accessible [ək'sesəbl]   *adj.* easy to approach, enter, or use
容易取得,容易获得

31. domestic [dəu'mestik]   *adj.* of or involving one's own country or specific country
本国的,国内的

32. competition [,kɔmpi'tiʃən]   *n.* the act of competing, rivalry
竞争

33. likely ['laikli]   *adj.* tending or inclined, apt
可能的

34. apt [æpt]   *adj.* having a tendency
易于……的,有……的倾向

35. sign [sain]   *n.* something that indicates or acts as a token of a fact, condition, etc., that is not immediately or outwardly observable
迹象

36. effect [i'fekt]   *n.* power or ability to influence or produce a result; efficacy
影响

37. upshot ['ʌpʃɔt]   *n.* the final result, outcome
结果

38. consequence ['kɔnsikwəns]   *n.* a result or effect of some previous occurrence
结果,后果

39. occupation [,ɔkju'peiʃən]   *n.* a person's regular work or profession
工作,职业

Phrase and Expression

1. take into account   将……考虑进去
2. be known as   被认为是……
3. lead to   导致,引向
4. according to   根据
5. as a result   因此
6. be likely to   可能
7. at the same time   同时
8. play a role in   在……中发挥角色(或作用)
9. be apt to   易于……; 倾向于……
10. at least   至少

 *Notes for Text*

1. One of the most popular definitions of recessions is that they are periods when real gross national product (GNP) has declined for at least two consecutive quarters.

译文：经济衰退最通行的定义之一是指一个国家在某些时期实际国民生产总值至少连续两个季度出现下跌。句中 that 从句是表语从句，when 引导的是定语从句，先行词是 periods. real gross national product (GNP)，实际国民生产总值。短语 at least 意为"至少"，其反义词是 at most(至多)；decline 意为"下滑，下降"；incline 意为"上升，增加"。

2. In 1990, real GNP declined between the third and fourth quarters and again between the fourth quarter of 1990 and the first quarter of 1991. Hence, there is general agreement that a recession did occur.

译文：1990 年，美国实际国民生产总值在第三和第四季度之间出现下滑，并且在 1990 年的第四季度和 1991 年的第一季度之间又出现下滑。因此，人们一致认为经济衰退确实发生了。句中 between 意为"在……之间"，一般指两者之间；hence 意为"因此"，表示因果关系，一般用逗号隔开。句型 there is general agreement that... 相当于 it is generally agreed that...，意为"人们普遍认为"。

3. For this purpose the National Bureau of Economic Research (NBER), whose chronology of recessions is widely accepted, uses monthly measures of production, employment, sales, and income, all expressed in real terms (after allowing for inflation).

译文：为此，美国国家经济研究局(NBER)广泛采用经济衰退年度表，对生产、就业、销售以及收入进行了逐月统计，所有数据都是按实际价值折算的(扣除通胀后)。whose 引导的是非限制性定语从句，先行词是 the National Bureau of Economic Research (NBER)，同时它又是句子的主语，谓语是 uses。句中 all expressed in real terms (after allowing for inflation)是过去分词当定语用，相当于 which are expressed in real terms。

4. The NBER found that the latest recession, from business cycle peak to trough, ran from July 1990 to March 1991.

译文：美国国家经济研究局(NBER)发现，最近的一次经济衰退，从经济周期的高峰到低谷，持续时间是从 1990 年 7 月至 1991 年 3 月。

5. Another problem with the two-consecutive-quarters definition is that there can be serious declines in economic activity even without two consecutive quarters of negative growth.

译文：有关连续两个季度下滑这个定义的另一个问题是即使没有连续两个季度的负增长，在经济活动中也可能存在严重的下滑。此句是表语从句，that 从句作 is 的表语。句中 negative growth 意为"负增长"。negative 意为"负的，消极的"；与之相对的是 positive，意为"正的，积极的"。

6. Suppose that in one period, real GNP declines 5 percent in the first quarter, rises 1 percent in the second, and declines 5 percent again in the third.

译文：假如在一个时期内，实际国民生产总值在第一个季度下滑5%，在第二季度上升1%，而在第三个季度又下滑5%。Suppose that 即假设，相当于连词 if；rise 意为"上升，涨"；give rise to sth. 意为"引起，导致某事物"。例：Her disappearance gave rise to the wildest rumors. 她失踪一事引起了流言飞语。

7. Obviously the first period shows a much more serious drop in GNP, but only the second period qualifies as a recession according to the definition.

译文：很显然第一个时期表明了国民生产总值下滑得更厉害，但是根据定义却只有第二个时期才可以被认为是经济衰退。短语 qualify as 意为"算得上，具有某种资格"。例：A stroll round the garden hardly qualifies as exercise! 在花园转转算不上锻炼！

8. These and other considerations have led the NBER to use a broader definition of recessions, which takes into account three dimensions of the decline in aggregate economic activity—its depth, duration, and diffusion across industries.

译文：出于对上述这些和其他方面的考虑，美国国家经济研究局（NBER）对经济衰退采用了一个更为广义的定义。那就是在总的经济活动中把经济下跌的三个维度考虑进去，即下降层面的深度、持续时间以及在行业之间的扩散情况。句型 take sth. into account/take account of sth. 意为"考虑；体谅"。例：When judging his performance, don't take his age into account. 评定他的表现时，不必考虑他的年龄。

9. One significant study by using three Ds approach indicates that recessions have been getting shorter and expansions longer.

译文：运用3Ds理论的一项重要研究表明经济衰退已经变得越来越短，而经济高涨却持续得越来越长。此句是宾语从句，that 从句作 indicate 的宾语。句中 approach 意为"方法；手段"。例：A new approach to language teaching. 语言教学的新方法。

10. The average recession during the past fifty years lasted eleven months, whereas the average recession was more than twice that long in the nineteenth century.

译文：在过去50年里平均经济衰退持续的时间为11个月，而在19世纪时平均经济衰退期却是这个周期的两倍多。句中 whereas 表转折，意为"而，然而"。句型 more than twice that long... 表示倍数，意为"是……两倍多"；twice as long as 意为"是……的两倍长"。

11. Expansions, on the other hand, now last about twice as long as they did in earlier times. A number of factors account for this trend.

译文：另一方面，高涨期现在是以前的两倍左右。很多因素都说明了这个趋势。A number of 作主语时，谓语动词要用复数；而 the number of 作主语，谓语动词要用单数。例：A number of students take part in the activity; The number of students of this school is on the rise. 短语 account for sth. 用来解释某事物的原因。例：His illness accounts for his absence. 他因病缺席。

12. One is the growing importance of the service industries, such as trade and transportation, where employment is usually more stable than in manufacturing.

译文：其中一个因素是服务业越来越显示出它的重要性，比如贸易和交通领域的就业情况一般比制造业更稳定。where 引导的是定语从句，先行词是 service industries。

13. As the more stable industries have grown in importance, this has made the whole economy more stable and less susceptible to prolonged and severe recessions.

译文：随着越来越稳定的行业变得越来越重要，这就使得整个经济更加稳定并且更不易受到持续时间长且严重的经济衰退的影响。句中 susceptible to sth. 作表语，指易受某事物影响或损害。例：plants that are not susceptible to disease，不易受病害侵袭的植物。

14. Also, the government has been playing a bigger role in moderating recessions, especially since the thirties.

译文：此外，特别是从 30 年代以来，政府在调节经济衰退中也发挥了越来越大的作用。句中 play a(n) big/important role in sth. 意为"在……中发挥作用"。例：English is playing a more and more important role in our daily life. 英语在我们的日常生活中发挥了越来越重要的作用。

15. Unemployment insurance has helped to reduce the loss of income during recessions, and monetary policy has been used to reduce interest rates and make credit more accessible.

译文：失业保险也有助于减少经济衰退期间的收入损失，并且通过使用货币政策来降低利率，使贷款更容易获得。句中 accessible 意为"可使用的，可接近的"。例：documents not accessible to the public，公众无法接触到的文件。短语 get/have access to sth. 意为"（使用某物或接近某人的）机会或权利"。例：Only high officials had access to president. 只有高级官员才有机会接近总统。

16. Financial markets in many countries are closely watched in other countries, and many investors are making investments on an international scale.

译文：很多国家的金融市场被其他国家密切注视着，很多投资商在国际范围进行投资。短语 on...scale 意为"以……的规模或程度"。

17. As a result ,periods of recession are likely to encompass many countries at about the same time.

译文：因此，经济衰退可能在同一时期出现在很多国家。As a result 意为"因此"；result from sth. 意为"由……引起或发生"。例：injuries resulting from a fall,因摔倒而受的伤。Result in sth. 意为导致；产生某种作用或结果. 例：Our efforts resulted in success. 我们的努力终于成功了。

18. This, in turn, has depressing effects on the United States by slowing the foreign demand for U. S. exports.

译文：这反过来通过放慢外国对美国出口的需求而对美国产生的影响是令人沮丧的。句中 demand for sth. 意为"需求……,需要……"。例：Demand for fish this month exceeds supply. 本月份鱼供不应求。

19. The upshot is that even though recessions are not as severe as they used to be, they have serious consequences in many directions.

译文：这样的结果就是即使经济衰退没有以前那么严重，但是它们却在很多方面造成了严重的后果。此句是 that 引导的表语从句，其中又包含了 even though 引导的让步状语从句。

20. Hence, it pays to keep close watch on them with all the daily, weekly, monthly, and quarterly data that are available for that purpose.

译文：因此，这就值得我们密切关注每日、每周、每月和每季度的专门统计数据。It pays to do sth. 意为"值得做某事"。例：It pays to be honest. 诚实不吃亏。

Exercise

I . Text comprehension questions.

1. What's one of the most popular definitions of recessions?

2. What kind of problems are there with the definition?

3. What factors account for the trend of recessions getting shorter and expansions longer?

4. Why does the author say that periods of recessions are likely to encompass many countries at about the same time?

5. Why does it pay to keep close watch on recessions?

Ⅱ. Decide whether each of the following statements is true (T) or false (F) or not mentioned (NM) in the text.

1. Weekly measures of production, employment, sales, and income are used by the National Bureau of Economic Research to know when recessions begin or end.

2. The three Ds refers to depth, duration, and diffusion across industries.

3. One significant study by using three Ds approach indicates that recessions have been getting longer and expansions shorter.

4. Expansions now last about twice longer than they did in earlier times.

5. Recessions will occur every four years.

6. Exports and imports have become less important to business enterprises.

7. Even though recessions are not as serious as they used to be, they have slight consequences in many directions.

8. We need to keep a close watch on recessions.

Ⅲ. Choose the best answer to each question with the information from the text.

1. Which of the following indicates the occurrence of recessions?

A. GNP has declined for at least three consecutive quarters.

B. GNP declines in this quarter and then rises in the next quarter.

C. GNP has declined for at least two consecutive quarters.

D. When the economy becomes bad.

2. What does the word "peak" mean in the phrase "from business cycle peak to trough" in

the text?

    A. The pointed summit of a hill.

    B. A point of greatest development, strength, etc.

    C. A mountain with pointed summit.

    D. To reach the highest point.

    3. Which situation is TRUE about the definition of recessions?

    A. Real GNP declined between the first and second quarters and between the fourth quarter of this year and the first quarter of the next year.

    B. Real GNP rose between the second and third quarters and then declined between the third and fourth quarter.

    C. Real GNP declined 3 percent in the first quarter, rises 2 percent in the second, and declines 3 percent again in the third.

    D. Real GNP declined 5 percent in each quarter.

    4. How long did the average recession last in the 19th century?

    A. 11 months.   B. 20 months.

    C. more than 22 months.   D. 10 months.

    5. Which is TRUE about the effect of recessions in the United States?

    A. It slows the foreign demand for U. S. exports.

    B. It helps to increase the demand for export.

    C. It can show weakness in the firm's competitive position.

    D. It causes recessions in other countries.

IV. Choose the word or phrase that is closest in meaning to the underlined one.

    1. In addition to the rising birthrate and immigration, the declining death rate contributed to the population growth.

    A. decreasing   B. inclining   C. descending   D. increasing

    2. If any of these symptoms occur while you are taking the medicine, consult your doctor immediately.

    A. occurrence   B. incur   C. happen   D. conclude

    3 The three consecutive years from 1983 to 1986, China launched a nationwide campaign to crack down on criminal offenses.

    A. conservative   B. successive   C. constant   D. consequence

    4. Then we collected all relevant technical data available in the country.

    A. assessable   B. apparent   C. arbitrary   D. obtainable

    5. People have all along been seeking to prolong life.

    A. extend   B. length   C. profound   D. protect

    6. He said it was only a joke, but I qualified it as a plot.

    A. quoted   B. referred   C. competed   D. qualification

    7. Advertisement is everywhere, and all of us are susceptible to it.

A. suspicious   B. successful   C. prone   D. probable

8. During the First World War, the German Army <u>encompassed</u> the city of his country.

A. surrounded   B. encountered   C. complained   D. competed

9. Among the most <u>significant</u> was his own record and ability as physician and pathologist.

A. progressive   B. attainable   C. important   -   D. possible

10. 2010 is coming but there is no <u>sign</u> that the economy is on the upturn.

A. signal   B. sigh   C. assign   D. indication

11. These findings <u>indicate</u> that further work is needed to re-evaluate the use of hydrogen in the treatment of this experiment.

A. show   B. insert   C. share   D. count

12. Sometimes the <u>consequences</u> of a poor decision are slight; at other times they are serious.

A. constancy   B. results   C. confidence   D. performances

V. Fill in the blanks with the phrases and expressions from the text. Change forms where necessary.

> play... a role in   be apt to   take into account   be likely to   as a result

1. When judging his performance, don't _____ his age _____.

2. It's nine o'clock and mother _____ come here any moment.

3. He _____ blurt out the whole truth, in cases where other people would have kept silence.

4. He neglected the traffic light, and _____, he was fined by the policeman.

5. English is now _____ an important _____ our life.

VI. Match the words with their definitions.

1. to grow smaller, diminish

2. to happen; take place; come about

3. to become less extreme or intense

4. to point out or show

5. liable to be affected by

6. the way or means of entering or leaving; access

7. to surround, to include entirely or comprehensively

8. collective, corporate

9. to attribute a quality to; characterize

10. the final result, outcome

(   ) moderate   (   ) decline   (   ) qualify

(   ) upshot   (   ) encompass   (   ) approach

(   ) indicate   (   ) occur   (   ) susceptible   (   ) aggregate

VII. Translate the following sentences into English.

1. 我们在作决定前应该考虑父母的建议。（take into account）

_____

_____

2. 他无法说明他旷课的原因。（account for）

_____

_____

3. 我听到传闻说公司很可能要破产。（be likely to）

_____

_____

4. 中国在国际事务上发挥了越来越重要的作用。（play a role in）

_____

_____

5. 他学习很努力。因此他很轻松地通过了期末考试。（as a result）

_____

_____

VIII. Oral exercises.

Students in groups of two will make conversations about recessions. In the conversation practice, some sentence patterns will be used. In this unit, students will use the following two sentence patterns：

I think it is a good idea to... 我认为……是个好主意

It seems / seemed that... 好像……，似乎……

Please follow example（1）and complete the following dialogue exercises. Student A and B will exchange roles upon completion.

For example（1）：

Student A：Do you think it is a good idea to know any knowledge about recessions?

Student B：Yes, I definitely think it is a good idea to do so.

Student A：Do you think it is a good idea to（provide monthly data for the public, stop economic activities during a recession, play a bigger role in recessions）.

Student B：Yes, I definitely think it is a good idea to do so（or No, I do not think so）.

Please follow example（2）and complete the following dialogue exercises. Student A and B will exchange roles upon completion.

For example（2）：

Student A: It seems that we should always keep close watch on recessions.

Student B: That is absolutely right (or That sounds strange).

Student A: It seems that (real GNP declines from time to time, the average recession was longer than in the 19th century, the economy recession happens periodically).

Student B: That is absolutely right (or That sounds strange).

Ⅸ. **Writing skills. Please look at the pictures, the words and phrases coming from the pictures are in relation to recessions. And then write 3 – 5 sentences to describe each of the pictures.**

The expressions in the brackets may help you to start your writing.

(There is/are ... in the picture; In the middle of the picture; Then let's look at the next picture; This picture is about ... ; The person on the right... ; From the picture, you can see... ; The central focus of this picture is... ; In the top left corner /bottom right corner of the picture, a man/woman/boy/girl... ; From her/his facial expression, I can assume that... ; From the... , I can tell that... ; Perhaps this man is about to...)

Picture 1 (a sad young woman, blank stare, weak, look for a job)

Picture 2 （a chart about the level of real output, trend, economy）

Picture 3 （no one there, a miserable sight, store）

Ⅹ. PPT presentation. Two students in a group will work together to prepare 2 – 3 pages of PPT slides to be presented in class. The topic for this unit is about America's great depression from 1929 to 1934. You will try to find some related pictures and explain the depression to your classmates.

Further Reading: Business Cycle

A business cycle is a sequence of economic activity in a nation's economy that is typically characterized by four phases—recession, recovery, growth, and decline—that repeat themselves over time. Economists note, however, that complete business cycles vary（变化）in length. The duration of business cycles can be anywhere from about two to twelve years, with most cycles averaging about six years in length. In addition（此外）, some business analysts have appropriated the business cycle model and terminology（术语）to study and explain fluctuations（波动）in business inventory and other individual elements of corporate operations. But the term "business cycle" is still primarily associated with（与……联系）larger （regional, national, or industry wide）business trends.

A recession—also sometimes referred to as a trough—is a period of reduced economic activity in which levels of buying, selling, production, and employment typically diminish（降低, 减少）. This is the most unwelcome stage of the business cycle for business owners and consumers alike. A particularly severe recession is known as a depression.

Recovery—also known as an upturn, the recovery stage of the business cycle is the point at which the economy "troughs" out and starts working its way up to better financial footing.

Growth—economic growth is in essence（实质上）a period of sustained（持续的）expansion. Hallmarks of this part of the business cycle include increased consumer confidence, which translates

into higher levels of business activity. Because the economy tends to(倾向于) operate at or near full capacity during periods of prosperity(繁荣), growth periods are also generally accompanied by inflationary(通货膨胀的)pressures.

Decline—also referred to as a contraction(收缩)or downturn, a decline basically marks the end of the period of growth in the business cycle. Declines are characterized by decreased levels of consumer purchases (especially of durable goods) and, subsequently, reduced production by businesses.

Exercise

I. Choose the best answer to each question with the information from the text.

1 Which of the following statements is TRUE about a business cycle?

A. Complete business cycles vary in duration.

B. The four phases of a business cycle repeat themselves again and again.

C. The duration of business cycles is 6 years.

D. Most business cycles average about 6 years in length.

2 What does the word "appropriate" mean in line 5?

A. Suitable.

B. Take something for one's own use, esp. without permission.

C. Proper.

D. Put something (esp. money) on one side for a special use.

3 Among the four phases of a business cycle, which phase do the business owners dislike best?

A. Recession.   B. Recovery.   C. Growth.   D. Decline.

4 In which phase does inflation most likely happen?

A. Recession.   B. Recovery.   C. Growth.   D. Decline.

5 Which one is NOT TRUE about the four phases of a business cycle?

A. The ability of buying, selling, production, and employment increase in the recession stage.

B. The economy becomes better and recovered in the recovery stage.

C. Consumers become confident and have higher level of buying in the growth stage.

D. It is the end of the period of growth in the decline stage.

II. Decide whether each of the following statements is true (T) or false (F).

1. There are at least four phases in a business cycle.

2. Economists note that complete business cycles are different in length.

3. The term "business cycle" is mainly irrelevant with larger (regional, national, or industry wide) business trends.

4. Trough means the highest point of a business cycle.

5. Consumers' purchases will decrease in the decline stage of a business cycle.

Unit Eleven Free Trade and Protectionism

Contents in This Unit

1. Two pre-reading discussion questions.
2. A text on free trade and protectionism.
3. New words and expressions.
4. Explanatory notes for the text.
5. Some exercises to build up your skills both in English and Business.
6. A PPT hands-on assignment to give you space for creation.
7. Further readings on free trade and protectionism.

Pre-reading Discussions for the text

Please discuss these questions in pairs. You may talk over the topics either in English or in Chinese according to your teacher's instruction.

1. Have you ever thought of the relation between free trade and economic growth? If yes, tell us the relation in details . You may write down some key words and phrases.

2. Do you think a highly competitive product will be durable to maintain its competitiveness? Discuss why you think so. You may write down the key words and phrases before you talk.

Text: Free Trade and Trade Barriers

The economic case for an open trading system based on multilaterally agreed rules is simple enough and rests largely on commercial common sense. But it is also supported by evidence: the experience of world trade and economic growth since the Second World War. Tariffs on industrial products have fallen steeply and now average less than 5% in industrial countries. During the first 25 years after the war, world economic growth averaged about 5% per year, a high rate that was partly the result of lower trade barriers. World trade grew even faster, averaging about 8% during the period.

The data show a definite statistical link between free trade and economic growth. Economic theory points to strong reasons for the link. All countries, including the poorest, have assets—human, industrial, natural, financial—which they can employ to produce goods and services for their domestic markets or to compete overseas. Economics tells us that we can benefit when these goods and services are traded. Simply put, the principle of "comparative advantage" says that countries prosper first by taking advantage of their assets in order to concentrate on what they can produce best, and then by trading these products for products that other countries produce best.

In other words, liberal trade policies—policies that allow the unrestricted flow of goods and services—sharpen competition, motivate innovation and breed success. They multiply the rewards that result from producing the best products, with the best design, at the best price.

But success in trade is not static. The ability to compete well in particular products can shift from company to company when the market changes or new technologies make cheaper and better products possible. Producers are encouraged to adapt gradually and in a relatively painless way. They can focus on new products, find a new "niche" in their current area or expand into new areas.

Experience shows that competitiveness can also shift between whole countries. A country that may have enjoyed an advantage because of lower labor costs or because it had good supplies of some natural resources, could also become uncompetitive in some goods or services as its economy develops. However, with the stimulus of an open economy, the country can move on to become competitive in some other goods or services. This is normally a gradual process.

Nevertheless, the temptation to ward off the challenge of competitive imports is always present. And richer governments are more likely to yield to the siren call of protectionism, for short term political gain—through subsidies, complicated red tape, and hiding behind legitimate policy objectives such as environmental preservation or consumer protection as an excuse to protect producers.

Protection ultimately leads to bloated, inefficient producers supplying consumers with outdated, unattractive products. In the end, factories close and jobs are lost despite the protection and subsidies. If other governments around the world pursue the same policies, markets contract and world economic activity is reduced. One of the objectives that governments bring to WTO negotiations is to prevent such a self-defeating and destructive drift into protectionism.

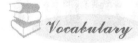

Vocabulary

1. multilateral [ˌmʌltiˈlætərəl] *adj.* of or involving more than two nations or parties
   多边的, 多国的

2. commercial [kəˈməːʃəl] *adj.* of, connected, or engaged in commerce
   商业的

3. evidence [ˈevidəns] *n.* ground for belief or disbelief; data on which to base proof or to establish truth or falsehood
   证据

4. steeply [ˈstiːpli] *adv.* in a steep manner
   陡峭地

5. average [ˈævəridʒ] *v.* to amount to or be on average
   平均为, 平均达

6. definite [ˈdefinit] *adj.* clearly defined; exact; explicit
   明确的, 确切的

7. statistical [stəˈtistikəl] *adj.* of or relating to statistics
   统计的, 以数据表示的

8. link [liŋk] *n.* the state of being connected
   联系, 连接

9. employ [imˈplɔi] *v.* to use as a means
   利用, 使用

10. compete [kəm'piːt]　　　　　*vi.* try to win something in competition with some-
one else
竞争

11. comparative [kəm'pærətiv]　*adj.* denoting or involving comparison
比较的

12. prosper ['prɔspə]　　　　　*v.* to thrive, succeed in a healthy way
繁荣,发达

13. liberal ['libərəl]　　　　　*adj.* not strict, free
自由的

14. unrestricted [ʌnris'triktid]　*adj.* not restricted or limited in any way
没受限制的,无限制的

15. motivate ['məutiveit]　　　　*v.* give an incentive for action, prompt
促进,激发

16. innovation [,inəu'veiʃən]　　*n.* the creation of something in the mind
创新

17. breed [briːd]　　　　　　　*v.* call forth
引起

18. multiply ['mʌltiplai]　　　　*v.* to increase or cause to increase in number,
quantity or degree
(使)增加

19. reward [ri'wɔːd]　　　　　*n.* profit or benefit resulting from some event of action
报酬,赢利

20. static ['stætik]　　　　　*adj.* not active or moving, stationary
静止的,不变化的

21. adapt [ə'dæpt]　　　　　*v.* to adjust(something or someone, esp. someone)
to different conditions, a new environment, etc.
(使)适应

22. gradual ['grædjuəl]　　　　*adj.* occurring, developing, moving, etc. in small
stages
逐步的,渐渐的

23. relative ['relətiv]　　　　　*adj.* not absolute or complete
相对的

24. current ['kʌrənt]　　　　　*adj.* of the immediate present
当前的,现在的

25. expand[ik'spænd]　　　　*v.* extend in one or more directions
扩展,扩张

26. resource[ri'sɔːs]　　　　　*n.* a source of economic wealth, esp. of a country
(mineral, labour, land, etc.)

资源

27. stimulus ['stimjuləs]
    n. something stimulates or acts as an incentive
    刺激物,促进因素

28. temptation [temp'teiʃən]
    n. the act of tempting or the state of being tempted
    诱惑,引诱

29. subsidy['sʌbsidi]
    n. a financial aid supplied by the government, as to industry, for reasons of public welfare, the balance of payments etc.
    补贴

30. complicate ['komplikeit]
    v. to make or become complex
    使复杂

31. legitimate [li'dʒitimit]
    adj. authorized, sanctioned by, or in accordance with law
    合法的,法定的

32. ultimate ['ʌltimət]
    adj. last, final
    最后的,最终的

33. bloated ['bləutid]
    adj. puffed up, as with conceit
    得意忘形的

34. inefficient [,ini'fiʃənt]
    adj. unable to perform a task or function to the best advantage
    无效率的,效率低的

35. despite [di'spait]
    prep. in spite of
    尽管

36. pursue [pə'sju:]
    v. carry out
    实施,贯彻

37. self-defeating [,selfdi'fi:tiŋ]
    adj. (of a plan, action, etc.)unable to achieve the intended result
    弄巧成拙的,适得其反的

38. destructive [di'strʌktiv]
    adj. causing destruction or much damage
    引起破坏(或毁灭)的,破坏性(或毁灭性)的

39. drift [drift]
    n. tendency, trend
    倾向,趋势

Phrase and Expression

1. base on 建立在……基础上,根据
2. rest on 建立在某事物的基础上;基于某事物
3. take advantage of 利用
4. concentrate on 集中精力于

5. in other words　用另外的话说

6. shift from...to...　从……到……转变

7. ward off　阻挡,防止

8. yield to　屈服于

9. siren call　诱惑,引诱

10. in the end　最后

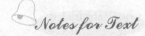 *Notes for Text*

1. The economic case for an open trading system based on multilaterally agreed rules is simple enough and rests largely on commercial common sense.

译文:创建以多国共同商定的规则为基础的开放贸易体系,这种经济案例现在十分简单,在很大程度上已经成为商贸常识。短语 rest on sth. 意为"建立在某事物的基础上;基于某事物"。例:His fame rests more on his plays than on his novels. 他的出名是靠他的戏剧,并不是靠小说。

2. Tariffs on industrial products have fallen steeply and now average less than 5% in industrial countries.

译文:工业品关税急剧下降,现在在工业国家里已经平均不到5%。句中 average 意为"平均为;平均值为;平均"。例:The rainfall averages 36 inches a year. 年降雨量平均为 36 英寸。On average 意为"按平均数计算"。例:We fail one student per year on average. 我们平均每年有一个学生不及格。

3. During the first 25 years after the war, world economic growth averaged about 5% per year, a high rate that was partly the result of lower trade barriers.

译文:在战后最初的 25 年里,世界经济平均每年以 5% 的速度在增长,这个高增长率在一定程度上是较低的贸易壁垒结果。句中 a high rate that was partly the result of lower trade barriers 是 5% per year 的同位语。短语 trade barriers 意为"贸易壁垒"。

4. The data show a definite statistical link between freer trade and economic growth. Economic theory points to strong reasons for the link.

译文:资料显示更自由的贸易和经济增长之间有一定的数据联系。经济理论为这种联系给出了充分的理由。短语 point to 意为"暗示(某事物的可能性);指示某事物"。例:All the evidences point to his guilt. 所有证据都表明他有罪。

5. All countries, including the poorest, have assets—human, industrial, natural, financial—which they can employ to produce goods and services for their domestic markets or to compete overseas.

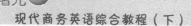

译文：所有的国家，包括最贫穷的国家在内，都拥有人力、工业、自然和金融方面的资产，并利用它们来为国内市场生产商品和服务，或参与国外竞争。Which 引导的是定语从句，先行词是 assets。短语 compete against/with sb. in /for sth. 意为"竞争；对抗；比赛"。例：Several companies are competing against/with each other for the contract. 几家公司正在为争取一项合同而互相竞争。

6. Economics tells us that we can benefit when these goods and services are traded.

译文：经济学告诉我们这些商品和服务的交换能让我们获益。短语 benefit from/by sth. 意为"得益于……"。例：He has not benefited from the experience. 他虽有体验却无长进。

7. Simply put, the principle of "comparative advantage" says that countries prosper first by taking advantage of their assets in order to concentrate on what they can produce best, …

译文：简单地说，"比较优势"原则指出，国家要富强首先就要利用他们的资产来专注于他们所能生产出来的最好的东西，……句中 simply put 是插入语，意为"简单地说"。take advantage of sth. /sb. 意为"利用"。例：He should take advantage of his native intelligence. 他应该好好利用自己天生的才智。短语 concentrate on sth. /doing sth. 意为"全神贯注，专心致志（于某事物）"。例：I can't concentrate on my studies with all that noise going on. 吵闹声不绝于耳，我无法集中精神于学习。

8. In other words, liberal trade policies—policies that allow the unrestricted flow of goods and services—sharpen competition, motivate innovation and breed success.

译文：换句话说，自由贸易政策——允许商品和服务自由流动的政策——增强竞争，激励创新和引向成功。句中 breed 意为"导致；造成"。例：Dirt breeds disease. 污浊导致疾病。

9. They multiply the rewards that result from producing the best products, with the best design, at the best price.

译文：通过生产出最好的产品，从中获得的报偿会成倍增加，而这些最好的产品当然有着最好的设计和最合理的价钱。句中 multiply 意为"增多，增加"。例：Our problems has multiplied since last year. 自去年以来我们的问题增多了。

10. The ability to compete well in particular products can shift from company to company when the market changes or new technologies make cheaper and better products possible.

译文：当市场发生变化或新的技术可以生产出物美价廉的产品时，那么在特定产品上所具有的强势竞争能力也会由于公司的不同而有所变化。这句话的主语是 the ability，谓语是 can shift；when 引导的是状语从句。短语 shift from. . . to. . . 意为"转向"。例：shift from extensive economy to intensive economy，从粗放经济转变为集约经济。

11. Producers are encouraged to adapt gradually and in a relatively painless way.

译文：这时候就要鼓励生产商逐渐地、相对不费力地去适应这种变化。短语 adapt to sth. 意为"适应"。例：Our eyes slowly adapted to the dark. 我们的眼睛慢慢地适应了黑暗的环境。

12. They can focus on new products, find a new "niche" in their current area or expand into new areas.

译文：他们可以致力于新产品，在当前的领域找到"缝隙市场"或扩展到新的领域。这是一个有三个谓语的简单句。句中"niche"意为"缝隙市场，利基市场"；focus on sth. 意为"集中（于某事物）"。例：I'm so tired that I can't focus on anything today. 今天我太累了，精神集中不起来。

13. A country that may have enjoyed an advantage because of lower labor costs or because it had good supplies of some natural resources, could also become uncompetitive in some goods or services as its economy develops.

译文：随着经济的发展，享有较低的劳动力成本或者享有一些丰富自然资源供给等方面优势的国家也能在一些商品和服务方面失去竞争力。本句中 that 从句是定语从句，修饰 a country，其中 because of... natural resources 是定语从句的两个并列原因状语；主句的谓语是 could also become。

14. However, with the stimulus of an open economy, the country can move on to become competitive in some other goods or services.

译文：然而，随着开放经济的刺激，这个国家能够继续前进而在别的商品和服务方面具有竞争力。其中 stimulus 是名词，意为"刺激物；促进因素"，stimulate 是及物动词，意为"刺激，激励（某人或某事物）"。例：Praise always stimulates him to further efforts. 表扬能激励他更加努力。

15. Nevertheless, the temptation to ward off the challenge of competitive imports is always present.

译文：尽管如此，避开有竞争力进口商品挑战的念想依然存在。短语 ward off sth./sb. 意为"避开"。例：ward off disease/danger，避开疾病/危险。

16. And richer governments are more likely to yield to the siren call of protectionism, for short term political gain—through subsidies, complicated red tape, and hiding behind legitimate policy objectives such as environmental preservation or consumer protection as an excuse to protect producers.

译文：为了短期的政治利益，比较富有国家的政府更有可能产生采取贸易保护制度的邪念——他们会通过补贴，复杂的法律文件和把隐藏在法定政策后的环境保护或消费者保护这些目的作为一个借口来保护生产商。短语 yield to sth./sb. 意为"屈服；让步"。例：She yielded to temptation and had another chocolate. 她禁不住诱惑，又吃了一块巧克力。短语 siren call 意为"诱惑"。

17. Protection ultimately leads to bloated, inefficient producers supplying consumers with outdated, unattractive products.

译文：贸易保护最终导致那些得意忘形的、效率低下的生产商给消费者提供一些过时的，没有吸引力的商品。短语 lead to sth. 意为"导致某种结果"。例：This misprint led to great confusion. 这个印刷错误导致很大的混淆。supply sb. with sth. /supply sth. to sb. 意为"向某人提供某物"。例：supply consumers with gas，electricity，etc. 为用户提供煤气、电等。

18. In the end, factories close and jobs are lost despite the protection and subsidies.

译文：最后，尽管有贸易保护和补贴，但是许多工厂还是倒闭了，许多工作也没有了。句中 despite 意为"尽管；不管"。例：Despite wanting to see him again, she refused to reply to his letters. 她尽管很想再见到他，但却不愿给他回信。

19. If other governments around the world pursue the same policies, markets contract and world economic activity is reduced.

译文：假如世界上其他国家政府也采取同样的政策，那么就会减少市场合同的签订和世界经济活动的进行。句中 pursue 意为"进行；追求；继续"。例：She decided to pursue her studies after obtaining her first degree. 她决定在获得学士学位之后继续深造。

20. One of the objectives that governments bring to WTO negotiations is to prevent such a self-defeating and destructive drift into protectionism.

译文：许多国家政府之所以参加世界贸易组织谈判，其中一个目的就是要阻止这种适得其反并具有破坏性的趋势进一步发展成为贸易保护主义。不定式 to prevent... 在这里作表语。

I. Text comprehension questions.

1. When did world trade grow even faster, averaging about 8%?

2. What does the principle "comparative advantage" say?

3. What are liberal trade policies?

4. Why does the author say that success in trade is not static?

5. How will the richer government protect the producers?

II. Decide whether each of the following statements is true (T) or false (F) or not mentioned (NM) in the text.

1. During the first 25 years after the First World War, world economic growth averaged about 5% per year.

2. Economics tells us that the trading of goods and services is beneficial to us.

3. Only the rich countries have human, industrial, natural and financial resources.

4. The rewards from producing the best products with the best design and at the best price can be increased through liberal trade policies.

5. From the passage we can find that success in trade needs competitiveness.

6. Producers can focus on new products, find a new "niche" in their current area or expand into new areas to adapt the shift.

7. Experience show competitiveness can not only shift from company to company but also shift between whole countries.

8. There is no temptation to prevent from the challenge of competitive imports.

III. Choose the best answer to each question with the information from the text.

1. What does "it" refer to in the sentence "But it is also supported by evidence"?

A. The economic case for open trade system.

B. Multilaterally agreed rules.

C. Commercial common sense.

D. The economic for an open trading system based on multilaterally agreed rules.

2. What are the possible benefits of liberal trade policies?

A. To sharpen competition.   B. To motivate innovation.

C. To breed success.   D. All of the above.

3. How can producers adapt the shift?

A. Gradually and in a relatively painless way.

B. Focus on new products.

C. Find a new "niche" in their current area.

D. Expand into new areas.

4. What's the meaning of "siren call" in the 6 paragraph?

A. Alarm.

B. An acoustic device producing a loud often wailing sound as a signal or warning.

C. Temptation.

D. A warning signal that is a loud wailing sound.

5. What is the author's attitude toward the protection?

A. Ironic.   B. Negative.   C. Positive.   D. Funny.

IV. Choose the word or phrase that is closest in meaning to the underlined one.

1. Our ultimate objective is the removal of all nuclear weapons.

A. major   B. final   C. terminal   D. basic

2. Many city vehicles have been adapted for use as school buses.

A. adjusted   B. managed   C. adopted   D. urged

3. There has been a gradual increase in the number of people owning cars.

A. abrupt   B. bit-by-bit   C. progressive   D. gentle

4. His words of praise were a stimulus for people to work harder.

A. move   B. stimulate   C. impetus   D. force

5. We need a definite answer to this question.

A. explicit   B. implicit   C. defined   D. obscure

6. The link between hard working and good performance on the exam is not static.

A. connection   B. join   C. bridge   D. drift

7. These products are of high quality and able to compete with other countries'.

A. contest   B competent   C. rival   D. contend

8. His business is still prospering even though the whole world suffers from the recession.

A. thriving   B. successive   C. productive   D. decaying

9. Despite the fact that she is short, she is an excellent basketball player.

A. Although   B. In spite of   C. Regardless   D. Notwithstanding

10. These anticancer drugs are effective but also destructive to white blood cells.

A. constructive   B. violent   C. opposite   D. devastating

11. Flies in food shops breed disease.

A. bring up   B. bring forward   C. bring in   D. bring about

12. The new bus routes benefit those who have no cars.

A. advantage   B. help   C. profit   D. satisfy

V. Fill in the blanks with the phrases and expressions from the text. Change forms where necessary.

| rest on   take advantage of   concentrate on   ward off   result from |

1. They _____ the old woman's ignorance to deceive her into buying false goods.

2. In 2009, how to _____ the influenza H1N1 virus is number one priority for the government.

3. The traffic accident _____ the driver's fatigue driving.

4. If you want to have a good performance in the exam, you should _____ what the teacher says in class.

5. He is not a man for you to _____, he always makes a hollow promise.

VI. Match the words with their definitions.

1. of, connected, or engaged in commerce

2. unable to perform a task or function to the best advantage

3. to make or become complex

4. puffed up, as with conceit

5. something stimulates or acts as an incentive

6. to increase or cause to increase in number, quantity or degree

7. any condition that makes it difficult to make progress or to achieve an objective

8. ground for belief or disbelief; data on which to base proof or to establish truth or falsehood

9. extend in one or more direction

10. not absolute or complete

(   ) stimulus   (   ) commercial   (   ) expand

(   ) complicate   (   ) inefficient   (   ) evidence

(   ) bloated   (   ) barrier   (   ) multiply   (   ) relative

VII. Translate the following sentences into English.

1. 行动应该有确凿的事实为依据。(base on)

_____

_____

2. 今天我们要集中讨论的问题是如何帮助无家可归的人。(focus on)

_____

_____

3. 更多的中国公司已经开始从出口转到了国内市场。(shift from...to)

_____

_____

4. 你将在生活中遇到许多罪恶，千万不可受其诱惑。（yield to）

_____

5. 在一定条件下，一件坏事可以产生好的结果。（lead to）

_____

_____

Ⅷ. Oral exercises.

Students in groups of two will make conversations about free trade and protectionism. In the conversation practice, some sentence patterns will be used. In this unit, students will use the following two sentence patterns：

We hold the opinion that...　我们认为……

The point is...　重点/关键是……

Please follow example（1）and complete the following dialogue exercises. Student A and B will exchange roles upon completion.

For example（1）：

> Student A：We hold the opinion that the economic case for an open trading system based on multilaterally agreed rules is simple enough and rests largely on commercial common sense.
>
> Student B：Yes, I can't agree more with you（or No, I don't agree with you）.
>
> Student A：We hold the opinion that（the economic growth was the result of lower trade barriers, there is a link between freer trade and economic growth, we can benefit when goods and services are traded, free trade policies brings about success）.
>
> Student B：Yes, I can't agree more with you（or No, I don't agree with you）.

Please follow example（2）and complete the following dialogue exercises. Student A and B will exchange roles upon completion.

For example（2）：

> Student A：The point is that liberal trade policies multiply the rewards that result from producing the best products, with the best design, at the best price.
>
> Student B：That is absolutely right（or That sounds strange）.
>
> Student A：The point is that（some governments often set up trade barriers, success in trade is not always static, they can focus on new products, we can always find new "niches" in the new areas, the protectionism is always present）.
>
> Student B：That is absolutely right（or That sounds strange）.

IX. Writing skills. Please look at the pictures, the words and phrases coming from the pictures in relation to trade protection below. And then write 3–5 sentences to describe each of the pictures.

The expressions in the brackets may help you to start your writing.

(There is/are . . . in the picture; In the middle of the picture; Then let's look at the next picture; This picture is about . . . ; The person on the right. . . ; From the picture, you can see. . . ; The central focus of this picture is. . . ; In the top left corner /bottom right corner of the picture, a man/woman/boy/girl. . . ; From her/his facial expression, I can assume that. . . ; From the. . . , I can tell that. . . ; Perhaps this man is about to. . .)

Picture 1 (earth, lock, key, chain)

_____

_____

_____

Picture 2 (old man, strong wind, snow, cold)

Picture 3 (brick, spade, short and young man)

X. PPT presentation. Students in small groups will try to study and understand what it means by non-tariff barrier, and prepare 4 – 5 pages of PPT slides to demonstrate a case of trade barrier.

Further Reading: Import Tariffs

An import tariff is a tax collected on imported goods. Generally speaking, a tariff is any tax or fee collected by a government. Sometimes tariff is used in a non-trade context, as in railroad tariffs. However, the term is much more commonly applied to(应用于) a tax on imported goods.

There are two basic ways in which tariffs may be levied(征收): specific tariffs and ad valorem tariffs.

A specific tariff is levied as a fixed charge per unit of imports. For example, the US government levies a 51 cent specific tariff on every wristwatch imported into the US. Thus, if 1,000 watches are imported, the US government collects \$510 in tariff revenue(税收). In this case, \$510 is collected whether the watch is a \$40 Swatch or a \$5,000 Rolex.

An ad valorem tariff is levied as a fixed percentage of the value of the commodity imported. "Ad valorem" is Latin for "on value" or "in proportion to(与……成比例) the value." The US currently levies a 2.5% ad valorem tariff on imported automobiles. Thus if \$100,000 worth of autos are imported, the US government collects \$2,500 in tariff revenue. In this case, \$2,500 is collected whether two \$50,000 BMWs are imported or ten \$10,000 Hyundais.

Occasionally both a specific and an ad valorem tariff are levied on the same product simultaneously(同时地). This is known as a two-part tariff. For example, wristwatches imported into the US face the 51 cent specific tariff as well as a 6.25% ad valorem tariff on the case and the strap and a 5.3% ad valorem tariff on the battery. Perhaps this should be called a three-part tariff!

As the above examples suggest, different tariffs are generally applied to different commodities. Governments rarely apply the same tariff to all goods and services imported into the country. One exception to this occurred in 1971 when President Nixon, in a last-ditch effort to save the Bretton Woods, system of fixed exchange rates, imposed(课税) a 10% ad valorem tariff on all imported goods from IMF member countries. But incidents such as this are uncommon.

Thus, instead of one tariff rate, countries have a tariff schedule(目录) which specifies the tariff collected on every particular good and service. The schedule of tariffs charged in all import commodity categories is called the Harmonized Tariff Schedule of the United States (HTS). The commodity classifications are based on(根据) the international Harmonized Commodity Coding and Classification System (or the Harmonized System) established by the World Customs Organization.

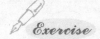

I. Choose the best answer to each question with the information from the text.

1 Which one is NOT TRUE about tariff?

A. A tariff is any tax or fee collected by a government.

B. Tariff can not be used in a non-trade context.

C. There are two kinds of tariffs: specific tariff and ad valorem.

D. A tariff is much more commonly applied to a tax on imported goods.

2. According to the passage, how much specific tariffs will be levied if the US imports 100 watches?

A. $51.　　　　B. $510.　　　　C. $25.5.　　　　D. $5.1.

3. Which one of the following statements is NOT TRUE according to the passage?

A. A specific tariff is levied as a fixed charge per unit of imports.

B. An ad valorem tariff is levied as a fixed percentage of the value of the commodity imported.

C. $2500 will be collected as ad valorem tariff whether two $50,000 BMWs are imported or two $10,000 Hyundais.

D. No matter what brand or price of watch is imported, the US government levies a 51 cent specific tariff.

4. Why does the author say that the example of president of Nixon is uncommon?

A. Because different tariffs are generally applied to different commodities.

B. Because governments rarely apply the same tariff to all goods and services imported into the country.

C. Because the Nixon government imposed a 10% ad valorem tariff on all imported goods from IMF member countries.

D. All of the above.

5. What's the function of tariff schedule?

A. To specify the tariff collected on every particular good and service.

B. To charge all imported goods.

C. To be clear about the charge of special imported goods.

D. To know the tariffs better.

II. Decide whether each of the following statements is true (T) or false (F).

1. Tariff is used as a tax on imported goods only.

2. The specific tariff on three $5,000 Rolex will be higher than on three $40 Swatch.

3. The higher worth the commodity imported is, the higher ad valorem tariff will be on it.

4. Government usually applies the same tariff to all goods and services imported into the country.

5. The commodity classifications are partly based on the international Harmonized Commodity.

Unit Twelve   Intellectual Property Rights

 Contents in This Unit

1. Two pre-reading discussion questions.
2. A text on intellectual property rights.
3. New words and expressions.
4. Explanatory notes for the text.
5. Some exercises to build up your skills both in English and Business.
6. A PPT hands-on assignment to give you space for creation.
7. Further readings on intellectual property rights.

Pre-reading Discussions for the Text

Please discuss these questions in pairs. You may talk over the topics either in English or in Chinese according to your teacher's instruction.

1. Do you have the habit of viewing the geographical indication of the commodity you buy? If yes, tell us why. You may write down some key words and phrases.

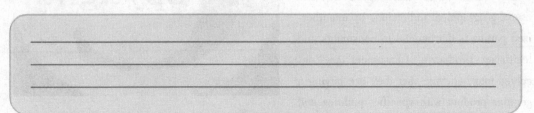

2. Do you care a lot about the trademark of a certain commodity? If yes, tell us why. You may write down the key words and phrases before you talk.

Text: Geographical Indication

A geographical indication is a sign used on goods that have a specific geographical origin and

possess qualities, reputation or characteristics that are essentially attributable to that place of origin. Most commonly, a geographical indication includes the name of the place of origin of the goods. Agricultural products typically have qualities that derive from their place of production and are influenced by specific local factors, such as climate and soil. Whether a sign is recognized as a geographical indication is a matter of national law. Geographical indications may be used for a wide variety of products, whether natural, agricultural or manufactured.

An appellation of origin is a special kind of geographical indication. It generally consists of a geographical name or a traditional designation used on products which have a specific quality or characteristics that are essentially due to the geographical environment in which they are produced. The concept of a geographical indication encompasses appellations of origin.

The use of geographical indications is not limited to agricultural products. They may also highlight qualities of a product which are due to human factors associated with the place of origin of the products, such as specific manufacturing skills and traditions. That place of origin may be a village or town, a region or a country. For example, "Bohemia" is recognized as a geographical indication in many countries for specific products made in the Czech Republic, in particular crystal ware.

A geographical indication points to a specific place, or region of production that determines the characteristic qualities of the product which originates from that place. It is important that the product derives its qualities and reputation from that place. Since those qualities depend on the place of production, a specific "link" exists between the products and their original place of production.

Geographical indications are understood by consumers to denote the origin and the quality of products. Many of them have acquired valuable reputations which, if not adequately protected, may be misrepresented by dishonest commercial operators. False use of geographical indications by unauthorized parties is detrimental to consumers and legitimate producers. Consumers are deceived into believing that they are buying a genuine product with specific qualities and characteristics, when they are in fact getting an imitation. Legitimate producers are deprived of valuable business and the established reputation of their products is damaged.

A trademark is a sign used by an enterprise to distinguish its goods and services from those of other enterprises. It gives its owner the right to exclude others from using the trademark. A trademark

will often consist of a fanciful or arbitrary name or device. A geographical indication tells consumers that a product is produced in a certain place and has certain characteristics that are due to that place of production. It may be used by all producers who make their products in the place designated by a geographical indication and whose products share specified qualities. Unlike a trademark, the name used as a geographical indication will usually be predetermined by the name of the place of production.

Geographical indications are protected in accordance with international treaties and national laws under a wide range of concepts, including special laws for the protection of geographical indications or appellations of origin, trademark laws in the form of collective marks or certification marks, laws against unfair competition, consumer protection laws, or specific laws or decrees that recognize individual geographical indications.

In essence, unauthorized parties may not use a geographical indication in respect of products that do not originate in the place designated by that indication. Applicable sanctions range from court injunctions preventing the unauthorized use to the payment of damages and fines or, in serious cases, imprisonment.

A number of treaties administered by WIPO provide for the protection of geographical indications, most notably the *Paris Convention for the Protection of Industrial Property* of 1883, and the *Lisbon Agreement for the Protection of Appellations of Origin and Their International Registration*. In addition, Articles 22 to 24 of the *Agreement on Trade-Related Aspects of Intellectual Property Rights* (TRIPS) deal with the international protection of geographical indications within the framework of the World Trade Organization (WTO).

If a geographical term is used as the common designation of a kind of product, rather than an indication of the place of origin of that product, then the term no longer functions as a geographical indication. When this has occurred in a certain country, then that country may refuse to recognize or protect that term as a geographical indication. For example, the term "cologne" now denotes a certain kind of perfumed toilet water, regardless of whether or not it was produced in the region of Cologne.

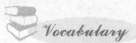
Vocabulary

1. specific [spi'sifik]   *adj.* explicit, particular, definite
                                        明确的,具体的,特定的

2. origin ['ɔridʒin]   *n.* a primary source
                                        起源,来源

3. characteristic [,kærəktə'ristik]   *n.* a distinguishing quality, or trait
                                        特征,特性

4. attributable [ə'tribjuːtəbl]   *adj.* capable of being attributed
                                        (可)归因于……

5. influence ['influəns]   *v.* impact, affect, to have effect on
                                        影响

6. recognize ['rekəgnaiz]   v. to give a formal acknowledgement of a status
                                认可

7. variety [və'raiəti]   n. the quality or condition of being diversified, various
                                各种，种种

8. appellation [,æpi'leiʃən]   n. an identifying name or title
                                名称，称呼

9. designation [,dezig'neiʃən] n. something that designates, such as a name or dis-
                                tinctive mark
                                指示

10. highlight ['hailait]   v. to bring notice or emphasis to
                                强调，突出

11. associated [ə'səuʃi,eitid] adj. related to
                                有关联的，相关的

12. determine [di'tə:min]   v. to decide
                                决定

13. originate [ə'ridʒineit]   v. come or bring into being
                                起源于，来自

14. denote [di'nəut]   n. indicate or designate
                                指出

15. acquire [ə'kwaiə]   v. to get or gain (something, such as an object, trait
                                etc.)
                                获得，得到

16. adequately ['ædikwitli]   adv. in an adequate manner or to an adequate degree
                                适当地，充分地

17. misrepresent ['mis,repri'zent] v. to represent wrongly or inaccurately
                                故意对……作错误的报道

18. false [fɔ:ls]   adj. deceitful
                                虚假的，欺诈的

19. unauthorized [ʌn'ɔ:θəraizd] adj. not having official permission
                                未经授权的，未经批准的

20. detrimental [,detri'mentəl] adj. harmful, injurious
                                有害的

21. deceive [di'si:v]   v. to mislead by deliberate misrepresentation or lies,
                                cheat
                                欺骗

22. genuine ['dʒenjuin]   adj. real, original
                                真的，非仿造的

23. imitation [,imi'teiʃən]   n. a copy or reproduction of a genuine article; coun-
                                terfeit

仿制品,赝品

24. distinguish [dis'tiŋgwiʃ]   *v.* to make, show or recognize a difference or differences
辨别,区别

25. exclude [iks'klu:d]   *v.* to prevent from being included
除外,排除

26. fanciful ['fænsiful]   *adj.* dubious or imaginary
想象的

27. arbitrary ['ɑ:bitrəri]   *adj.* based on or subject to individual discretion or preference or sometimes impulse or caprice
任意的, 随意的

28. certification [,sə:tifi'keiʃən]   *n.* a document that attesting the truth of a fact or statement
证明

29. decree [di'kri:]   *n.* an edict, law made by someone in authority
法令

30. sanction ['sæŋkʃən]   *n.* the penalty laid down in a law for contravention
处罚,制裁

31. injunction [in'dʒʌŋkʃən]   *n.* an instruction or order issued by a court to a party to an action, esp. to refrain from some act
强制令

32. imprisonment [im'priznmənt]   *n.* putting someone in prison or in jail as lawful punishment
拘禁,监禁

33. administer [əd'ministə]   *v.* apply formally, perform
实施

34. framework ['freimwə:k]   *n.* a structural plan or basis of a project
体系,框架

Phrase and Expression

1. derive from   来自于,起源于
2. consist of   由……组成
3. due to   由于,因为
4. in particular   特别,尤其
5. depend on   依赖,依……而定
6. deprive of   剥夺,使丧失
7. in accordance with   依照,根据
8. in essence   本质上,基本上
9. in respect of   关于,至于

10. range from. . . to. . .　在……与……间变化

11. in addition　此外

12. regardless of　不管，不顾

1. A geographical indication is a sign used on goods that have a specific geographical origin and possess qualities, reputation or characteristics that are essentially attributable to that place of origin.

译文：地理标志是指用于商品上，标示该商品来源于某个特定的地区，并且其品质、声誉或其他特征主要是由该原产地所决定的一种标志。本句为复合句，主句为主系表结构。表语 a sign 由过去分词短语 used on goods 修饰作定语。表语部分包含两个由 that 引导的定语从句，前者修饰先行词 goods，后者修饰先行词 characteristics。

2. Agricultural products typically have qualities that derive from their place of production and are influenced by specific local factors, such as climate and soil.

译文：农产品通常都具有来自原产地的品质，并且受到当地具体因素，比如气候和土壤的影响。由 that 引导的从句直到句子结束是定语从句，修饰宾语 qualities；derive from 与 are influenced 是定语从句中的两个并列谓语。derive from 意为"源自，源于"。例：Thousands of English words derive from Latin. 大量英语单词源自拉丁语。

3. Whether a sign is recognized as a geographical indication is a matter of national law.

译文：一个标志是否被认为是地理标志已经是国家法律的问题。本句是个复合句，whether. . . indication 是主语从句；be recognized as sth. 意为"被承认；被认可"。例：He is recognized as the lawful heir. 他被公认为合法的继承人。

4. It generally consists of a geographical name or a traditional designation used on products which have a specific quality or characteristics that are essentially due to the geographical environment in which they are produced.

译文：它通常由一个地理名称或一个产品的传统称号组成，而这个产品所具有的特定品质或特征通常是由它们被生产时的地理环境所决定的。本句是个包含多层定语从句的复合句，即定语从句套定语从句。第一层，used on products 是过去分词短语作定语修饰前面的宾语；第二层，which have a specific quality or characteristics 定语从句修饰先行词 products；第三层，that are essentially due to the geographical environment 定语从句修饰先行词 quality or characteristics；第四层，in which they are produced 定语从句修饰先行词 geographical environment。短语 consist of 意为"由……组成（只能用在主动语态中）"。例：The committee consists of ten members. 委员会由十个人组成。

5. The concept of a geographical indication encompasses appellations of origin.

译文：一个地理标志的概念包括了原产地的名称。encompass 意为"包含；包括"。例：The general arts course at the university encompasses a wide range of subjects. 大学文科包括的科目范围很广。

6. They may also highlight qualities of a product which are due to human factors associated with the place of origin of the products, such as specific manufacturing skills and traditions.

译文：它们也可以突出跟产品原产地相关的人为因素引起的产品品质，比如具体的制作技术和传统。句中 associated with 是过去分词作定语，修饰 human factors，相当于 which are associated with；associate with 意为"将……与……联系起来"。例：Whisky is usually associated with Scotland. 威士忌常使人联想到苏格兰。

7. For example, "Bohemia" is recognized as a geographical indication in many countries for specific products made in the Czech Republic, in particular crystal ware.

译文：例如，在很多国家，"波西米亚"被认为是用来标示产于捷克共和国的某些特定产品，特别是水晶制品的一个地理标志。句中 in particular 意为"尤其；特别"。例：The whole meal was good but the wine in particular was excellent. 这餐很美味，尤其是酒特别好。

8. A geographical indication points to a specific place, or region of production that determines the characteristic qualities of the product which originates from that place.

译文：地理标志指出了一个具体的地方或生产的区域，这就决定了源自于那个地方的产品的特定品质。短语 originate from sth. 意为"始自某事物"。例：The style of architecture originated from the ancient Greeks. 这种建筑风格起源于古希腊。

9. Since those qualities depend on the place of production, a specific "link" exists between the products and their original place of production.

译文：由于这些品质是由产地所决定的，所以在产品和它们的原产地之间就存在一个具体的"链接"。本句是个复合句，由 since 引导原因状语从句。短语 depend on 意为"依赖，取决于"；be dependent on 意为"依赖于；取决于"。

10. Many of them have acquired valuable reputations which, if not adequately protected, may be misrepresented by dishonest commercial operators.

译文：很多地理标志已经获得了可贵的声誉，假如不加以很好的保护，它们可能会被一些不法商人所歪曲。本句是个复合句，which 引导的定语从句修饰宾语，即先行词 valuable reputations；另外，if not adequately protected 是过去分词短语在从句中作条件状语。

11. False use of geographical indications by unauthorized parties is detrimental to consumers and legitimate producers.

译文：未被授权的单位虚假使用地理标志有损于消费者和合法的生产商的利益。Be detrimental to sb./sth. 意为"有害的；不利的"。例：We must resist the activities that are detrimental to children's interests. 我们必须抵制有损孩子们利益的活动。

12. Consumers are deceived into believing that they are buying a genuine product with specific qualities and characteristics, when they are in fact getting an imitation.

译文：消费者会受到蒙骗，以为他们买的是具有特定品质和特征的正品，而其实他们买的却是仿制品。句中 genuine 意为"真的，非伪造的"；imitation 意为"仿制品"。

13. Legitimate producers are deprived of valuable business and the established reputation of their products is damaged.

译文：合法生产者会因此失去宝贵的业务，他们的产品所建立起来的声誉也会因此受到损害。短语 deprive sb./sth. of sth. 意为"剥夺某人（或某事物）某事物"。例：deprive of one's civil rights，剥夺某人公民取利。

14. A trademark is a sign used by an enterprise to distinguish its goods and services from those of other enterprises.

译文：商标是企业用来区别于其他企业的商品和服务的标志。distinguish A from B 意为"区别/辨别 A 与 B"。例：The twins are so alike that no one can distinguish one from the other. 这对孪生子长得很像，无人能分辨出谁是谁。

15. Geographical indications are protected in accordance with international treaties and national laws under a wide range of concepts, ...

译文：依据国际条约和国家法律，地理标志在相当广泛的领域中受到了保护。In accordance with 意为"与……一致；依照；根据"。例：I am in accordance with you in this matter. 在这件事情上，我和你是一致的。另外，in accordance with one's wishes 意为"按照某人的愿望"。

16. In essence, unauthorized parties may not use a geographical indication in respect of products that do not originate in the place designated by that indication.

译文：从本质上讲，假如产品不是来自于标志上指示的地方，未经授权的单位不能使用该地理标志。短语 in respect of sth. 意为"就某方面而言"。例：The book is admirable in respect of style. 这本书风格极佳。

17. Applicable sanctions range from court injunctions preventing the unauthorized use to the payment of damages and fines or, in serious cases, imprisonment.

译文：可用的制裁包括用以阻止未经授权使用地理标志的法院禁令以及损害赔偿和罚款，对情节恶劣者可以进行监禁。句中 range from...to... 意为"在……和……之间变化或变动"。例：Their ages range from 25 to 50. 他们的年龄在 25 至 50 岁之间。

18. A number of treaties administered by WIPO provide for the protection of geographical indications, most notably the *Paris Convention for the Protection of Industrial Property* of 1883, and the *Lisbon Agreement for the Protection of Appellations of Origin and Their International Registration*.

译文：许多由世界知识产权组织（WIPO）实施的公约规定了对地理标志的保护，最为著名的就是 1883 年的《保护工业产权巴黎公约》和《保护原产地名称和国际注册里斯本协定》。Administer 意为"实施；施行；执行"；administer the law 意为"执法"。

19. If a geographical term is used as the common designation of a kind of product, rather than an indication of the place of origin of that product, then the term no longer functions as a geographical indication.

译文：如果一个地理术语被用来作为某一类产品的通用名称，而不是用来指示该产品的原产地，那么这个术语就不再具有地理标志的作用。短语 rather than 意为"（要）……而不……"，用法相当于 instead of。例：I think I'll have a cold drink rather than coffee. 我想喝冷饮，不想喝咖啡。

20. For example, the term "cologne" now denotes a certain kind of perfumed toilet water, regardless of whether or not it was produced in the region of Cologne.

译文：例如，"科隆"这个术语现在指的是某种香味的花露水，而不管它是否是在科隆地区生产的。短语 regardless of 意为"不理会；不顾"。例：He continued speaking, regardless of my feelings on the matter. 他不顾及我在此事上的感情继续往下说。

Exercise

I. Text comprehension questions.

1. What is geographical indication?

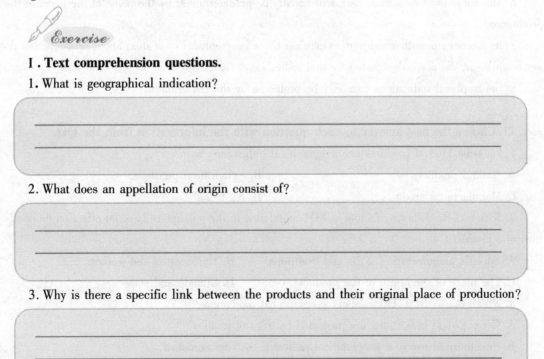

2. What does an appellation of origin consist of?

3. Why is there a specific link between the products and their original place of production?

4. What is a trademark?

5. What treaties were administered by WIPO to protect geographical indications?

II. Decide whether each of the following statements is true (T) or false (F) or not mentioned (NM) in the text.

1. Geographical indication can only be used for agricultural products.

2. Agricultural products have qualities that differ from their place of production and are affected by specific local factors such as climate and soil.

3. Appellation of origin belongs to the concept of a geographical indication.

4. False use of geographical indications by unauthorized parties is harmful only to consumers.

5. Trademark can give its owners the right to prevent others from using the trademark.

6. The name used as a trademark will usually be predetermined by the name of the place of the production.

7. In essence, unauthorized parties may not use a geographical indication about products that do not originate in the place designated by that indication.

8. Geographical indications can only be protected by the government.

III. Choose the best answer to each question with the information from the text.

1. For what kind of products can geographical indications be used?

A. Natural products.   B. Agricultural products.

C. Manufactured products.   D. A, B and C.

2. Which of the following factors is NOT mentioned in the passage to have an effect on the qualities of a product?

A. Specific manufacturing skills and traditions.   B. The mood of the workers.

C. The place of the origin of the products.   D. Climate and soil.

3. Which one is NOT TRUE about geographical indications?

A. Geographical indications are protected by a lot of treaties.

B. Unauthorized use of a geographical indication will be punished.

C. The use of a geographical indication gives its owner the right to exclude others from using it.

D. A geographical indication denotes the origin and the quality of products.

4. What's the purpose of the example of "Bohemia"?

A. To highlight human factors such as specific manufacturing skills and traditions.

B. To tell us that "Bohemia" is very famous.

C. To emphasize that "Bohemia" made in the Czech Republic.

D. There is no special meaning in taking this example.

5. What punishments are mentioned in the passage if unauthorized parties use a geographical indication?

A. The payment of damages.　　　　　　B. Fines.

C. Imprisonment.　　　　　　　　　　　D. A, B and C.

IV. Choose the word or phrase that is closest in meaning to the underlined one.

1. The president <u>highlights</u> the importance of his visit to China.

A. emphasizes　　　B. lightens　　　C. advance　　　D. encourage

2. It is said that his book <u>originated from</u> the real life of a general.

A. resulted from　　B. derived from　　C. led to　　D. resulted in

3. Nowadays a lot of people are <u>deceived</u> into buying some useless goods under the influence of advertising.

A. received　　　B. delayed　　　C. forced　　　D. cheated

4. We can <u>acquire</u> knowledge not only from the book but also from the experience.

A. inquire　　　B. gain　　　C. possess　　　D. find

5. He told me that this medal was made of <u>genuine</u> gold.

A. real　　　B. sincere　　　C. true　　　D. realistic

6. Their voices are so similar that I can't <u>distinguish</u> them from each other on the phone.

A. investigate　　B. reveal　　　C. tell　　　D. demonstrate

7. They wanted to <u>exclude</u> all boys from attending their club.

A. prevent　　　B. separate　　　C. determine　　　D. persuade

8. Poor eating habits are <u>detrimental</u> to health.

A. convenient　　B. harmful　　　C. fatal　　　D. beneficial

9. We often <u>denote</u> danger by red letters.

A. describe　　　B. recognize　　　C. sign　　　D. show

10. Since you are an adult now, you should <u>depend on</u> yourself instead of your parents to solve problems.

A. be independent of　　B. rest on　　　C. rely in　　　D. care about

11. The form of aid he chose to <u>administer</u> was entirely original with himself.

A. manage　　　B. supervise　　　C. control　　　D. perform

12. Think carefully about what you say: your view could be easily <u>misrepresented</u> by the press.

A. disguised　　B. vanished　　　C. distorted　　　D. interpreted

Ⅴ. Fill in the blanks with the phrases and expressions from the text. Change forms where necessary.

in particular	consist of	deprive of	in accordance with	range from. . . to

1. The atmosphere _____ more than 70% nitrogen(氮气).

2. _____ international trade, both parties, once entering into a contract, should be liable for its execution.

3. The price of beer _____ $1.3 _____ $2 in this pub.

4. He is _____ part of his wages as a punishment of being late for work.

5. One dish _____ pleased the guests.

Ⅵ. Match the words with their definitions.

1. not having official permission

2. the quality or condition of being diversified, various

3. an identifying name or title

4. a structural plan or basis of a project

5. dubious or imaginary

6. to mislead by deliberate misrepresentation or lies

7. a copy or reproduction of a genuine article; counterfeit

8. to give a formal acknowledgement of a status

9. capable of being attributed

10. based on or subject to individual discretion or preference or sometimes impulse or caprice

( ) attributable   ( ) deceive   ( ) unauthorized

( ) framework   ( ) variety   ( ) appellation

( ) arbitrary   ( ) fanciful   ( ) recognize   ( ) imitation

Ⅶ. Translate the following sentences into English.

1. 这两件东西外表相同但本质不同。（in essence）

2. 这种产品质量好但是数量不足。（in respect of）

3. 很多英语单词源自于拉丁文和希腊文。(derive from)

_____

_____

4. 眼下的一切迹象都表明这两个国家将很快重新开战(谈判)。(point to)

_____

_____

5. 由于天气很冷,我们无法去植树。(due to)

_____

_____

Ⅷ. Oral exercises.

Students in groups of two will make conversations about geographical indications. In the conversation practice, some sentence patterns will be used. In this unit, students will use the following two sentence patterns:

I don't get very excited about... 我对……不怎么感兴趣

1 wonder / was wondering if... 我想知道……,我在想是否……

Please follow example (1) and complete the following dialogue exercises. Student A and B will exchange roles upon completion.

For example (1):

Student A: I don't get excited about whether there is a geographical indication for the product when I buy it.

Student B: I think it is understandable to do so(or I don't think it is understandable to do so).

Student A: I don't get excited about (whether the qualities are influenced by specific local factors, whether the qualities depend on the place of production, false use of geographical indication, the concept of a geographical indication).

Student B: I think it is understandable to do so(or I do not think it is understandable to do so).

Please follow example (2) and complete the following dialogue exercises. Student A and B will exchange roles upon completion.

For example (2):

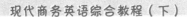
Student A: I wonder if a trademark gives its owner the right to exclude others from using the trademark.

Student B: Sorry, I don't know(or There is no telling).

Student A: I wonder if (a trademark consists of a fanciful or arbitrary name or device, geographical indications are protected by law, the unauthorized parties false using a geographical indication will be punished or not, false use of geographical indications by unauthorized parties is detrimental to consumers and legitimate producers).

Student B: Sorry, I don't know(or There is no telling).

IX. **Writing skills. Please look at the pictures, the words and phrases coming from the pictures in relation to intellectual property rights below. And then write 3 – 5 sentences to describe each of the pictures.**

The expressions in the brackets may help you to start your writing.

(*There is/are . . . in the picture; In the middle of the picture; Then let's look at the next picture; This picture is about . . . ; The person on the right. . . ; From the picture, you can see. . . ; The central focus of this picture is. . . ; In the top left corner /bottom right corner of the picture, a man/woman/boy/girl. . . ; From her/his facial expression, I can assume that. . . ; From the. . . , I can tell that. . . ; Perhaps this man is about to. . .)*

Picture 1 （ a warning sign, a pirate, horrible look）

_____

_____

Picture 2 （a skeleton, a video disk, two knives）

_____

_____

_____

Picture 3 （a poster, two disks, expensive, cheap, genuine, imitation）

_____

_____

_____

Ⅹ. **PPT presentation. Students in small groups will try to study and understand what intellectual property rights are, and prepare 4 – 5 page of PPT slides to demonstrate cases which violates intellectual property rights.**

Further Reading: Trademarks

Trademarks or marks are words, symbols, designs, combinations of letters or numbers, or other devices that identify（识别） and distinguish（区分）products and services in the marketplace. When trademarks are presented to the public via（通过）advertising, marketing, trade shows, or other means, they become one of a company's most valuable assets—potential（潜在的）customers identify a company by its trademark. Because certain trademarks immediately create an image of quality goods and services to potential buyers, they are valuable assets that should be protected.

When trademarks are registered（注册）at the state, federal, or international levels, their owners are provided the maximum legal protection for company names and/or company products. Thus, in creating or selecting company names and trademarks, a major concern is to design names and trademarks that may be registered with U. S. Patent Office. Today, the feasibility（可行性）of designing names for products and services as well as trademarks for them is not likely because millions of trademarks are already registered.

The creation of trademarks involves the development of symbols or other devices to identify products and services in the marketplace. Guidelines(指导方针)exist for creating trademarks. Individuals who are developing trademarks must avoid generically descriptive(描述的,叙述的)and misleading terms as well as foreign translations. As soon as a tentative(尝试的)trademark has been developed, its creators should consult a patent attorney for assistance making it sufficiently distinctive (特殊的,不一般的)to be registered.

Exercise

I. Choose the best answer to each question with the information from the text.

1. What are trademarks?

A. Trademarks or marks are words, symbols, designs, combinations of letters or numbers, or other devices that identify products and services in the marketplace.

B. Trademarks or marks are words, symbols, designs, combinations of letters or numbers, or other devices that distinguish products and services in the marketplace.

C. Trademarks or marks are words, symbols, designs, combinations of letters or numbers, or other devices that allow others to use them freely.

D. A and B.

2. Which means is NOT mentioned in the passage when trademarks are presented to the public?

A. Advertising.　　　　B. Newspapers.　　　　C. Marketing.　　　　D. Trade shows.

3. Why does a trademark become one of a company's most valuable assets?

A. Because a certain trademark immediately creates an image of quality goods and services to potential buyers.

B. Because a trademark can identify and distinguish products and services in the marketplace.

C. Because a trademark is unique.

D. A and B.

4. What's the major concern in creating or selecting company names and trademarks?

A. To design names and trademarks that may be registered with U. N. Patent Office.

B. To design names and trademarks that may be registered with his own country's Patent Office.

C. To design names and trademarks that may be registered with U. S. Patent Office.

D. All of the above.

5. Which one of the following is NOT TRUE about trademarks?

A. Trademarks are valuable assets that should be protected.

B. When trademarks are registered at the state, federal, or international levels, their owners are provided the minimum legal protection for company names and/or company products.

C. The creation of trademarks involves the development of symbols or other devices to identify products and services in the marketplace.

D. Individuals who are developing trademarks must avoid generically descriptive and misleading

terms as well as foreign translations.

II. Decide whether each of the following statements is true (T) or false (F).

1. Trademarks can help to identify and distinguish products and services in the marketplace.

2. Certain trademarks immediately create an image of quality goods and services to potential buyers.

3. Trademarks are not valuable assets that should be protected.

4. Today, the feasibility of designing names for products and services as well as trademarks for them is possible though millions of trademarks are already registered.

5. There are no guidelines existing for creating trademarks.

GLOSSARY

a focus group	（销售）讨论组
a panel of	一个小组委员会
above all	首先，尤其是，最重要的是
accessible [ək'sesəbl] adj.	容易取得，容易获得
according to	根据
account for	解释，说明
acquire [ə'kwaiə] v.	获得，得到
activist ['æktivist] n.	行动主义分子，积极分子
adapt [ə'dæpt] v.	（使）适应
adaptable [ə'dæptəbl] adj.	有适应能力的
adequately ['ædikwətli] adv.	适当地，充分地
administer [əd'ministə] v.	实施
agenda [ə'dʒendə] n.	议事日程，（会议的）议程表
aggregate ['ægrigeit] adj.	总数的，总计的
aggressive [ə'gresiv] adj.	积极进取的，活跃的
agreement [ə'gri:mənt] n.	协定，协议，契约
all in all	总而言之
alter ['ɔ:ltə] v.	改变，变样
ambiguity [,æmbi'gju:iti] n.	含糊不清，模棱两可，不明确
amongst [ə'mʌnst] prep.	在……之中，在……之间
anniversary [,æni'və:səri] n.	周年纪念，周年纪念日
apart from	与……脱离，与……区别
apparel [ə'pærəl] n.	衣着，服饰
appellation [,æpi'leiʃən] n.	名称，称呼
appreciate [ə'pri:ʃieit] v.	欣赏
approach [ə'prəutʃ] n.	方法，途径
apt [æpt] adj.	易于……的，有……的倾向
arbitrary ['ɑ:bitrəri] adj.	任意的，随意的
arise from	由……引起，产生
articulate [ɑ:'tikjulit] vt.	明确有力地表达
as a matter of	事实上
as a result	因此
as a whole	整体来看
as well as	也
as well	也，同样

assemble [əˈsembl] v.	汇编,组装
assess [əˈses] v.	评估
asset[ˈæset] n.	资产
assistance [əˈsistəns] n.	帮助
associated[əˈsəuʃi,eitid] adj.	有关联的,相关的
assume [əˈsjuːm]vt.	假定,假设,臆断
at a global level	在世界级别上,在全球一级
at least	至少
at the point of	在……时
at the same time	同时
attorney[əˈtəːni] n.	代理律师
attributable[əˈtribjuːtəbl] adj.	(可)归因于……
attribute [əˈtribjuːt] n.	特性
authority[ɔːˈθɔrəti] n.	权力,权威
available[əˈveiləbl] adj.	可用的,可得到的
average[ˈævəridʒ] v.	平均为,平均达
barrier[ˈbæriə] n.	障碍,隔阂
base on	建立在……基础上,根据
be apt to	易于……; 倾向于……
be associated with	与……有关
be based on	取决于;以……为基础
be contrary to	与……相矛盾
be inferior to	在……之下;次于;不如
be known as	被认为是……
be likely to	可能
be similar to	与……相似
beneficial [ˌbeniˈfiʃəl] adj.	有益的
benefit[ˈbenifit] vi.	得益
bloated[ˈbləutid] adj.	得意忘形的
breed[briːd] v.	引起
bribe[braib] n.	贿赂
bulk[bʌlk] n	主体,绝大部分
call for	要求,需要
capital[ˈkæpitəl] n.	资本,资金,本金
cash flow	现金周转
casualty [ˈkæʒjuəlti] n.	死者,伤者
catalog [ˈkætələɡ] n.	目录册
category [ˈkætiɡəri] n.	种类,类别
celebration[ˌseliˈbreiʃən] n.	庆祝;庆祝会(仪式)

census ['sensəs] n.	统计数, 记录
cents-off deal	降价销售
certification[ˌsəːtifiˈkeiʃən] n.	证明
characteristic[ˌkærəktəˈristik] n.	特征, 特性
chronology[krəˈnɔlədʒi] n.	年表
circumstance ['səːkəmstəns] n	环境, 条件, 情况
claim [kleim] n.	权利, 所有权
colonial [kəˈləunjəl] adj.	殖民时期的
combined with	与……混合
come into play	开始活动, 投入使用, 起作用
come up with	想出, 提出
commercial[kəˈməːʃəl] adj.	商业的
commit. . . to. . .	把……交付给, 委托于
comparative[kəmˈpærətiv] adj.	比较的
compete[kəmˈpiːt] v.	竞争
competition [ˌkɔmpiˈtiʃən] n.	竞争
complicate[ˈkɔmplikeit] v.	使复杂
concentrate on	集中精力于
confidentiality [ˈkɔnfiˌdenʃiˈæləti] n.	机密
conflict [ˈkɔnflikt] n.	(信念、意见、利益等)严重分歧, 冲突
conflicting [ˈkɔnfliktiŋ] adj.	相矛盾的; 冲突的
conflicting interests	利益冲突
confuse with	把……和……混淆
consecutive[kənˈsekjutiv] adj.	连续的
consequence [ˈkɔnsikwəns] n.	结果, 后果
consideration [kənˌsidəˈreiʃən] n.	考虑因素, 要考虑的事
consist of	由……组成
context [ˈkɔntekst] n.	环境
contract[ˈkɔntrækt] n.	合同, 契约
contradict [ˌkɔntrəˈdikt] vt.	与……矛盾, 同……抵触
contrary [ˈkɔntrəri] adj.	相反的, 相违背的
controversy[ˈkɔntrəvəːsi] n.	争议, 纠纷
cope with	与……相适应, 对付, 应付
coupon [ˈkuːpɔn] n.	(购物)优惠券
cover [ˈkʌvə] vt.	涉及, 包含
credit [ˈkredit] n.	信贷
creditor [ˈkreditə] n.	债权人
criterion [kraiˈtiəriən] n.	标准
current[ˈkʌrənt] adj.	当前的, 现在的

cutout['kʌtaut] *n.*	剪贴画
date to	追溯到
de facto [di:'fæktəu] *adj.*	实际上存在的
deal with	讨论,处理,涉及,对付
deceive[di'si:v] *v.*	欺骗
decline[di'klain] *n.*	缩小,衰弱,降低
decree[di'kri:] *n.*	法令
define [di'fain] *vt.*	定义,解释
definite['definit] *adj.*	明确的,确切的
definition[ˌdefi'niʃən] *n.*	定义,释义
demographic [ˌdemə'græfik] *adj.*	人口统计学的
demonstrate ['demənstreit] *vt.*	证明,演示
denote[di'nəut] *n.*	指出
depend on	依赖,依……而定
deprive of	剥夺,使丧失
derive from	来自于,起源于
deserve[di'zə:v] *vt.*	应受,应得,值得
designation[ˌdezig'neiʃən] *n.*	指示
despite[di'spait] *prep.*	尽管
destructive[di'strʌktiv] *adj.*	引起破坏(或毁灭)的, 破坏性(或毁灭性)的
determinant [di'tə:minənt] *n.*	决定因素
determine[di'tə:min] *v.*	决定
detriment ['detrimənt] *n.*	损害,不利
detrimental[ˌdetri'mentəl] *adj.*	有害的
devise [di'vaiz] *v.*	制定,设计
diagrammatic [ˌdaiəgrə'mætik] *adj.*	图式的
diffusion [di'fju:ʒən] *n.*	传播,扩散
dilute[dai'lju:t] *vt.*	削弱,减轻,降低
dimention [di'menʃən] *n.*	方面
disclosure[di'skləuʒə] *n.*	揭露,披露,公开
discount ['diskaunt] *n.*	折扣
discriminate against	歧视
discrimination [dis,krimi'neiʃən] *n.*	差别对待;歧视
dispense [dis'pens] *v.*	分发
distinctive [di'stiŋktiv] *adj.*	区别性的
distinguish[dis'tiŋgwiʃ] *v.*	辨别,区别
distribution [ˌdistri'bju:ʃən] *n.*	销售,销售量
distribution chain	销售过程

domestic [dəu'mestik] *adj.*	本国的,国内的
drift [drift] *n.*	倾向,趋势
due to	由于,因为
duration [djuə'reiʃən] *n.*	持续时间
economical [,i:kə'nɔmikəl] *adj.*	实惠的
effect [i'fekt] *n.*	影响
elect [i'lekt] *v.*	选择
employ [im'plɔi] *v.*	利用,使用
encompass [in'kʌmpəs] *v.*	包括
end up with	以……而结束
engage in	从事
enhance [in'ha:ns] *v.*	提高
entail [in'teil] *v.*	使……必要
entity ['entiti] *n.*	实体,本质
entrant ['entrənt] *n.*	参赛人
entrepreneur [,ɔntrəprə'nə:] *n.*	企业家
environmental [in,vaiərən'mentəl] *adj.*	环境的
essentially [i'senʃəli] *adv.*	本质上;根本上,基本上
ethics ['eθiks] *n.*	道德准则,行为准则
evaluate [i'væljueit] *v.*	评价, 估计
even as	正当
evidence ['evidəns] *n.*	证据
except that	除了
exclude [iks'klu:d] *v.*	除外,排除
expand [ik'spænd] *v.*	扩展,扩张
expertise [,ekspə:'ti:z] *n.*	专门知识或技能
explicit [ik'splisit] *adj.*	明确的,详述的,明晰的
exposure [ik'spəuʒə] *n.*	暴露,揭发
facilitate [fə'siliteit] *vt.*	使变得容易,促进
facilitator [fə'siliteitə] *n.*	服务商
fall into	分成,变成,落入
false [fɔ:ls] *adj.*	虚假的,欺诈的
fanciful ['fænsiful] *adj.*	想象的
favorable ['feivərəbl] *adj.*	有利的
feedback ['fi:dbæk] *n.*	反馈
fend for oneself	自己谋生,照料自己
focus group	小组讨论
focus on	以……为焦点;集中于
forbid sb. from doing	禁止某人做某事

foreign-born	出生在国外的
formalize ['fɔ:məlaiz] vt.	使成为正式;使具有一定形式
framework ['freimwə:k] n.	体系,框架
frequent-flyer	飞机常客
fuel [fjuəl] vt.	激起,刺激,保持……的进行
gaining steam	增加势头
generate ['dʒenəreit] v.	产生
genuine ['dʒenjuin] adj.	真的,非仿造的
geographic [dʒiə'græfik] adj.	地理的
give away	赠送
give birth to	生(孩子),产生
global ['gləubəl] adj.	全球的, 全世界的
gradual ['grædjuəl] adj.	逐步的,渐渐的
gross [grəus] adj.	总的
handout ['hændaut] n.	免费散发的, 印刷品
harmonious [hɑ:'məunjəs] adj.	和谐的;协调的
hence [hens] adv.	因此,所以
highlight ['hailait] v.	强调,突出
illustrate ['iləstreit] vt.	表明,阐明,表示,显示
imitation [,imi'teiʃən] n.	仿制品,赝品
impact [,impækt] n.	影响力
impending [im'pendiŋ] adj.	即将发生的,逼近的
imply [im'plai] vt.	暗示,意味
imprisonment [im'priznmənt] n.	拘禁,监禁
in a positive light	以积极的角度
in accordance with	依照,根据
in addition	此外
in case	假使,以防(万一), 以免
in combination with	与……结合(联合)
in conjunction with	连同,与……共同
in contrast to	与……相反
in essence	本质上,基本上
in other words	用另外的话说
in particular	特别,尤其
in relation to	与……相关
in respect of	关于,至于
in response to	作为对……的答复;作为对……的反应
in some circumstances	在某些情况下
in terms of	就……而言;根据

in the end	最后
indicate ['indikeit] v.	指出，表明
indistinguishable [,indis'tiŋgwiʃəbl] adj.	难以识别的
inefficient[,ini'fiʃənt] adj.	无效率的，效率低的
inferior [in'fiəriə] adj.	不如的；较差的
influence['influəns] v.	影响
influx ['inflʌks] n.	流入，涌入
inherit [in'herit] vt.	继承（传统、遗产、权利等）
in-joke['in,dʒəuk] n.	（圈内人才领会的）小范围或内部笑话
injunction[in'dʒʌŋkʃən] n.	强制令
innovation[,inəu'veiʃən] n.	创新
innovative [inəuveitiv] adj.	有创意的
instill[in'stil] v.	逐渐使某人获得
integrate into	与……成为一体
integration [,inti'greiʃən] n.	一体化
intellectual[,inti'lektʃəl] adj.	需用智力的；用脑力的
intellectual property	知识产权
interactive[,intər'æktiv] adj.	相互影响的
interest['intrist] n.	利益，私利
interstate[,intə'steit] n.	州际的
intuitive [in'tju:itiv] adj.	有直觉力的；凭直觉获知的
inventory ['invəntəri] n.	存货清单
issue['iʃju:] n.	问题，议题，争议
launch[lɔ:ntʃ] v.	开始从事，发起，发动
laureate ['lɔ:riət] n.	得奖人
lead to	导致，引向
legitimate[li'dʒitimit] adj.	合法的，法定的
liberal['libərəl] adj.	自由的
likely ['laikli] adj.	可能的
link [liŋk] n.	联系，连接
live on	继续存在；靠……为生；
lobby for	为争取……而游说
logo['ləugəu] n.	公司标志
make use of	使用
marketing mix	销售组合
meaningful ['mi:niŋful] adj.	意义深长的，有意义的
merchandise ['mə:tʃəndaiz] n.	商品
military ['militəri] adj.	军事的，军用的，军人的
ministerial[,mini'stiəriəl] adj.	部长的，大臣的，公使的

miscellaneous [ˌmisə'leiniəs] *adj.*	各种各样的
misrepresent['mis,repri'zent] *v.*	故意对……作错误的报道
moderate ['mɔdərət] *v.*	使减轻(缓和),节制
monetary ['mʌnitəri] *adj.*	货币的,金钱的
motivate['məutiveit] *v.*	促进,激发
mug[mʌg] *n.*	圆筒形有柄大杯
multilateral[ˌmʌlti'lætərəl] *adj.*	多边的,多国的
multiply['mʌltiplai] *v.*	(使)增加
narrow down	使……缩小
negative['negətiv] *adj.*	负的,消极的
negotiate[ni'gəuʃieit] *v.*	谈判;协商;商定
negotiation[ni,gəuʃi'eiʃən] *n.*	协商,谈判,磋商
net [net] *adj.*	净的
nevertheless [,nevəðə'les] ad*v.*	然而,不过
niche[nitʃ]	缝隙市场,利基市场
notion['nəuʃən] *n.*	观念,概念,看法
numerical [nju:'merikəl] *adj.*	数字的,用数字表示的
objectionable[əb'dʒekʃənəbl] *adj.*	有异议的
obligation [,ɔbli'geiʃən] *n.*	义务,责任
obstacle ['ɔbstəkl] *n.*	障碍(物),妨碍
occupation[,ɔkju'peiʃən] *n.*	工作,职业
occur [ə'kə:] *vi.*	发生,出现
offensive [ə'fensiv] *adj.*	过时的
offset ['ɔfset] *v.*	补偿
on. . . grounds	以……为由
opportunity [,ɔpə'tju:nəti] *n.*	机会,时机
organization[,ɔ:gənai'zeiʃən]	组织;机构
oriented ['ɔ:rientid] *adj.*	有兴趣趋向的,定向的
origin['ɔridʒin] *n.*	起源,来源
originate[ə'ridʒineit] *v.*	起源于,来自
originator [ə'ridʒəneitə] *n.*	创始人
out of necessity	迫不得已,出于需要
overall ['əuvərɔ:l] *adj.*	全面的
overriding[,əuvə'raidiŋ] adj	最重要的;高于一切的
pad [pæd] *vt.*	虚报(账目)
painstakingly ['peinz,teikiŋli] ad*v.*	刻苦地;煞费苦心地
participate[pɑ:'tisipeit] *v.*	参与
partnership['pɑrtnəʃip] *n.*	合伙企业
pass out	分发

patent[ˈpeitənt] n.	专利权
patriotic [ˌpeitriˈɔtik,ˌpætriˈɔtik] adj.	爱国的,有爱国心的
patronage [ˈpætrənidʒ] n.	顾客,常客
peak[piːk] n.	顶点
perceive[pəˈsiːv] v.	认为,感知
personality [ˌpəːsəˈnæləti] n.	人格
personality traits	个性品质
pharmaceutical [ˌfaːməˈsjuːtikəl] adj.	制药的
phenomenon [fiˈnɔminən] n.	现象,迹象,特别的事情
pivotal [ˈpivətəl] adj.	关键的
play a role in	在……中发挥角色(或作用)
play an important role in	起重要作用
point-of-purchase display	销售现场广告;采购点促销
positive[ˈpɔzətiv] adj.	积极的,肯定的
predecessor [ˈpriːdisesə] n.	前身
predetermine[ˌpriːdiˈtəːmin] v.	预先确定
predictable[priˈdiktəbl] adj.	可预言(预报)的,可预见的
premium [ˈpriːmiəm] n.	赠品
presentation [ˌprezənˈteiʃən] n.	发布会
productivity [ˌprɔdʌkˈtivəti] n.	生产率,生产能力
profitable [ˈprɔfitəbl] adj.	有益的,有好处的
prolong[prəˈlɔŋ] v.	拉长,延长
promotion[prəˈməuʃən] n.	宣传,促销
promotional[prəˈməuʃənl] adj.	促销的
pronounceable[prəˈnaunsəbəl] adj.	可发音的
property [ˈprɔpəti] n.	所有权;版权
proprietor[prəˈpraiətə] n.	所有者,业主
prosper[ˈprɔspə] v.	繁荣,发达
protest[ˈprəutest] n. & v.	抗议;对……提出异议;反对
provide[prəˈvaid] v.	提供
publicity[pʌbˈlisəti] n.	宣传
purpose [ˈpəːpəs] n.	目的;意图
pursue [pəˈsjuː] v.	实施,贯彻
put...aside	把……放在一边;撇开,不予理会
work out	锻炼,训练
qualify [ˈkwɔlifai] v.	把...称为
qualitative [ˈkwɔlitətiv] adj.	定性的, 性质(上)的; 质量的
range from...to...	在……与……间变化
rationale [ˌræʃiəˈnɑːl] n.	根本原因

rebate ['ri:beit] *n.*	折扣
receptionist [ri'sepʃənist] *n.*	接待员
recession [ri'seʃən] *n.*	经济不景气,经济衰退
recipient [ri'sipiənt] *n.*	接受者
recognize ['rekəgnaiz] *v.*	认可
redeem [ri'di:m] *v.*	偿还
redress [ri'dres] *n.*	补偿,补救
reduction [ri'dʌkʃən] *n.*	降价
refund [ri:'fʌnd] *n.*	返还现金
regardless of	不管,不顾
register ['redʒistə] *n.*	记录器
regulate ['regjuleit] *vt.*	管理,控制,制约
relate to	涉及
relative ['relətiv] *adj.*	相对的
reluctant [ri'lʌktənt] *adj.*	勉强,不情愿的
reputation [,repju'teiʃən] *n.*	荣誉
resource [ri'sɔ:s] *n.*	资源
respectively [ri'spektivli] *adv.*	各自的,分别的
respond to	作出反应,应对
rest on	建立在某事物的基础上;基于某事物
result in	作为结果,因此
retail ['ri:teil] *n.*	零售
retrieve [ri'tri:v] *vt.*	寻回,恢复,挽回
reward [ri'wɔ:d] *n.*	报酬,赢利
rival ['raivəl] *n.*	竞争对手
rural ['ruərəl] *adj.*	(有关)乡村生活的
sales efforts	推销工作,销售活动
sanction ['sæŋkʃən] *n.*	处罚,制裁
scale [skeil] *n.*	规模
scarce [skɛəs] *adj.*	稀有,缺乏
scarf [skɑ:f] *n.*	围巾;披肩;领巾
segment ['segmənt] *n.*	部分,份,片,段
segmentation [,segmən'teiʃən] *n.*	分割,分隔
self-defeating [,selfdi'fi:tiŋ] *adj.*	弄巧成拙的,适得其反的
severe [si'viə] *adj.*	严重的
share [ʃɛə] *n.*	股份
shift from... to...	从……到……转变
sign [sain] *n.*	迹象
significant [sig'nifikənt] *adj.*	重要的

siren call	诱惑,引诱
skeptic ['skeptik] n.	怀疑者,怀疑论
so-called	所谓的,号称的
sole[səul] adj.	唯一的,单独的
solely['səulli] adv.	单独地;唯一地;仅仅
solvent['sɔlvənt] adj.	有偿付能力的,无债务的
sort out	整理;弄清楚,解决
specialize in	专攻,精通
specific[spi'sifik] adj.	明确的,具体的,特定的
stable ['steibl] adj.	稳定的
state patent	国家专利局
static ['stætik] adj.	静止的,不变化的
statistical[stə'tistikəl] adj.	统计的, 以数据表示的
steeply['sti:pli] adv.	陡峭地
stimulus['stimjuləs] n.	刺激物,促进因素
subdivide[ˌsʌbdi'vaid] vt.	再分
subsidy['sʌbsidi] n.	补贴
suffice [sə'fais] vi.	足够
suffice it to say	只要说……就够了;无须多说;可以肯定地说
suggestive[sə'dʒestiv] adj.	引起联想的
susceptible[sə'septəbl] adj.	易受影响的
sweepstake ['swi:psteik] n.	抽奖
tactic['tæktik] n.	方法,策略
tailor ['teilə] vt.	调整,使适应
take advantage of	利用
take into account	将……考虑进去
target group	目标群体
tariff ['tærif] n.	关税,关税表
taxation[tæk'seiʃən] n.	税,税收
temptation[temp'teiʃən] n.	诱惑,引诱
think nothing of	不把……放在心里,轻视
three-of-a-kind	三张相同的牌
title ['taitl] vt.	(给书籍、乐曲等)加标题,定题目
trait [treit] n.	显著的特点
transparent[træns'pærənt] adj.	透明的,含义清楚的
trend[trend] n.	趋势,倾向
trivial ['triviəl] adj.	琐碎的,不重要的
trough[trɔf] n.	低谷,低谷期,萧条期
turn out ...	结果是……;原来是……

typeface [taipfeis] *n.*	字体
ultimate ['ʌltimət] *adj.*	最后的,最终的
unauthorized [ˌʌn'ɔ:θəraizd] *adj.*	未经授权的,未经批准的
underprice [ˌʌndə'prais] *v.*	以低价与……竞争
under the control of	在……控制下
undertake [ˌʌndə'teik] *vt.*	从事
unrestricted [ˌʌnris'triktid] *adj.*	没受限制的,无限制的
upgrade ['ʌpgreid] *vt.*	提高,改善
uprising [ʌp'raiziŋ] *n.*	起义,暴动
upshot ['ʌpʃɔt] *n.*	结果
Uruguay ['juərugwai] *n.*	乌拉圭(国名,位于南美洲)
utilize ['juːtiaiz] *v.*	利用
variable ['vɛəriəbl] *n.*	变量
variety [və'raiəti] *n.*	各种,种种
vary ['vɛəri] *vi.*	变化
vary between	在……之间变化
venture ['ventʃə] *n.*	商业活动,(为赢利而投资其中的)企业
version ['vɔ:ʒən] *n.*	版本;形式
vertical ['vɔ:tikəl] *adj.*	垂直的
vertical integration	垂直管理
vigilant ['vidʒilənt] *adj.*	警觉的,警惕的
violate ['vaiəleit] *vt.*	违背,违犯,违反
wants and needs	需求
ward off	阻挡,防止
warranty ['wɔrənti] *n.*	保证
weight [weit] *n.*	影响
well-chosen ['wel'tʃəuzən] *adj.*	精选的;适当的
wholesale ['həulseil] *n.*	批发
widowhood ['widəuhud] *n.*	孀居,守寡
withdraw [wið'drɔ:] *vi.*	撤回,退出
within agreed limits	在商定的范围内
yield to	屈服于